# CENNITA LOW

# BIG BAD WOLF

A COS commando novel

# AUTHOR'S NOTE 2008

When I first joined RWA (Romance Writers of America), I didn't know a thing about publishing. I went to my first conference and stood in line for an appointment with available editors. Unlike the many writers around me, I had no idea which editor was accepting for what line; in fact, I didn't know about publishing houses having different lines, that was how ignorant I was. In those days, there were business cards pinned on a board and we picked the editors with the time slot under their names. I basically went "inny-meeny-miny-mo" with my pick. The writers around me were no different from those today—every one of them eagerly waiting their turn to sell their manuscripts, armed with knowledge about each editor's likes and dislikes ("this one doesn't like male names for their heroines," one advised me when I told her my heroine's name was Jaime) and full of encouragement of each other.

The editor I picked was one from the Silhouette Intimate Moments line. You know what? I had no idea what that was. I knew I'd read many, many Harlequin and Silhouette books but I never looked at the lines; I went by authors. In a small voice, I asked a few women around me for author names who wrote for that line, a question that brought me several raised eyebrows, let me tell you. Being around romance writers is the best thing in the world—we're a helpful and friendly bunch. Those girls took me under their wing and gave me the quickest half hour coaching about interviews with editors and hot plot summaries ever.

"Spies are hot right now! And give your heroines different jobs!"

I took that to heart when I walked in for my first interview. Spies? I love spies! Heroine with a different job? Do I have one! I decided I'd make the heroine a roofer. I figured it'd catch the editor's attention and besides, I knew a lot about roofing (ha). The editor liked my spiel enough to ask to see the partial of the manuscript. I think I about peed in my pants.

So, that's how Big Bad Wolf got written. My first manuscript. I entered it into the Golden Heart (RWA's national contest for unpublished writers) that year and it finaled in 1999. To this day, Big Bad Wolf holds a special place in my heart.

Because of my current publishing delay, I wanted to give something back to the readers who have been so supportive and patient with me. Big Bad Wolf, in essence, has the beginning nugget of ideas that became the COS covert world. In the following weeks, I'll be rewriting and updating the story and posting it as a gift to you. I hope you'll enjoy it as much as I enjoyed writing a tale about a roofer girl and the spy who fell in love with her.

DEDICATION
To my friend, Jaime, whom I miss very much.

To Ranger Buddy who taught me much more than roofing.

## ACKNOWLEDGEMENT

Special thanks to Monique who gave me much invaluable techy help. Jed says you're a good asset.

I also want to thank all my wonderful GLOW fans, especially those in my YAHOO group and my blog visitors, who have given me so much support through the years. Your encouraging emails kept me going, in spite of the delays and problems. Your friendship is a cherished part of my writing life.

# Chapter One

*Here comes trouble.* That was the first thought that crossed Jaymee Barrow's mind when she saw him walking around the job site. There were men all around her, already busy at work at eight in the morning, men half-naked and sweaty, of all shapes and sizes, but none had the same effect on her as this stranger.

She was a woman used to men. Having grown up among them, she understood them better than her few girlfriends. She had learned from personal experience to spot trouble of the male kind a mile away. It was still early but she was already perspiring from carrying supplies up and down the ladder. She impatiently flicked away a drop of perspiration at the end her nose, pausing in the middle of getting ready for work, her nail gun in one hand, squinting her eyes as she watched the tall man talk to Joe, the electrician, then Stan, the plumber. They both shook their heads and the stranger moved on, coming closer toward her. Her finger lightly squeezed the trigger of the nail gun as he approached.

He was tall and whipcord lean. The tee-shirt he wore clung to his muscular shape like a second skin, damp from the searing Florida summer heat, emphasizing an impressive chest and a long torso that invited eyes to drift lower, which hers did, all the way. The faded jeans hung low on his hips, molding and hugging his thighs and legs, doing strange things to her heart rate as she continued staring. Here comes trouble, the voice in her head repeated, as if in warning.

The stranger tapped one of Jaymee's men on the shoulder. "The plumber there told me to ask for Jay. Which man is he?"

She stiffened. He was asking for her?

Her workers snickered. Lucky, the man whose shoulder the stranger tapped, gave a gap-toothed smile. "You want the boss?" he qualified, as if to make sure.

"Yeah."

"You can find Jay by the blue truck."

"Thanks."

Jaymee couldn't shake off the feeling of impending disaster. She knew what he would do next, and he didn't fail her. He stopped right in front of Dicker and spoke to him. This close, the slow drawl of his gravelly voice sent shivers down her spine. "Are you Jay?"

Dicker threw back his head and laughed. The stranger frowned. Jaymee coughed politely. Pointedly. She waited until he turned around, and cocked her head to one side when he looked down at her. She decided that she didn't like the height disadvantage.

His eyes were gray. No, blue. Or in between. However, there wasn't anything in between about the intensity of his gaze. He looked at her and her insides suddenly felt like the inside of a burning tar kettle. Jaymee blinked, feeling suddenly quite dizzy. What was wrong with her? He was just a man, like any other, but her heart didn't seem to agree as it suddenly accelerated to a gallop.

"Jay?" he asked, a frown puckering his forehead.

Jaymee nodded, unable to say a word. Something exuded from him that she couldn't yet pinpoint; it was a new thing, something that prickled and made her want to jump into her truck, lock it and drive off like the devil was after her. She shook off such fanciful thoughts, and belatedly tried to find her tongue. He was just too damn tall, that was all.

"Can I help you?" To her disgust, her voice came out breathy and slightly husky.

"You're Jay." It was more a statement than a question. The tone of his voice, as had his expression, had now turned skeptical. "The boss."

She usually handled similar situations with light amusement. It was, after all, very rare to find a woman roofer. A woman roofer/boss at that. That was why it was easier to be Jay. Homeowners and people seemed to react differently to Jay, the contractor than Jaymee, the contractor. However, his whole demeanor irritated her, and thus her answer came out sharper than intended.

"I'm Jay," she agreed, and after a slight pause, added, "the boss. How can I help you?"

He considered her for a moment, then shrugged. "I'm looking for work, any kind of labor. Do you have any job openings?"

Jaymee stared up at him. He had incredibly long eyelashes, she noted vaguely. Rugged and strong-jawed, with full sensuous lips that were slightly crooked. His hair was long and untidy, like most construction workers, and a devilish lock, black as night, fell across his forehead. Her eyes traveled down the length of him again—strong, wide shoulders, powerful biceps. She looked at his large hands. Long, artistic fingers. Clean nails. If he could roof, she thought, then she could build a rocket ship.

He just patiently stood there under her perusal. When her eyes met his again, she found mockery glinting back at her. The man was probably used to being treated like some piece of mouth-watering meat, and she was quickly disgusted with herself. She met his eyes directly, unflinchingly, refusing to let him see how he affected her.

"I don't think, Mr...?" She paused.

"Langley. Nicholas Langley."

"Mr. Langley," Jaymee said, "I don't think you have any, or enough, roofing experience. Do you?"

Nicholas Langley shrugged again. "I'm a quick learner and a good worker," he said, "and a damn good carpenter."

"So why don't you apply to be one?" Jaymee asked. "The pay's better."

"The two companies I asked already have a full crew and the third wants me to move. I've just gotten in town, and I'd rather stay here a while."

Dammit, she needed a carpenter. She needed a whole crew, with the lack of good help around here these days, and ordinarily, would hire the man on the spot. But he didn't look like a carpenter either.

"How do you fare working in hundred-degree heat?" She wanted to scare him off.

"No problem."

"What do you know about roofing?"

"That it's hot work."

"Can you shingle at all?"

"I can swing a hammer."

"We use nail guns now, Mr. Langley," she wryly told him.

"I'm good with guns."

Jaymee shivered slightly at his voice. Self-assured and deceptively potent, like good brandy, it had the same heated effect on her stomach. She sighed inwardly. She was shorthanded, having fired Rich and Chuck yesterday. She couldn't afford to be picky. Against her better judgment, she asked, "When can you start?"

"Now."

She arched a brow at him. "You need tools first," she told him, then looked down at his feet, "and you have on the wrong kind of shoes."

Nicholas Langley looked down and tapped one hiking shoe on the dusty ground. "What's wrong with them?"

"The sole will mark and scuff up the shingles," Jaymee explained. "You need soft sole rubber, preferably canvas shoes. Like these." She lifted her leg up, so he could see her shoes.

"OK." His eyes traveled from her shoes up her calf and then her thigh. She hastily put her foot down.

"Why don't you start in the morning?" she suggested. "Bring your tools here. We start around eight. I can't pay you shingling rate until I see what you're capable of doing. The labor rate isn't much but once you can lay shingles fast, you get paid by the square."

"Fine." The man wasn't much of a talker, she concluded. "Mind if I hang around and watch for a bit?"

"Be my guest," she answered, and extended a hand. "Nice meeting you."

She hoped that Nick Langley wouldn't return in the morning. Most of them didn't. Roofing wasn't exactly a much sought-after job.

His grip was firm and his palm felt surprisingly hard. She eyed him thoughtfully. Well, maybe her would-be new laborer could work after all. Those were the calluses of an outdoor man. And those muscles must come from somewhere.

She couldn't help it. A soft sigh of appreciation escaped her lips as she watched him turn around and wander off, showing her the other side of his too-good-to-be-true anatomy. Abruptly, she returned to the chore of getting ready. The man was no ordinary laborer, that was for sure. That strange tingling feeling bothered her again, and she tried to figure out what it was about Nicholas Langley that was making her nervous.

"Just an ordinary man," she muttered very softly.

\*

Leaning against a tree, the man known as Killian watched the woman on the roof with hooded eyes. "Nick" was one of his many identities, usually when he was playing drifter or portraying an easy-going front. The lady had taken him by surprise in more ways than one, something that very rarely happened. Besides the obvious, she was also projecting an energetic stillness that was intriguing. He had been deliberately laid-back and unassuming, and yet her awareness of him was palpable, to the point of nervousness. Why was he making her nervous?

He wondered what made her choose to be, of all things, a roofer. She didn't seem strong enough for such hard work. He liked the gentle tone of her voice when she spoke, a far cry from the crew from the old days when he worked in construction.

Not that there was anything wrong with being a roofer, he thought, studying her nimble movements as she moved across the roof. She obviously knew her job very well, barely pausing while she laid the shingles in diagonal fashion, the nail gun flashing in the sun as it moved across the shingle in rapid rat-tat-tat.

The sun beat down relentlessly, and Nick made a note to remember to bring along a cooler for his new job in the morning. A corner of his mouth quirked up in amusement. He remembered the way she had looked at him when she questioned his experience. It was easy to read her mind. Jay, the boss lady, didn't want him to work for her. It was in the tone of her voice, the hopeful look in her eyes that he would reconsider the heat and change his mind to go seek a better job.

He knew that she could tell he wasn't a construction worker. Those quick dark eyes of hers had settled for a long moment on his hands and the slight wrinkle of her nose betrayed her certainty. He glanced down at his hands and shoved them into his jeans pockets. He was getting careless. His nails were too clean.

Nick continued eyeing the woman on the roof as he contemplated his next move. He needed money to survive and construction was the easiest way to get quick cash in this town. He couldn't go for the higher skills, or they would start asking for past employment history and too much information. His safest bet was as cheap labor to cover expenses for another month or two. There were plenty of transients in Florida and he wouldn't rouse anyone's interest.

Jay turned around when she reached the peak of the roof, and her lycra-clad behind showed off a decidedly shapely derriere as she finished nailing the top row. Nick's eyes narrowed a fraction. She was going to be trouble. Her ass, for one thing, roused his interest. Very much.

But he hadn't the time to explore all the possibilities, not when he was still in the dark as to what had happened after he'd bailed out from his boat before it exploded. He needed to find out whether he was still thought to be alive, needed to know who was out for his blood. Being unsure of the situation, he hadn't withdrawn any cash or used his credit cards; he couldn't successfully evade by leaving a trail of recorded cash. So he had made do with what he had; he had taken his hidden Jeep and drove inland.

But it was time to get in touch with one or two in his unit. He needed a computer and a phone for a few days. His eyes became slits in the bright sunlight. No, he hadn't the time to see what made Jay the boss lady tick. He needed to figure out whether someone inside had betrayed his team before he went back in. He shifted his weight from one foot to the other. He supposed he could waste a few more minutes watching that cute little ass at work.

*

It was past dinnertime when Jaymee got home. The house was a mess. Taking off her shoes and socks, she strode into the kitchen, and ignoring the dirty dishes, she poured herself a glass of juice. From the window above the kitchen sink, she could see the sun disappearing behind the tall pines on the other side of the lake, giving the water a final quick shimmer for the day. The grass needed mowing, she noted, arching her back muscles tiredly.

"You didn't call to let me know whether you were going to be late," a voice said from behind her. "There's a sandwich in the fridge."

"Thanks," Jaymee said, turning around to look at her father. "You could have washed the dishes, you know."

He shrugged, sitting at the kitchen table. "Didn't feel like it." He took a swallow from the long-necked bottle in his wrinkled work-worn hand.

He probably didn't feel anything at all. "How many beers did you have today, Dad?" She sat down on the other chair at the table. "You're going to give yourself another stroke."

"That would make you happy, wouldn't it?" he asked, and coughed hard. "Then you could just up and go."

It was fortunate that she also couldn't feel a damn thing, she thought, as she studied the man who sat there carelessly drinking himself into oblivion. Very little could hurt her these days.

"It's been eight years," she quietly reminded him, "and I've almost gotten your business back in the black. It would be a shame, don't you think, to die on me when I'm just about to finish paying off every dime I owe you?"

"Damn right," her father agreed. "My daddy always taught us to pay for our mistakes, and that's how things are done. Your bad judgment near destroyed the business my daddy and I built, girl, and don't you forget it."

"My bad judgment," Jaymee countered, emphasizing through clenched teeth, her face a frozen mask, "was foisted on me by you. You used to like him, remember? Enough to encourage him to come after me."

"Don't you go putting blame of your mistakes on me," the older man exclaimed, then started to wheeze again. When the coughing subsided, he continued, "You liked his pretty face and damn near gave away the business with your shenanigans. Killed your ma. Left me unable to work."

She wasn't in the mood to defend herself. She had grown immune to her father's brand of punishment in the past eight years. And perhaps she was partly guilty for some of the bad luck that had fallen on the Barrows, and that was why she had slaved for eight years. To pay her debts for past mistakes, she repeated her father's litany. It wouldn't be too long now — two years, maybe sooner — now that she had gotten the Hidden Hills subdivision account, and the business would be in the clear again. Then she could leave.

Finishing her drink, Jaymee got up and turned the water on at the sink, clanking the dirty dishes loud enough to drown out the drunken accusations behind her. She was simply not in the mood to go on being the scapegoat. Maybe it was because she was so near to her goal that she was losing her usual calm acceptance of her father's anger. A year and a half, she promised herself. If she pushed, she would be free in a year and a half. The Hidden Hills subdivision account had fallen into her lap like a sudden lottery windfall, and with Excel Construction promising her at least three houses a week, twenty thousand dollars as projected profit wasn't too difficult a goal.

She frowned at the memory of firing Chuck and Rich. She couldn't afford to let them go, but they were simply doing shoddy work these days, hoping that she didn't notice. Catching them "undernailing" the shingles was the last straw. With the strict regulations after the hurricanes these days, a failed inspection for improper nailing could cost her thousands of dollars in fines. So now she was two men short and one house behind. Then she remembered Mr. Roofer Wannabe. How could she have forgotten, when he had spent the better part of the day following her every move? She couldn't forget those eyes. The incredible long lashes. The easy smile with the knowing eyes, the kind that she usually avoided meeting because she knew what they did to a woman's logic.

Nicholas Langley. Jaymee silently mouthed his name as she piled the dishes into the dishwasher. She wondered how long he would last. Wannabes like him usually lasted a day, three at the most. They weren't interested in sweating it out in this kind of weather for so little money, so they were gone after the first paycheck.

Nothing like roofing to equalize all men, she thought, a slight grin forming on her lips. They could be beach bums, young surfer boys, college kids on vacation, or like this Langley, transient workers. However, once she put them through the routine of walking up and down a six/twelve pitched roof on their knees for a couple of days, they all usually made their exits in the same way—in a big hurry. And sometimes, limping, she added, her grin becoming wider.

She was quite sure that Mr. Langley was going to show up for the first day. While he'd been studying her, she'd also been keeping him within sight all day, and it hadn't escaped her notice when he'd picked up a shingle wrapper from the ground and took it with him when he left. She had grinned then too, hiding it under the shadows of her wide-brimmed cap. Mr.

Langley was going to read the instructions off the wrapper on how to lay shingles. Somehow, that pleased her. At least, the man was trying.

After wiping her hands dry, Jaymee proceeded to get the vacuum cleaner out of the closet and dragged it into the living room, leaving her father at the kitchen table.

"Aren't you going to eat?" he called after her.

She plugged the cord in and turned the machine on, the high screechy sound keeping out his voice. If Mr. Langley was willing to learn, she concluded as she pushed the vacuum back and forth, then she supposed she should give him a chance. Even if he meant trouble.

*

Nick showed up for work the next day, looking just as good as he did the day before. Jaymee wrinkled her nose. Well, at least he had the sense to keep his pants on, she noted with morose resignation, as she looked at her new helper. He had gotten out of his Jeep with the lazy grace of a prowling animal on the hunt. The hair on the back of her neck had stood up the instant his eyes met hers and he gave her a knowing, careless smile.

Uh-oh. That was what her warning system had been trying to tell her all yesterday. She should have known, she privately groaned. With those blue-gray eyes, why hadn't she paid attention? Wolf. She had seen his kind before.

The temperature was already in the mid-eighties, even at that early hour, and the wet sheen of perspiration gleaming off his exposed skin made her suddenly aware of how much skin and muscle there was on Nicholas Langley. He was wearing one of those muscle tank tops, revealing wide shoulders that rounded off into beautifully sculpted arms. A light sprinkling of black hair temptingly beckoned above the low neckline. Her eyes moved lower, helplessly drawn to the length of him, taking in the long, long legs to his feet. Like she'd called it. Hot. And getting hotter.

It didn't help that he stood there like some cadet under inspection. He was, she realized, mocking her. It was there in those wolf eyes, with their strange, intense light gleaming at her.

"Are the shoes right?" he inquired politely.

She hadn't missed the new shoes. "Show me the bottom," she said.

"The bottom of my shoes?" he asked, as if to make sure.

Jaymee glanced up at him sharply and saw that the gleam in his eyes was now full-fledged laughter. Her chin jutted up. "Yes," she told him in her firmest tone, and hastily stepped back when he moved unexpectedly in her direction, bumping into the tailgate of her truck. To her dismay, he put a hand right next to her, braced his weight on it, and obediently lifted up a foot for her inspection.

If she moved six inches forward, she would be up against his chest. Her senses were on overload, amped-up and uncomfortable. She didn't like her reaction at all, not one bit. She didn't like how he had managed to make her feel small and helpless. Didn't like that she noticed the way the muscles rippled in his forearm that was bearing his weight. Didn't like the delicious scent of male and cologne that crowded her mind like an instant logic-erasing spell. Hated, hated, those blue-gray eyes giving her their own lazy perusal.

"Does it look good to you?" he asked, still polite.

She was sure that they weren't talking about the same thing, but Jaymee hadn't stayed unattached at the advanced age of thirty without good reason. She knew men and all their rotten little games, and had been given an excellent lesson in the particular area of wolves in sheep clothing. She considered that the one main important point under the topic of Past Experience in her resume toward singular living.

Breathing out easily, she replied, "Looking good won't help you, Langley, when you're slip-sliding off a roof." She gave a brisk nod. He smelled too damn good for a roofer. Time to make him sweat. "You can put your foot back down. Your shoes look fine. You can start by taking the toolboxes and air hoses up onto the roof."

It wasn't easy to sound businesslike when she was talking to an expanse of male chest, but she didn't think leaning back and looking up would give her any advantage. Moving sideways, she eased out of the warmth of his male body and made her escape with a pretended air of looking busy.

Nick followed the sway of those enticing hips for one moment longer before turning to look into the back of the truck. If he weren't careful, he was going to get himself fired before he'd even started on his new job. He didn't know why he took such perverse delight in trying to rile up Jay Barrows, but the deliberate cool and distant attitude of hers was like an itch just out of reach.

Hoisting three coiled air hoses onto one shoulder, he picked up a box of nails under his free arm, his mind still on his new boss. She might not know it, but Jay Barrows affected him too. He'd watched her a long time yesterday. She was cool as the ocean breeze in the summer heat, working with silent determination while others wiped away their sweat, and seemed to be all business, rarely smiling. However, Nick had been trained to look for the weak links in his opponent's armor; it was his job to break in, examine, and leave his mark.

Erase, replace, destroy. That was his core job in his unit. There were nine of them, and each was programmed in one specialty, although essentially, they had been trained for one thing.

Nick put that subject out of his mind for now. He would worry about getting his hands on a computer later. Right now, he had to concentrate on his newly-chosen line of work. After reading the instructions on the shingle wrapper he'd picked up the day before, he now had a basic understanding of how to install shingles on a roof, but suspected that on-the-job training was very different from mere words written by some technical writer. He, the Programmer, should know that.

And he was proven right.

A few hours later, perspiration pouring down his face, stinging his eyes, his tank top drenched into a useless rag, he marveled at the inhuman coolness of his boss. The other roofers, Dicker and Lucky, were taking a cigarette break, sitting on top of several bundles of shingles, but Jay Barrows was methodically laying her shingles one after another, moving in a crab-like manner across the roof.

His current duty was to tear open a bundle of shingles and put several within her reach all the way up the roof, so that she didn't have to stop to get the shingles herself. She had given him a utility knife with a hooked blade, showing him how to cut "starters" out of the fiberglass shingles for each row.

She was a good teacher. Instead of explaining and instructing in the sweltering heat, she went straight to work, leaving it up to him to watch her, pointing out ways to do things quicker in short sentences. Too much explanation usually distracted from physical work and roofing, he quickly found out, was all about working efficiently and constantly.

The starter shingles went on first, over the drip edge, then the first course, six inches or so off the left side. Each time, her nail gun flew over the shingles with a precision and speed that belied the difficulty of being in such a cramped and awkward position while wielding the tool attached to the air hose. All in humidity-drenched hundred-degree heat.

"We break for lunch in half an hour," Jaymee said, as she continued laying shingles without looking up. "You can stay on the site or go to a diner. Up to you."

"What do you do?"

She gave him a brief glance, then resumed nailing. "I go to a diner. It's good to get out of the heat."

The heat had turned her ponytail into a mass of unruly curls, and Nick felt the urge to run his fingers through them, to feel what those little corkscrews were like.

"Can I come along? I'm still quite lost around town." It was a small lie, but he wanted to see that delectable mouth chewing on food.

Jaymee hesitated. It would be ungracious to refuse. "Sure," she told him, and changed the subject. "Get me a lead boot for the plumbing pipe from that box, will you?"

He was a good worker, she thought. He hadn't complained about the heat yet, and followed every order without question, an essential requirement while roofing and dying of thirst. The latter was somehow surprising to her, as he didn't strike her as someone who took orders easily. It was there behind that lazy grace—a man who did things his way—and she had the feeling that he was merely biding his time.

For what, she hadn't the faintest idea, but one thing was certain. Nicholas Langley definitely had never been a construction worker. Why was he working as a laborer? There were only a few reasons people picked her kind of work. They were uneducated, or addicted to drugs and thus couldn't find a steady job, or they started really young and had made this their livelihood, or they were running from the law. The first three reasons didn't fit. Nick Langley appeared educated and his body certainly didn't look abused. He didn't look like some roofing apprentice, since he was probably a few years older than she was, which left one last alternative theory.

Somehow, he didn't fit the description of a hardened criminal either, but Jaymee had seen them come and go enough these past years to know not to be surprised. Perhaps Langley was a criminal. That would make perfect sense, since she, Jaymee Barrows, was attracted to the criminally inclined, and would do well to remember her debts from that one mistake.

Nick lifted a brow when she finally waved him to stop, stood up and stretched. "Lunch?" he asked hopefully. He was getting hungry.

"Lunch," she agreed, then disengaged the nail gun from the hose. She pulled out the foam plugs that protected her hearing.

"I need to get some of those," Nick remarked.

Jaymee smiled. More proof that he wasn't in construction. Roofers rarely bothered about hearing protection in Florida. Most of them were partially deaf by the time they turned forty.

"I have some extra ones. I'll give them to you after lunch." She walked to the ladder leaning against the roof and turned to the other two roofers. "Coming to lunch, Dicker?"

"Nah, I'm going to stay here. Brought my own today."

"We'll be here when you get back," the other man said.

"OK. I have to go pick up some more roofing cement, so I'll probably take longer today," Jaymee told them. "Make sure you cut the valleys before the sun heats them too long. The last time we left them till the end, the whole side of the white roof had tar stains, and the builder complained."

"OK, boss."

Nick watched with interest when Jay pulled off her tee-shirt after she got down from the roof, displaying a colorful bikini. She went to the tap on the side of the house and sluiced her body with water to cool off, wiping herself with the shirt. Now that was a great idea. He proceeded to take off his tank top and did the same, putting his head under the gush of water as well. That felt wonderful, cleaning off the dust and the sticky sweat.

Jaymee swallowed hard. She shouldn't be looking, but God, the man was nothing but sleek muscles. His body was lean and hard, the same dusting of fine dark hair arrowing down to an "outie" belly button, just above the top of his jeans.

"Maybe it would be better if I wore shorts tomorrow," Nick interrupted her wayward imagination.

Jaymee blinked. Shorts. Meaning naked thighs and calves. Shaking her head, she said, "You'll regret it. The fiberglass shingles'll cut up your knees in no time, and it'll also burn you every time you kneel down. Remember, the shingles are baking in the sun."

Nick nodded. He should know that by now. Every time he held on to one too long, the heat had burned his fingertips. No wonder she wore gloves. She, he noted, was golden all over, at least where he could see. There wasn't an ounce of fat on her, and that scrap of cloth she had on right now barely covered unexpectedly full breasts. She wasn't shy about walking on the job site like that, obliviously passing the other men who were looking at her like they would like her for lunch.

As far as he could tell, she was unmarried and unattached. Perhaps she was looking for a man. His eyes narrowed a fraction. No. She hadn't sent any such signals to any of the men she'd talked to all morning. She had been serious and totally businesslike. Jay Barrows was obviously unaware of any male attention, except for his. He hadn't missed the heat that showed up in her lively eyes now and then when she looked at him, which was often, heat that would disappear as quickly as it flared up. She was fighting it, and for some reason, it made him want to add fuel to that fire.

Donning a fresh tee-shirt, Jaymee beckoned to him to climb into her truck. "Don't you have another shirt to wear?"

"It'll dry in the sun," Nick said, shrugging. Jaymee sighed, then pulled another shirt out from behind her seat. She threw it onto his lap. "I doubt your shirt would fit," he wryly commented, indicating her smaller size.

"All my tees are in large and extra large sizes," she countered, starting up the truck. "Unless you're a three hundred-pound football player, you'll fit."

"Why the large size?" It fit fine, although the printed message—'I'm woman. I'm strong. I'm tired.'—didn't.

"Comfort. I like my clothes loose about me." She looked at the message emblazoned across his chest and laughed in surprised amusement. "I'm sorry. That's the only clean shirt I have left."

Nick liked the sound of her laughter. It was a low bubbly chuckle, like a child's. "I hope you aren't inviting other workers to lunch," he said. "I hate to declare that 'I am woman' at first introduction." The dimples appearing in her cheeks were captivating. He wanted to make her smile like that again. "Where are we going?"

"We're going to Hungry Boys," Jaymee announced, still grinning, "a great diner. Full of macho men at lunch. You'll like it. Of course," she added considerately, giving him a sidelong glance, "you might be too tired—"

He looked down at his shirt again. "It all depends," he said lightly.

Dangerous ground, she told herself. She endeavored to change the subject. "So, Langley, where were you before you arrived here?"

"Nick."

"Hmm?"

"Call me Nick. Or Nicholas, if you like."

"OK, Nicholas."

Interesting. She didn't choose Nick, like most people would. "Is Jay your real name?"

"No." She frowned. Maybe he didn't want her to know anything about him. "And you're changing the subject."

"What is it?"

Two could play at being obtuse. "What, you mean the subject?"

"You know perfectly well that I was asking about your real name." The thread of mockery in his voice was unmistakable. "Is it a roofing secret?"

"A roofing secret?" She was beginning to enjoy bantering with him.

"Yeah, like why not cutting the valleys would leave stains on the roof," Nick replied.

Jay pulled into the parking lot of Hungry Boys. She got out and rolled up the window. "If you leave the valley uncut in the summer," she explained, "the sun melts the tar strip on the underside of the shingle that laps onto the roof."

"Ah, I get it. The sun bakes it and the tar sticks on the roof, staining it." He locked up his side of the truck and fell in stride with her.

"Strong, as well as smart," Jaymee quipped. "The men are going to love you in there."

"Then I'm going to have to place myself in your care," he calmly retorted. "I can't fight them off all by myself."

Somehow, she had the impression that he wouldn't have any problems fighting off anyone, male or female. At the entrance, she held out a protective hand, a grave expression on her face.

"Walk behind me then, Nicholas. The best way to ward off unwanted attention is to let them know you belong to me."

She strode in through the doors without a backward glance.

## Chapter Two

Stupid, stupid, stupid. What the hell made her say that?

Hungry Boys was its usual crowded noon business. Jaymee liked it there—the food was a disgustingly generous portion for a decent price and just the way she liked it, with no thought for one's health. And the desserts would defeat the most voracious appetite.

They both sat at the counter. Two tall glasses of iced tea immediately appeared in front of them and the waitress patiently waited as they drained them of the sweet liquid.

"Thanks, Mindy." Jaymee smiled. "You're an angel."

Mindy, a tall platinum blond with bold eyes, refilled the glasses. "I'm the angel among the animals," she acknowledged, grinning back, then slid a long look at Nick. "And what type of animal is he?"

Jaymee chose to ignore the question. "What's the special today?"

Her friend wasn't the type to back away when something caught her interest. Mindy turned to Nick, jutting out her generous bosom. "Do you want to have the special today? It's definitely for a hungry boy."

Jaymee sighed. She recognized that particular look. Mindy was going to have her claws in her new worker and no one was going to stand in the way. Somehow, the idea didn't please her, but before she could say anything, Nick drawled, "I'll take what the boss is having."

Mindy's eyes narrowed. "The boss, huh?" she scoffed at Jaymee. "Baked chicken and vegetables. Chicken rice soup."

"I'll take it," Jaymee told her.

"And you, sweetheart?" Mindy's bright red lips pouted prettily. Jaymee rolled her eyes.

"Sounds good," answered Nick, returning an easy smile, amusement lacing his low, gravelly voice.

Mindy scribbled the order down and handed a straw to Jaymee, poking it right under her nose. "Looks good too, girlfriend," she said loudly, then disappeared.

She allowed the embarrassed silence to hang as long as she could, then finally mumbled, "Sorry, Mindy is just a joker."

The last thing she wanted was for him to think that she was after him.

"That's OK. After all," he solemnly reminded her, "I needed to establish that I belonged to you."

Her tan couldn't hide the deep blush staining her cheeks. She shouldn't have joked with him. Now he was too familiar with her, and that was always a no-no in her book about wolves. She decided to change the subject back to him again.

"Tell me, what exactly do you do? I know it's not construction." She looked at those elegant hands. If not for the calluses, they could have been a surgeon's hands, with those long artistic fingers that made her look down forlornly at her own short ones.

"I do all kinds of things," Nick answered. "It all depends on where I am." He wasn't technically lying.

Jaymee took a sip of her tea. He was hiding something, and must have been doing it for some time, sliding easily out of answering questions with hardly a pause. She didn't want to pry, rarely cared about her workers' sordid pasts, but his deliberate evasions challenged her. It had been too long since she had been so intrigued.

"What sort of things?" she probed. "And where were you when you were doing them?"

Nick's slate-colored eyes were a few degrees cooler as he contemplated her. "I survive," he said, quietly, remembering the fiery explosion that nearly killed him. He grimly wondered about the others. Had their boats blown up too? "I always survive, no matter where I am."

Before she could push further, the food arrived, all at once—soup, meal, vegetables, potatoes. Mindy arranged the dishes in front of them. "Anything else?" she asked.

"No, thanks, Min," Jaymee said, digging into her food.

"You eat too much," observed the waitress.

"I'm a hungry woman," retorted Jaymee, slurping up her soup.

Mindy's eyes twinkled back at her. Leaning forward, she jerked her head meaningfully in Nick's direction and stage-whispered, "You're hungry for the wrong thing."

Jaymee choked on her soup. Nick obligingly patted her on the back. To her relief, the waitress left them alone for the rest of the meal, only coming back to refill the glasses with iced tea, casting obvious glances at Nick. Jaymee ignored her and concentrated on eating her lunch in a hurry to avoid another comment from her friend.

Nick ate quietly, studying the woman next to him. That temporarily put off her questions. She was persistent when she decided on something, and downright as good at evading questions as he was. She sidestepped any gestures to get closer to her like a seasoned defensive tackle. It was fear that lurked in her eyes whenever he manipulated their conversation off safe topics. It was the kind of wariness that was very seductive to a man like him, who made it his business to find out what put fear in the opposition.

It wasn't just that obstinate touch-me-not façade she put up that attracted him. He wasn't sure what it was about her that made him want to find out more. He had a weakness for tall, leggy blondes, and she definitely didn't fit that description, but every time she threw him one her wide-eyed challenging looks, his body tightened up in male response.

She wasn't exactly beautiful. Her eyes were small and slightly tilted at the corners, but they were bright and inquisitive like a bird's. A strange muddy color, sometimes hazel, sometimes almost green. She had an expressive nose that she wrinkled whenever she was thinking, and a willful pouty mouth, the kind that belonged to a woman used to getting her own way. Her hair, that unruly mop that was always secured behind her, was thick and irresistibly unmanageable. Just like the owner. All willful and unmanageable passion held back by a dirty, frayed ribbon. He wondered what it would be like to snap that ribbon, and let loose all those glorious emotions that she was desperately keeping under control. It was that edgy wariness that added fuel to this strange urge growing in him—to go after and pounce. He blinked at the image those words brought up, recalling quite easily the toned body under the baggy tee-shirt and the surprising swell of her breasts.

Jay Barrows was a contradiction in demeanor and attitude. Her body language was carefully asexual. Everything about her was concentrated on being efficient and professional. Yet he still noticed those little feminine things about her—the way she took off her shirt to clean herself, like any typical woman would after a hot workout, the way she moved, and most telling of all, definitely the way she kept him at a distance. Again, he felt the urge to find out what made her tick.

They were almost done with their meal when someone came to stand between them at the counter. "How are you supposed to make money wasting time sitting on your butt?" The voice was slightly slurred.

Jaymee stiffened and slowly whirled her stool around to face the intruder. Nick looked at the weather-beaten face with the bloodshot eyes. The telltale odor betrayed the old man's condition, even though he appeared steady enough, glaring down at Jaymee.

"I'm having lunch," Jaymee calmly stated the obvious.

"You can't eat at the job? Do you think you can get work done driving around town in that truck?" the man sneered. Nick considered interrupting, but Jay's reaction stopped him. Somehow, he knew that she wouldn't just take that kind of talk from anyone. Therefore, this older man must be—what, a relative? When Jay still didn't say anything, the old man continued, "And what is this about firing Chuck and Rich? They've been working for me since you were still Miss High and Mighty College Student. How are you going to get work done shorthanded?"

"I was wondering when you'd show up. I have a few errands to run and I felt like eating here," she finally cut into the tirade. "As for firing Chuck and Rich, it's none of your damned business. Everything's taken care of."

"It's my business and don't you forget it, Jaymee girl!"

Jaymee, Nick repeated silently. Jaymee Barrows.

"You need to go home, Dad," Jaymee quietly said.

"Don't talk down to me!" His voice was higher now, attracting attention.

Nick came to a decision. "Come on, let's go," he said, standing up.

Jaymee knew that any minute now, her father was going to go into one of his rants. She hadn't told him about her decision to fire the old-timers precisely to avoid this. She nodded and caught Mindy's quick eyes.

"Go, sweetie. I'll put it on the tab," Mindy called from the other end of the counter. She then turned to glare at Jaymee's father, but her voice was sweet. "Want something to eat, Bob? Coffee, perhaps?"

Jaymee didn't wait for his reply as she walked out, after leaving a tip. She knew her father well; he wasn't done yet. She suspected that those two former workers had probably shared a couple of drinks with him and talked about the past, and that usually led to more drinking and bitter memories. Suddenly, the bright sunshine outside the diner felt like hell on earth. She wondered what her new help was thinking as he walked silently beside her.

"Don't you walk off like you own the business, Jaymee Barrows!" Bob Barrows called at them, a little out of breath. He stopped in front of the blue truck and coughed long and painfully. "I have a right," he said, in between horrible wracking noises.

Jaymee sighed. "Go home, Dad. We'll talk later, all right?" She gentled her voice. Sometimes that worked. "I'm going to the supply place to pick some materials up, then I'll be back at work. You just rest up and don't worry about the business."

Bob snorted. "Don't worry? You destroyed the business once. I'm going to keep an eye on you so you don't do it again." He finally caught sight of Nick standing by. "Who's this?"

"He's the new help." She didn't bother to introduce Nick.

"I get the picture now. A pretty face." Bob's face turned purplish with anger. "You let a pretty face take the place of two valued workers. You're going to ruin my business, you are."

He walked threateningly toward Jaymee, only to be blocked by Nick's six-foot plus body. "Nice to meet you, Mr. Barrows," stated Nick, pleasantly.

Bob Barrows looked up at the tall man, and undaunted, poked a finger into Nick's chest. "You can't lie to me, boy. You ain't nothing but a distraction for my daughter. I can tell you ain't even a worker, and she has work to do. She promised me! She promised to…"

"Dad!" Jaymee's voice was arctic in spite of the melting heat, cutting off whatever Bob was going to reveal. "I'm getting into the truck and driving off now. If you don't go home, I'll be late for work. Do you understand me?"

That seemed to get the old man's attention. "Work. Yes, work. Go to work," he muttered and turned away. "You just keep working, Jaymee, and pay the debts."

"Should he be driving?" Nick asked, as he got into Jaymee's truck.

"He drove here. He can drive back," she bitterly replied, and started the truck. She was mortified. Everybody in town knew about the Barrows' story, so it wasn't like it was a big secret, but somehow, she didn't want Nick Langley to know. She didn't want those see-too-much eyes to look at her with pity. Suddenly, she wished she could just forget the sense of duty that had forced her to endure her father's bitterness.

Nick could feel the ice forming back around her, that armor that made her so machine-like at work, but could see the hurt in her hazel eyes and in the slight trembling of her hand as she shifted gears.

"Want to talk about it?" he invited.

"None of your business, Langley," snapped Jaymee, her eyes on the road. Then she sighed. "I'm sorry my father was rude to you. He isn't well."

"Is that the reason he thinks you're ruining his business?" He knew that he was treading on forbidden territory, but for some reason, Jaymee Barrows was fast becoming more than a passing interest. Besides, one curious cross-examination deserved another.

She braked a little too hard at the red light. Tossing her head back, she flashed angry eyes at him. He noted that they were green now.

"Look, leave the subject alone," she grated, her voice slow and even. "It has nothing to do with you. You just started a job. Do it right, and I'll pay you well, Langley."

"It doesn't hurt to have a friendly ear sometimes," he casually commented.

"I don't need anything friendly from you. Everything is under control. You work. I pay. The work gets done. Badabing, badaboom. Get it?" The honk from behind told her that the light had changed back to green, and she cursed before accelerating jerkily.

Her fury was an interesting contrast to the cool and controlled woman with whom he'd been working all morning.

"Nothing is ever so simple," he pressed on, wanting to add fuel to the fire, wanting to push her.

Jaymee felt like screaming. She wanted to be alone, to calm down, but every sentence the man beside her uttered seemed to rile her further. He was just trying to be friendly and concerned, a small voice reasoned, but that made her even more furious. She pulled into the parking lot at the supply warehouse, tires squealing.

"What are you, a psychologist out of a job?" she lashed out. "Do you think it fun to try to analyze and understand me from a mere conversation? What, you're so bored, you have to push and probe and pretend to make psychobabble conclusions?"

She was a lot closer to the truth than she realized, Nick thought. When under extreme danger, like disengaging an explosive, he liked to relieve the pressure by analyzing it. Sometimes, it added to the "fun." His team sometimes didn't agree. Unable to help himself, he grinned.

"Yeah," he admitted, not getting out of the truck.

Jaymee stared at his lips. She watched the crooked wolfish smile slowly appearing on his lips. Confident. Cocksure. Somewhere in her mind, a warning siren started. She'd seen that smile before on another male face, one she'd thought she—

"Yeah, what?" she demanded, but she kept staring at that smile.

"Yeah, I want to probe and push." He paused and moved closer, his body heat surrounding her, trapping her like invisible bands of steel. His head dipped and, pausing a few inches from her upturned face, he added, "I want to see what turns Jay Barrows into Jaymee Barrows."

He had found her out. All thought disappeared when his head descended. She sat still as his lips touched hers, her heart roaring like a speeding train. She was prepared to fight and resist, but his lips were gentle against hers, soft and persuasive.

Nick didn't deepen the kiss, only slanted his head for more access into her sweet mouth. It was an impulse that he chose not to resist. He didn't know why he felt the need to comfort her as well as hold her, but she drew a strange reaction from him. Her response was making promises to him that he knew she wasn't consciously giving. There was an enticing innocence about the way she sat there and kissed him back, and he knew, there and then, with absolute certainty that he was going to take Jaymee Barrows to bed sooner or later.

Later. After he'd straightened out some things.

He reluctantly lifted his head, his breathing uneven. He smiled into eyes so slumberous that he wanted to start kissing her again. "Better?" he asked.

Jaymee could only stare back at him. She hadn't been kissed in—God—years. Her last date was exactly a year and three months ago, a blind arrangement forced on her by Mindy, an awkward, uncomfortable experience that she vowed she'd never repeat. She'd decided then that she could live without dating until she got her life straightened out, and here she was, kissing a stranger. And probably a criminal on the lam.

"I ought to fire you," she told him. It was difficult to sound boss-like when one's voice sounded breathy and aroused.

Nick cocked his head, those long eyelashes unbelievably sexy as he watched her through half-closed eyes. "You shouldn't. You're shorthanded," he reminded her.

That was like a wake-up call. She had a house to finish. "It won't matter if we both die of heat stroke in this truck," she retorted with a nonchalance she didn't feel. "Come on, I've got to get busy."

She didn't let him get through her armor again that day, and Nick was wise enough not to try. She kept the atmosphere thoroughly businesslike, giving him chores that had him climbing up and down the ladder. As the day ended, she let him do a couple of the last rows of shingles, showing him how to cut the rake of the roof. The other two roofers left at four, as most construction workers did, but Jaymee Barrows, he discovered, was either a workaholic or a woman on a mission. She kept on working till almost six. He stayed on, even after she told him that he could leave any time. She didn't object.

Jaymee had to get the house done, no matter how late it would be when she finished. She was one roof behind, and couldn't put off the builder from insulating it tomorrow. Used to working past normal working hours alone, she was pleasantly surprised to find her new help willing to stay on. Of course, this was just day one. He could be gone after a few days of this.

With focused effort, she tried to keep the memory of his lips on hers at bay. That kiss unnerved her more than the confrontation with her father. She had thought herself quite able to control her emotions after eight years of practice, but in less than ten hours, this stranger had managed to get under her shield where she sometimes yearned to be touched.

Instantaneously, she ruthlessly pounced on that admission. Yearn. Oh no, not yearn. Jaymee Barrows did not yearn for anything from a man. Ever. Especially from someone who looked like this man. He would be a mistake, her second mistake. The cost of her first one had been high—her father's health, her mother's death, and more than one hundred thousand dollars in the hole, courtesy of her father's business acumen. Nick Langley could cost her everything else.

Behind the dumpster, and out of sight, Jaymee touched her lips. He could cost her what she thought she had mended with super glue—her heart and her pride. She wasn't going to allow the past to repeat itself.

*

By the end of the week, on payday, Nick was feeling the soreness of previously unused muscles. He was a superb athlete, trained to swim for miles to escape enemy land, able to climb up cliffs to avoid being detected by dogs, and had undergone covert programs to shift physical and mental pain when tortured. However, a man's body, he admitted, wasn't created by the Almighty to squat and kneel for untold hours on end, dragging a tool attached to hundreds of feet of heavy air hoses. Especially, he added, a long, lanky body that had to bend more than normal to nail a shingle.

In that short week, he'd discovered that his kneecaps could protest with noisy complaints after a daily regimen of eight hours of being squashed into kneepads and being subjected to crawling like a toddler up a slope. The arches of his large feet, clad in soft-sole rubber, ached from the constant pressure of his weight pushed on the front. He imagined that those ancient Chinese women who bound their feet probably felt like this, as he ignored the pain and kept on laying shingles. The fingertips of his left hand were raw from constantly scraping against the fiberglass shingles as he pulled them apart to be nailed. And, his nose was sunburned. That was the most difficult part, ignoring the heat and continuing to work with speed as the day got hotter and hotter.

His boss, the cool Jay Barrows, was totally unaffected by the weather. She watched over him like a hawk, spotting every mistake he made. She was a tyrant, a pint-size general, approaching each roof like a battle in a great war. After only four days, Nick had a healthy respect for her. She might look tiny next to him and could barely carry a five-gallon can of roof cement across the length of the roof, but the lady could outwork every man around her, with a horse thrown in for good measure.

She had been so very polite all week, except that one time he messed up and walked all over the shingles with tar under his shoes. He had trekked black prints up a whole side of the roof's hip before she noticed, and the colorful language she'd used while tearing off the whole row of shingles would have put his fellow operatives to shame. He still grinned at the memory. Wouldn't Command just love to see a tape of one of their top commandos standing meekly while being dressed down with heavy sarcasm by a barely five foot-two termagant?

The thought of Command sobered him. Getting paid tonight would give him some cash. It wouldn't be enough to buy cheap electronics and the hardware he needed, but it would be a start. He wished that he could just use his credit card and buy a damn laptop. He shrugged. If necessary, he would build a crude system, if he had to. He rejected the easy use of a phone, since phones could be traced, and he hadn't any control of the fiber optics without his usual toys. And emails would be monitored as well. His agency had a super-computer that would trace his exact location within minutes and right now, he didn't want to be found.

No, he would bide his time. Knowing Command, they would give him a reasonable amount of time before deciding that he was dead. Or before sending a tracker on his trail, he added, rubbing his jaw. Damn, he didn't like trackers, mean S.O.Bs who shot first and asked later.

The little house at the end of the dirt trail came into view as he followed Jay's earlier instructions. The property was a few acres, surrounded by a wooden fence. He could see some sort of a lake behind the house. Parking the Jeep next to the familiar blue truck, he slowly got out, looking around. Behind him, two other trucks pulled in. Dicker and Lucky were in one of the vehicles. Two other men got out of the other mud-splattered truck. Nick nodded at Dicker and Lucky.

"Hey, Langley," greeted Dicker. "Getting your first paycheck, huh?"

"Yeah." The two roofers didn't talk to him much, and he never encouraged them.

"How do you like roofing?" asked Lucky, lighting a cigarette. "The sun tough on you?"

"It's all right," Nick answered, taking in the two approaching strangers. They were, undoubtedly, roofers; they had tar all over their clothes. They nodded at him, but didn't seem very friendly.

"This is the new man we've been telling you about, Chuck," Dicker said, gesturing at Nick. "Nick, this is Chuck and that's Rich. They used to work for Jay just prior to you showing up."

Lucky's gap-toothed smile was positively wicked. "Yeah, you boys can forget about convincing Jay to give you another chance. Nick here replaced both of you."

The one named Chuck spat to one side. "Sure, that's for one week. How long do you think he's going to last?" He looked suspiciously at Nick. "You ain't no roofer, man. How long are you going to stick around?"

Nick shrugged.

"Not much of a talker, are you?"

"Oh, he talk," Lucky said, still grinning. "He talk fine with Jay. I think he's learning lots from Jay."

"Well, I just want my check for what she owes me," the other man, Rich, said. "Miss High and Mighty thinks she can do everything herself her way. She's welcomed to it."

They all walked up the trail toward the house. Nick followed along as they went the back way, instead of up the front porch. Dicker turned to him.

"Boss doesn't like us walking in the front with our dirty shoes all tarred up. Her office is at the back, next to the kitchen. That's where we get paid." He looked at Nick up and down. "Of course, you're all cleaned up regular, aren't you? Look at that, boys, no tar on him at all."

The four of them studied Nick like he was some alien. He returned their stares, unperturbed.

"He ain't no roofer," Chuck repeated. "She's going to call us back as soon as he's gone."

"Not if you keep leaving things half done, like you'd been doing," Lucky declared.

"She's just plain bitchy," said Chuck, and spat again. "We weren't doing nothing particularly wrong. We've been working for her daddy before she even knew how to hold a hammer, let alone swing it. Now she gone and fired us."

"Yeah, and just because she got to run the company doesn't mean she could just treat us like dirt," Rich agreed.

"Well, boys, she's the boss right now," Dicker told them.

"Well, Dickhead, I beg to differentiate from your opinion," retorted Chuck.

"Ha! Differentiate from your opinion," snorted Lucky. "You sound mighty educated with them big phrases, Chuckie. Now, if you can only remember to nail six nails in the shingles instead of two—"

"Shut up! Shut up, man!" Rich yelled, losing his temper. He was the one to keep an eye on, Nick decided.

Dicker climbed up the back porch steps. "You better keep it down now."

"What, is she afraid her daddy might hear? We already done told him she got rid of us and he wasn't too happy about that," Chuck sneered. "He told us that he would help us get our jobs back." He gave Nick a hard look. "What do you think of that, boy?"

Chuck wasn't that much older than Nick, probably by four or five years, with a balding pate and a beer belly protruding over his pants. "Surf rats. College smarty pants," he went on. "You all think you know everything, don't you?"

Nick leaned lazily against the banister. "Sounds to me like you two tried to cheat with some shoddy work," he drawled. It was easy to put two and two together from the other men's conversation and it was even easier to push these men's buttons. "I'd say that firing you was a justifiable action on her part, nothing dirty or bitchy about that."

"Justifiable action." Lucky sat down on the porch steps, his gap-toothed laugh coming out in hiccups. "I want to see you try to differentiate your opinion with Langley, Chuckie. Maybe you can give him some justifiable actions." He hugged his knees, laughing so hysterically even Dicker smiled.

Rich put a threatening hand on Lucky's head. "The only action you..."

"What's going on out there?" Jaymee's voice broke them apart. She was behind the screen door. "Rich, Chuck, if you want to collect your last check, I suggest you don't cause my porch any damage. Come on in and give me your bills. Be careful where you step, please. I just had the carpet cleaned in the office."

She pushed open the screened door, a scowl on her face. She was wearing shorts for once, and Nick got to appreciate her bare legs. They were shapely, toned from all the time she squatted down, and he noticed that they weren't as tanned as her arms, which made sense, since she was constantly in those long tight pants at work. Her bare feet revealed pretty pink toenails, which for some inexplicable reason, made his mouth water. You're losing it, boy-o, getting hot about painted toenails.

It wasn't that, he amended, as he entered the kitchen, a surprisingly large room. It was the woman herself who turned him on with the little unexpected displays of her feminine side. One moment she was tough as nails, throwing bundles of shingles around like they weighed nothing, then he would catch a whiff of the flowery perfume she wore. Another moment, she would ignore a cut as she kept on laying shingles, blood trickling unheeded down her arm, and then he would see her adjusting her bikini and rubbing suntan lotion over her arms and shoulders. Today, she had been covered in dust and dirt from climbing under the overhang of a dormer to pound down a nail, hair disheveled, face smeared, curses streaming from her lips, and now, she was soft and clean, delightfully dainty, wearing a very feminine flowery blouse. And God, such pretty, sweet, enticing painted toenails. She was driving him crazy.

Her study was a small room stacked with boxes and file cabinets. It smelled vaguely of her, as if she spent a lot of time there. A sofa was against one wall, and two of the roofers went to sit on it. The others pulled two of the kitchen chairs into the room. Jaymee walked to the desk by a big picture window and sat down—Nick froze in mid-step—in front of two computers.

"Sit down, Nick," she said, frowning when he just stood there.

Nick tore his gaze from the computers and looked around. He was too big to sit on the sofa with the two men, and there weren't any more chairs in the room.

Jaymee sighed and relinquished her big office chair. "Here, take this. I'll be moving around signing checks anyway." When he hesitated, she impatiently pounded the arm of the chair and ordered, "Sit! I'll sit on the desk if I have to."

Nick sank down into the large leather chair, softened from constant use. He immediately thought of her tight little ass sliding on and off it as she did her paperwork every night.

Jaymee picked up her checkbook and turned on one of the computers. "I'll pay you two first, Chuck and Rich, and will print out a record for you to keep. I'll send you all the appropriate forms at the end of the year."

"Didn't your daddy talk to you?" asked Chuck, a sullen expression on his face.

"He did," Jaymee answered, "and I said no."

"Where's he? I want to talk to him!" Rich loudly demanded.

"He isn't here," Jaymee informed him curtly, "and you were talking to the wrong person. I don't need your kind of work giving my business a bad name. Let's just get this done, Rich. Give me your bills and I'll sign you a check and a bonus."

The two men were angry, but they could see that they were wasting time. So they did what they were told, muttering between themselves. Jaymee started a program on the computer, then punched in some numbers. While the printer started, she signed the checks and handed them over.

"After all these years I've worked for your daddy..."

"It ain't right, the way you treat us..."

Jaymee took the sheets from the printer and gave them to the two men. "Don't lose these," she said over their voices. "I've added a bonus in your checks. 'Bye."

She folded her arms and raised her eyebrows, leaning a hip against Nick's chair. She wasn't aware that she was touching his forearm.

Chuck looked back and forth from Jaymee to Nick. "I see what's going on," he said, as he and Rich walked out. "Let's go, Rich. You and I ain't pretty enough for Miss Barrows."

Nick felt the temperature in the room drop as the two men left. From the study, they could hear part of the disgruntled conversation of the two departing roofers as they slammed the screen door shut.

"You know about her and pretty boys..."

"Ain't her old man gonna get another stroke if she bought another high lift..."

Laughter. Silence. Dicker shifted in his seat. "Never mind them, boss," he told Jaymee. "You don't need to dwell on nothing they've been saying, insinuate-like."

"It's OK. What do I owe you this week, Dicker?" Jaymee asked, picking up her pen.

Dicker gave her a bill, then Lucky did the same. "Come on, Luck, I need to get me some bait to go on my fishing trip this weekend," he said. "'Night, Jay."

"'Night, Dicker. Catch a good one."

"Will do. 'Night, Langley."

"'Night."

Jaymee realized suddenly that Nick and she were alone, something she had avoided the last few days.

# Chapter Three

Nick rotated the chair and watched Jaymee as she entered some numbers into the program. On rollers, it slid silently into position behind her, until she stood between his open thighs. "Need a seat?" he asked.

Jaymee slowly turned around, managing not to fall onto his lap as she gripped the table behind her. She tried to sound cool as she looked down at him, but her heart rate was, as always, when he got too near, speeding up with maddening awareness. "You need to give me a bill for my records."

He made her nervous this evening. There was a different air about him as he watched her with those deceptively lazy eyes.

Nick shook his head. "I'd like to be paid in cash." He placed his hands on her hips, holding her.

Her knees were going to buckle. "Are you a criminal?" she asked lightly.

As if he would admit it, even if he was one. He shook his head.

"A tax dodger?"

"Negative."

"An escaped convict?"

"Nope."

"An illegal alien, then?"

His smile was wicked, sexy. "Which accent do you want me to put on for you?"

Jaymee folded her arms protectively over her chest. That smile was dangerous to a woman's peace of mind. "I'm entitled to an explanation."

She had paid cash to some past employees before, those whom she knew were transient workers who had no address for her to contact at year's end. The construction industry was seasonal and laborers came and went.

However, Nick Langley called to her like no one had for a long time. His mystery fed her curiosity. She wanted to solve it, and hopefully, eliminate this senseless attraction she felt. All week, she had kept him at arm's length, not wanting him to make more of that kiss in the truck. It frightened her, the way he made her feel. He'd caused her to forget herself and every one of her self-imposed rules. She wanted to use her head this time because the last time she followed her heart, she'd been conned into believing that the man to whom she'd give it to was sincere. She knew better now. Men like Nick Langley didn't stay sincere for long, and certainly wouldn't stay around for long after they got what they wanted.

When he remained silent, she pressed on, "Well?"

"I'm trying to straighten some stuff out," Nick said, a smile teasing his lips. "It's nothing criminal, so you don't have to worry about helping a convict, but I just need some time."

"Some time for what? What exactly do you do, Nicholas?"

That crooked smile was awfully distracting and she refused to succumb to the temptation of bending over and kissing those lips.

"Construction?" he asked, his blue-gray eyes twinkling.

Jaymee gave a snort. "Yeah, you're just the typical construction man."

"And what does a typical construction man look like? What does he have that I don't?" He flexed an impressive bicep at her, questioningly wriggling his brows.

Jaymee wanted to run her hand over the arm, to feel its hard strength. Then she wanted to—she cut off her thoughts abruptly.

"Nails too clean, shoes too clean." She counted each item off on a hand. "Owns a pretty new Jeep, paid off, you told me—that, Mr. Construction Man, is a big telltale clue. Paid off? Do you know how much a new Jeep costs? And lastly," she gestured grandly, then, not able to help herself, she ran a light finger on his bare arm and whispered, "No tattoos."

She was good, a worthy opponent indeed. "Do you always stereotype people?" asked Nick quizzically. "Are you a stereotypical roofer?"

Jaymee frowned. "You know, mister, I can see right through you," she told him.

"Oh?" Nick leaned back comfortably, lacing his hands behind his head. He was beginning to enjoy this bait and wait exercise with his new boss.

"You always pretend to answer my questions, but all the time you try to divert me by putting me on the defensive. Not so?"

Oh, she was good. "Why would I do that?"

"You men are all the same, talking all the time like I'm not here. I've grown up among men all my life, Nicholas. I know how they think, what they do, why they talk the way they do. They talk differently when women are around them, except that I'm around them so much, they forget I'm a woman sometimes. I know every which way they talk down to women, every half-truth they utter to them, to each other."

"Ah," Nick said sagely, "an expert in evasive tactics."

Jaymee looked startled for a second, a slight frown on her face. "Evasive tactics?" she repeated, then nodded, pleased. "Yes, I like that. I'm an evasive tactic expert."

Nick grinned at her. If she only knew.

"So, back to the original subject, what exactly do you do?"

He noticed that she didn't say that she wasn't going to pay him in cash, which told him plenty about her decision already. He relaxed. "I'm good with electronics. You know," he placed his hands on the table on each side of her body, and tapped a long finger against the keyboard, "computers. Radios. Stuff like that." Missiles. Bombs. Satellites. He continued in silence.

Jaymee studied him for a few moments. Those long elegant fingers and artistic hands. Yes, she could see him playing with electronic things, assembling, wiring, rearranging. Clever, knowledgeable fingers. She shook off the sudden torrid images of those hands on her body. She wanted to laugh and cry at the same time. Her imagination, so long buried under piles of debts, had suddenly decided to stir from its coma.

She wasn't, by nature, a prying person, and since he had answered her question, she was satisfied enough to let it go for now. Maybe he would tell her more later, when he finished straightening out whatever needed straightening out, but right now, at this moment, she needed to understand why she was reacting in this way.

"OK, I'll help you out," she told him, and smiled at his surprise at her sudden capitulation. "Let me get my figures into my program, and turn the computer off." She waited a beat. "You have to move and give me room, Nicholas."

"What's wrong with my lap?"

Jaymee looked down her nose. "Get your own laptop."

He laughed, his teeth very white against his new tan. "Done," he said, and without warning lifted her onto his lap, turning her to face the computer on the desk. The big arms closed securely around her waist as he scooted the chair closer toward the table.

Jaymee swallowed hard. Reaction? How about internal combustion? The numbers on the screen didn't make sense. She'd probably messed up the whole program, as she tried to concentrate on the task instead of his roaming hands. They seemed to be everywhere, around her waist, on her thighs, up her back. Then they were pulling her blouse that was tucked into her shorts. Her brain refused to work any longer.

"Stop it," Jaymee huskily commanded, and almost slammed her palms down on the keyboard when his hands touched flesh. They glided across her quivering stomach, his fingers teasing the top of her shorts, one finger lazily exploring her belly button, before moving higher. She clutched those clever hands just before they reached their target.

"Stop it," she said again, trying to push them back down.

"Don't you like it?" he whispered into her ear, that gravelly voice low and seductive.

Too much. She hadn't been touched or caressed for.... In a last ditch effort, she moved to scramble off his lap, but her body went on strike when his teeth caught her earlobe. The sudden shot of electricity from that sensitive spot caused her to arch her hips in helpless response, seeking to make a live connection. She began to tremble.

"Yes, you do, Jaymee. Tell me." Nick's thumbs curled under her lacy brassiere and stroked the underside of her suddenly sensitive breasts.

Jaymee grit her teeth. No, she would not. "Yes."

The admission came out in a moan—helpless and unsure. She didn't protest when he undid the front clasp of her bra with a practiced ease that she took note of before he diverted her attention by possessively cupping her released flesh. Her eyes closed to savor the intimate sensations his touch generated.

Nick couldn't see her face but her soft moan was sexier than any words. She was softer than the Egyptian cotton of his favorite shirts and utterly enchanting in the way she responded to him. Her breasts eagerly spilled into his hands, heavy and baby smooth, her nipples turning pebble hard as he played with them.

Her restless hips were doing wonderful things to his body as she arched and squirmed in his arms.

Jay Barrows had all but disappeared. In her place was Jaymee, a passionate bundle of womanhood, far more exciting than how he'd imagined her at night, and Nick desperately wanted this woman. He wanted to keep her in this state of aroused need, just to see this part of her revealed, and he was glad, possessively, triumphantly glad, that she was showing it to him. He knew, bone deep, that she didn't—hadn't been—out of control in a long, long time.

Jaymee melted into his chest and lifted her chin. He didn't need a second invitation, placing his lips on hers. His kiss was tender and exploring. Somewhere among the exploding sensations, a part of her felt the restraint he was exercising, as if he didn't want to frighten her. Hooking an arm around his neck, she pulled him closer, trying to get closer, wanting more, making a sound of protest when he broke off the kiss.

She opened her eyes with great reluctance. The animal heat in his gaze made her heart beat faster. His eyes roved her flushed face with a predatory gleam.

"Kiss me like you mean it," she recklessly said, ignoring the moment of reprieve he was giving her.

"If I do, Jaymee, it won't be a simple romp on an office chair. Are you prepared to give me what I want?" His voice was gentle, even though his eyes glittered with suppressed emotion. In a slow caress, his hand moved over her thudding heart. "I want what your heart's promising me. I want you wild and crazy under me. You'll have to take off that leash you've put on yourself."

Jaymee couldn't say a thing. She should be, but she wasn't at all shocked that this stranger understood her so well. He had seen through her enough to know where to pierce her armor, and he was telling her that if she let him make love to her, she would lose the thing at which she worked so hard, her control. And she knew, without a doubt, that sleeping with him would mean relinquishing a lot. He had already proven it moments ago, and that was with him holding back his own needs. He would be the kind of lover who'd take everything, control everything, and expect total surrender, in the pursuit of mutual pleasure. Nothing less would do. It was there in his eyes, in the quiet expectancy of his strong body so close to hers.

He stared down at her solemnly, as if he could read her racing thoughts. "I want you to think about it, sweet Jaymee," he continued in that deceptively gentle tone, "because if you let me have you, I won't allow you to hide anything from me. There'll be no stopping once I start because I want you very much. I won't even listen, baby, if you change your mind, because I'll be unleashed too. It's been a while since I've felt this way too."

They were quiet words but still caused her to tremble with fear and longing. Unleash the wolf. She understood exactly what he was warning her of. If she said yes, it wouldn't be the tender controlled kisses and soft caresses. It would be wild. It would be powerful. It would be...heaven.

All that would probably kill her.

She didn't realize that she had spoken aloud. "No, sweet Jaymee," Nick said, shaking his head as he traced her lips with one long finger. "I'm going to free you. You've locked yourself inside that delectable body for too long. It's nice. It's safe. I'm neither."

Oh, she agreed. He was neither nice nor safe. The feral gleam in his slate eyes gave her fair warning. There was a humming heat emanating from his body, like a race engine idling, waiting, and she could feel the power of a waiting predator inside this man. There was nothing safe about him at all, not the hands that continued stroking her, or the hard flesh beneath her nudging intimately.

"So, if I say no, you're going to let me go," she stated, her breath catching when his thumb scraped a sensitive nipple.

"For now," he agreed. "I'll give you a little time to get used to me."

"Get used to you?" Jaymee frowned. "What about get to know you?" But she already knew the answer. He didn't stop her when she sat back up, adjusted her blouse, and added, "You aren't staying long, are you?"

Nick gave her a considering look. "No."

At least he was honest. Not like.... She clamped down on her past with the usual iron determination. She hated to be reminded—yet, of course, while she continued to pay for that mistake, she was reminded—of it every day. One was supposed to learn from one's mistakes, unless there was some sort of mental retardation, which, she told herself with wry amusement, was probably what was wrong with her. She was actually going to repeat history and fall into the arms of the wrong type of guy. Time to change the subject.

"In that case, I'd better get your tax records updated all the time," she said in a calm, logical voice. "That way, I won't be caught without records of labor hours if I ever get audited." She leaned forward, still sitting on his lap, and punched in a command. "I'll fiddle with the program later. Let me make some notes and then I'll pay you so you can go enjoy your weekend." She reached for a legal pad lying a few feet away.

Despite his discomfort, Nick had to smile. If he ever needed a partner during a mission, he would surely take Jaymee Barrows. She was one cool customer, able to adapt to situations with an innate perception that had caught him off-guard several times already, and nothing—nothing—escaped those bright eyes. When she'd looked at him, he'd noticed that they were no longer green, but an unrevealing mix of flecked brown and gold. He was learning to read her moods and found how subtly manipulative those colors were as he caught himself adjusting his behavior and reaction whenever he saw a change. Right now, that dark flat look managed to prick his conscience about taking her while offering nothing in return. Now that, he acknowledged with a certain awe, was power. No one, male or female, had ever managed to do that to him in all his years in covert work. The trained part of him was already preparing for battle, even with a woman who hadn't any idea of her power over him, and he decided to make a quick retreat, so he could analyze the situation.

Besides, there was something else on which he had to get his hands, besides Jaymee's irresistible body. He looked at the computer over her shoulder as she made notes on her writing pad. When she tried to get off his lap again, he held her still, his hands returning to her waist.

"No. Not yet."

"You're being presumptuous. I don't play games."

Nick nuzzled her neck and rested his chin on her shoulder, looking at the computer screen. "Games can be fun, Jaymee. You get to know how the other person thinks, see what they do. Like right now, I keep wondering what you'd do if I pulled that barrette off your hair and ran my fingers through that thick mane. Why do you keep it tied up all the time, anyway?"

"I don't feel like being mistaken for a broom," she muttered, "and if I cut it, I look like Shirley Temple on speed." She sighed. "I've got work to do."

"Computer stuff?"

"That, and other things."

"Why do you have two computers?"

"One of them is brand new," Jaymee said, pointing to the other computer on the desk, "and it's a piece of crap."

"What do you mean?"

She liked the way his chin rested on her shoulder. He smelled of soap and clean male scent, his thick black hair tickling her ear. "I bought it off the Internet so I could transfer my files to a computer with more memory and then I wasted a whole day on the damn thing because the files won't open! Some stupid message kept appearing, saying that some program is running that I've to close, but there wasn't any program on! Anyway, the screen would then freeze up. I almost pushed the stupid thing off the table after five hours of playing with it."

"Why didn't you call up the company that sold it to you?"

The look she gave him told him that she didn't appreciate him thinking her so dumb. "Of course I did. Some technical support line. I don't have the time during their hours to sit here and talk mumbo-jumbo with some expert. It's a lost cause." She clicked the icon to close the program. "As long as this works, I'll just make do till I have time to fix the other one."

"Maybe I can help."

That got Jaymee's attention. She tried to twist around to look at him.

"I suggest you don't, ah, move your cute little ass so much, sweetheart," he drawled, "or that little time I promised you will be withdrawn sooner than expected."

Jaymee felt the warmth rushing to her cheeks, but she was secretly pleased with his masculine reaction. She was so out of practice, she'd forgotten how heady feminine power could be. Without considering the consequences, she moved her bottom experimentally and smiled with wonder at the hard nudge that answered back. She repeated it, too totally immersed in her delight to notice that the man holding her was looking down at her with exasperation mingled with lust.

Nick wanted to focus on the computer, but damn, the woman was downright irresistible. It was obvious that she hadn't allowed herself so close to a man for a long time. She seemed to have no idea that doing what she was doing was courting danger, that she couldn't expect a red-blooded man not to throw her onto the sofa behind them and have his way with that sweet body. But something held him back, even as his body painfully requested release. He wanted her to get used to him, didn't he? Maybe he'd spoken too soon because she certainly was taking him at his word. He growled in agonized pleasure as one particular squirm rubbed him the right way.

That little moan startled Jaymee back into reality. Oh my God, what had come over her? Her face flushed even redder. "I…." She licked her lips, not knowing quite how to explain her outrageous behavior.

"It feels good, babe," he said, although he sounded a trifle tortured.

"I'm sorry, I don't..." She shrugged helplessly, then looked around for an excuse. Better change the subject. "The computer. Yes, you did say you know computers. Do you mean you can fix it?"

There was a short pause. Jaymee made sure she sat very still.

"Would you like me to check it out?" He was laughing at her; she could hear it in his voice. "I can probably find out whether it's a hardware or software problem. That would narrow down the possibilities."

"Right. Of course," she said. "Will you let me get off now? Then you can look at the computer a lot better. I'll turn it on for you."

He gave a sexy soft laugh. "You turn on everything, Jaymee." Pushing back the chair, he watched her make her escape. "Sorry, couldn't resist that."

Jaymee didn't want to play word games or any other type of games with him. His double entendres were too clever by far, and his behavior was making it difficult for her to think straight. Already, her out-of-control imagination was playing games in her head, as she saw herself dressed in red and saying, "What sexy hands you have, Nick Langley," to which the big bad wolf replied, "The better to seduce you with, dear Jaymee."

"Turn it on, Jaymee." She looked down at him. "I mean the new computer."

The laughter in his voice sent her scurrying to find the master switch of the surge protector connected to the second computer. She could feel sweat forming at the back of her neck as she snapped the switch on. She couldn't believe that she had stared at the bulge in his pants, that she had come this close to actually smirking out loud, "What a big..." What was wrong with her? She had to get away from him for a few minutes, to gather herself again.

"Excuse me for a bit," she said, trying not to sound flustered. "I'll be right back. Want a drink? Beer? Soda?"

"A beer sounds great," answered Nick agreeably, half-regretting that he had to let her go. He was very close to finding the trigger to this mysterious woman, but the answer to his prayers was sitting on the desk in front of him. Seducing Jaymee would have to wait. As soon as she closed the door behind her, he drew the chair close to the table and got to work.

*

In the restroom, Jaymee rubbed her heated face with a damp cloth. She'd gone insane. Somehow eight years without a man had built into a pressure cooker of crazed lust without her knowledge, and a man with hungry eyes and incredible hands had, wittingly or unwittingly, taken off the tight cover.

She stared into the mirror, seeing the strange wild glitter in her own eyes, the unnatural rosiness of her cheeks. Lust. She lusted after this new man in her life and his hot tough body. And he wanted her just as badly. His body told her so, and his words were just as brutally honest. It'd be a simple affair and no more, something to which she'd never agree. Never. She bit down on her lower lip. She wouldn't, right?

She groaned aloud in the little room and rewetted the cloth to wipe her face again. She couldn't hide the truth any longer. She would. She would settle for an affair if that was what Nick wanted. Or she could try to fight it. It'd be, she decided with firm grimness, just a matter of determination. She refused to be Red Riding Hood, being seduced by his eyes and hands and...and...other big parts.

There were other fairy tales that had big bad wolves in them. "I'll be the third little pig instead," she told her image in the mirror. "I'll be the smart little pig that built the house of stone."

She nodded, as if her solution was some brilliant strategy of war. The wolf couldn't get that little pig in that story. Then she grinned at the ridiculousness of her thoughts.

Feeling a modicum of control returning, she turned off the lights and reentered the kitchen. She eyed the closed door to her study, then went to get some beer from the refrigerator. An electronic background, she noted, meant someone with training, maybe even a degree. What was he doing laboring as a roofer in a town in the boondocks? It just didn't add up. What was it he had to straighten out, and why was he in hiding? She really didn't want to help him, if he had done anything illegal. The less she knew the better. Let him leave soon. He was far too threatening to her world.

Nick didn't look up when the door opened, his fingers flying over the keyboard as he played with the computer's operating system program. He could detect her floral scent as she came closer, and nodded his thanks when a bottle of beer appeared in front of him. Taking a swig, he sank deeper into the chair and scanned the screen. He was beginning to like the chair a lot.

Jaymee looked at the screen. Those lines looked like nonsense to her, but Nick appeared to know what they meant as he grunted and typed something, then moved the cursor around.

"What's the problem, do you know?" she questioned, pulling up a chair alongside his. "What are these things?"

"I'm just directing some basic self-testing programs," he explained. "The computer can zero in on where the problem is. It looks promising. If it's software, it's fixable without anything being taken apart."

"Oh." Whatever. If he fixed it, she would be eternally grateful. She had cried at the possibility of spending more money to replace whatever was wrong with it. "Can you really fix it?"

Of course he could. The Programmer ate computer chips for breakfast, and, he added after giving his companion a brief glance, sexy roofers for dinner. "It might take a while. I've nothing to do this weekend, so if you want, I can come back and play with it." And get to his connections.

"You'll have to tell me when. I won't be home much."

"Going somewhere for the weekend?" He wondered what she did for fun.

"No, I'll be in and out, but if you tell me when it's convenient for you, I'll be here."

"How about eleven in the morning? Then you can feed me lunch."

Jaymee nodded. "Fine. How much are you charging me to fix it?"

Nick shrugged. "Let me work on it first." He eyed her with outrageous wickedness, and added, "I'm very negotiable about payments."

She was determined to stick to business. "Cash, then," she said, gulping down her milk. "If I'm not home when you arrive, just wait in the back porch."

Turning off the computer, Nick stood up, stretching his back. His knees creaked and popped in protest. Hearing it, Jaymee tried to hide a grin. Week one for Roofer Wannabes was always a painful experience.

"You think it's funny, don't you?" He made a threatening step toward her and she quickly pulled the two kitchen chairs between them. "You like seeing me in pain."

Jaymee tugged the chairs behind her as she went back into the kitchen. "Is the big construction man in pain?" she mocked back, feeling safe with the chairs as protection. "Come, come. What about those tough muscles?"

Nick finished his drink and put the empty bottle in the sink. He watched her arrange the chairs at the small table before walking to the counter. Pulling out the top drawer, she withdrew some cash.

"Come on," she said, "I'll help you to your Jeep, poor limping thing."

"It is getting dark and scary outside," he agreed. "Hold my hand?"

Her voice was Southern sweet in the semi-darkness. "I hope the mosquitoes eat you up, Langley."

# Chapter Four

Nick showed up at the little house early on purpose. Jaymee's truck was where she'd parked it the night before, so she was either home or hadn't used it to go wherever she had to be. Walking down the path, he admired the clumps of hibiscus bushes in full bloom. He didn't really look last evening, but the property was quite picturesque, especially in the backyard with the view of the lake.

A wooden picnic table stood under an elm oak with dipping branches. He recognized Jaymee's shirts on a clothesline nearby. The lake was quite big, shared by surrounding properties, and he could see an upside down canoe on the bank.

If he stood quietly at the porch, he could hear the lazy buzz of summer all around — the bees and the frogs competing, the creaky clothesline, the hushing whispers of leaves as they rubbed each other, even the occasional watery plop from the lake. Nick paused for a long moment on the steps. He could see it very well. A laughing Jaymee sitting at that picnic table with her three kids quarreling and fighting in this backyard. They would all have curly dark auburn hair like their mother's, with the same green and brown eyes, and be just as feisty, probably just as stubborn; and in the middle of all that bedlam, Jaymee would raise her laughing eyes at him and —

He almost fell off the steps. He had no business fantasizing about Jaymee Barrows like that. It wasn't like him to make up scenarios that could never be. The moment Command found out that he was alive, the instant he was briefed about the situation, he would be gone, with new orders. And Jaymee would still be here, running her small business like it was part of a grand plan. She'd meet a safe man, someone who would give her those things she wanted, and it'd be his eyes she'd seek over the noisy chatter of her children.

Nick calmly crushed the aluminum can in his hand, and turning away from the backyard, he tapped on the back door. It was Bob Barrows who came to answer, his gaze turning suspicious at the sight of the visitor.

"She ain't here."

"She told me to meet her here," Nick informed him. He wondered what it was that made this old man so hostile toward his hard-working daughter. "I was just making sure that she isn't home yet."

"She's busy enough without you taking up her time," Bob said, not opening the door any wider. "You ain't no good for her, man. Why don't you just leave her be, so she won't get her heart broken?"

"That's a strange way of caring about your daughter, isn't it?" Nick politely asked. And because he wanted more details about Jaymee's past, he added, "Could it be that you're just making sure there's no possibility of her abandoning the business, and therefore, you?"

Bull's eye, Nick thought, as he took note of the man's sharp intake of breath. The old guy's switch, he disdainfully concluded, was pathetically easy to find. He knew that there was more to the story. Jaymee apparently wasn't knuckling under a bullying father; she was doing this of her own free will, and he intended to find out the reason.

"Well, is that Miss High and Mighty's story to you?" Bob Barrows' runny eyes narrowed into malicious slits. "You may fall for all that college knowledge she pretends to have, but if she was so smart, how come she's in the hole she's in?"

"Why don't you tell me?" Nick leaned nonchalantly against the railing.

A crafty smile fanned the wrinkles on the old man's face. "I can still see pretty good with my old eyes. You want my daughter, don't you? You got that same look Danny boy had whenever he cast his wicked eyes in her direction."

Bob pushed open the screen door and came out, shuffling his feet as if he wasn't sure how far the floor was. He squinted up at Nick.

Sloshed. Probably been so since last night. Nick studied him for a second. "Who is Danny?"

Sitting down slowly in the rocking chair, Bob gave him that shifty, knowing look again. "Why, her fiancé, of course." And he laughed, enjoying Nick's surprise. "I knew I could get you with that one, boy! She already got herself a pretty boy, she doesn't need a second one."

Nick was unprepared for the surge of anger that swamped him. A fiancé. He hadn't expected that piece of information at all. Reason told him that the old man was lying, but his own reaction to the news, even if it were untrue, jarred him. This wasn't him at all. The Programmer rarely acted on emotions. Through the years, he'd gotten used to efficiently studying a system and taking it apart, and out of habit, he did it to people around him. It helped him put distance between him and his targets. This jumble of emotions—anger and yes, jealousy—startled him.

Before he could probe Bob further, he heard footsteps coming from the side of the house, then Jaymee rounded the corner, with her usual fast strides. She stopped abruptly at the sight of him and her father, looking from one to the other as if to gauge what was happening. Wearing rumpled clothing and with her hair in its usual untidy ponytail, she looked tired.

Nick narrowed his eyes. She looked like she'd just gotten out of bed. He squeezed the crushed aluminum in his hand tighter.

"Hi," Jaymee greeted, climbing the porch steps. "'Morning, Dad. Feeling better?"

Her father just grunted, rocking the chair, his eyes half closed.

"Hi," Nick said.

"Come on into the house. I need a glass of water. God, it's hot today."

Jaymee frowned slightly, sensing that something wasn't right. Nick had followed her silently into the kitchen and watched her pour water into two glasses. He was angry about something. She could feel it, even though his face was cool and unreadable.

Nick waited till she drank down the glass of water. "You look tired." He studied at her disheveled appearance again. Wherever she'd spent the night, she hadn't taken her truck with her, which meant someone had picked her up and dropped her off. The seed of suspicion put a scowl on his face. "Busy morning?"

She was looking away, so he didn't bother hiding his black stare.

"Hmm," she agreed, yawning on cue. "Nothing a cup of coffee won't fix, though. Go ahead and make yourself comfortable in the study. I'll be right there as soon as I wash up."

He wanted to grab her by the shoulders, turn her around and demand to know where she'd spent the night. Was it with this Danny person? Without a word, he did as she told him, sitting himself in front of the new computer. He didn't wait for her, turning on the machine.

Jaymee quickly ran a brush through her tangles and pulled at her clothes in an effort to look less unkempt. Normally, she wouldn't care what she looked like, but then, she hadn't acted normal since Nick showed up. She gave herself a critical lookover in the mirror. She made a face. She wasn't a fresh-faced twenty year-old any more. Eight years of the kind of work she did had dissolved the baby fat around her face, leaving her far too lean and hollow-cheeked. There was nothing there to attract a man. Boring hazel eyes. Boring lips. Bad hair. She sighed. Maybe some lipstick would help. And definitely keep that tangled mess of hair off her face.

The sound of fingers tapping on the keyboard came from the study as she crossed the kitchen, her hands busy securing the pin in her hair. She could hear the rocking chair outside the kitchen window, and she stuck her head out to check on her father. He had dozed off, as was his mid-morning habit. Good. She didn't want him confronting Nick again. He probably hadn't even noticed him standing on the porch.

"Any progress?" she asked, walking in and standing beside Nick.

She had no idea what he was doing as he kept typing senseless sentences. It must be the right thing since the computer seemed to be talking back to him, flashing messages on its screen and blipping encouraging noises.

"Mmmhmm."

Several minutes of silence went by before she tried again. "Is it a serious problem?"

"No." She found his fast-moving fingers absolutely fascinating.

"Can I do anything?"

"No."

Jaymee sighed. He was treating the damned machine like some long lost lover, and what was more, it was responding to his touch with a lot more enthusiasm than an inanimate object ought to have. It was obviously a female computer. "Well, I guess I'll fix us something to eat and do some chores. Holler if you need me."

"OK."

She studied him a moment longer. So much for freshening up. What'd it be like to be at the receiving end of that unwavering concentration? At that moment, he raked an impatient hand through those dark, luxuriant too-long locks, muttered something back to the machine, and went back to typing. His eyes hadn't left the screen since she came in. All that lipstick, she mournfully sighed again. Wasted.

When she left the room, Nick heaved an answering sigh of his own. Frustration dominated the jumbled emotions he felt. Frustration and anger. It was disconcerting. He had, before him, what he needed—easy access to spend time online and break through firewalls so he could leave a message for his contact privately—and he should be feeling elated at his good luck. Instead, all he wanted to do at the moment was lock the study door and kiss a certain woman into telling him her secrets. The memory of the taste of her mouth called him, and the thought of her kissing somebody else after he left her the night before felt like a 100-lb weight on his chest.

Everything about her told him that she was a loner, unattached, and had been for awhile, but he could be wrong. Maybe she did have a fiancé somewhere and he just hadn't shown his face around the job sites, that was all. And maybe the fiancé would have his face smashed in, if he ever did.

Nick took a deliberate deep breath and exhaled. She was interrupting his focus. With resolute grimness, he pushed everything to the back of his mind, allowing only thoughts about the computer to remain. He was almost done playing with the operating program. Fixing what was wrong was easy enough, but he needed to rewrite parts of the program for his needs.

Just as he'd suspected, Jaymee wasn't using DSL or wireless. He'd come prepared for that. Looking under the desk, he disengaged the phone line that hooked up the older computer to the wall outlet. Then he stood up and checked the back of the new computer and found the phone line dangling loose. Holding the line in his mouth, he pulled out a small plastic packet from his back pocket and poured its contents onto the table. Several tiny flat microchips the size of fish flake food scattered out.

Nick cocked his head, listening intently for Jaymee's movements outside the study. He heard her moving around the sink area. Making lunch, from the sounds of it. Pulling out a pair of tweezers from the other back pocket, he used them to pick up a chip. He released the line he was holding in his mouth into his other hand, and with a quick practiced twist, he inserted the microchip into the connector, firmly pressing it into place. He plugged it into the outlet in the wall.

It took another five minutes before his link went through. He hesitated when the password was requested. If he gave it, Command would know that he was alive, and so would anyone else monitoring his password. They wouldn't be able to read his message, but they'd know that he wasn't dead, and after the narrow escape from his boat, he had a feeling that his demised condition was very important to the enemy. If he'd been betrayed from the inside, then their attempt to kill him had failed.

No. He would have to break in. There were only a few personnel in his agency who could trace or recognize his encryptions, and really, only one who knew how to decode it, and then disguise a similar message back to him. Step by step, his mind took him through the logistics. Override the security checkpoints. Invade through disguise. Disrupt by merging simple commands. Then make sure only one person would come across it.

He plucked at his lips as he manipulated the command strings that moved across the screen in rapid succession. He had no idea when the man for whom he left the code would come across the message, and he was going to need another excuse to play with the computer.

Swiftly, he removed all traces of his activities and returned the screen to MENU. Jaymee probably wouldn't know that he was breaking into the government's most secured lines even if she was watching him, but Nick didn't want to bet too heavily on that. His boss had a way of grasping a situation very quickly.

"Lunch is ready! Nick?"

"Yeah, I'm almost done," he called back as he finished up.

*

Jaymee couldn't figure him out. It was her source of pride since her unfortunate brush with the deceptive side of the male gender that she'd learned to read every one of them and put them in their rightful category. Through the years, she and Mindy had exchanged notes. There was the Bear, the one she could leave at a job site as long as there was honey, the promise of better pay if the job was done that day. There was the Rabbit, the worker who hurried, hurried, hurried to finish a job. From her list of restaurant adventures, Mindy, in her typical droll sense of humor, had added in the Drunken Monkey, the Snake, and the Peacock. But he wasn't any of those.

There was one more in her list, the most dangerous animal of all because he was the most deceptive, knowing when to hide under sheep's clothing and be nice, only to turn around and devour women like her. And nothing about Nick Langley had convinced her that he was anything but a wolf, out on a hunt, only after a good time.

But sometimes she wondered whether she was wrong. She couldn't figure out why he was in her world at all, and most important, why he wanted her. Unlike before, she didn't have any money or assets now to interest a wolf. Eight years of eluding men had taken away any confidence of how she could affect any male interest.

She flashed him a smile. "How's it going?"

Nick sat down at the kitchen table. "Almost done. I need a Philips screwdriver to open up the case. I might as well check everything while I'm at it."

Jaymee put the plate of cold chicken salad and a glass of milk in front of him. "Go ahead. I'm just glad that the computer isn't a lemon."

Nick smiled at the food in front of him. How long had it been since a woman fed him cold chicken salad and milk for a meal? It was an uncomfortably homey gesture, and warm pleasure blunted the anger he'd been carrying.

"It's not a Z-28," he agreed, lifting a fork, "but it'll take you where you want to go."

He watched her take a sip of milk from his glass. Nice lipstick. Tempting lips.

"Let me get my dad to join us," Jaymee said, heading for the screen door. "Dad! Dad! Come in and eat your lunch."

She turned to Nick and warned, "Just ignore his bad manners, all right?"

Nick nodded. Bob shuffled in, giving a wide yawn. He cast a resentful look at Nick.

"Still here? I thought you said he was your laborer, Jaymee, not your bodyguard."

Jaymee set a place for him, then took the middle seat. "He's fixing the new computer." She gestured. "Here, take your medication and get some food in you."

"I don't want milk," the old man growled.

"Sorry, beer and medication don't go together," she calmly informed him. "If you end up in the hospital this time, I'll have to mortgage the house to pay the bills, and then you won't get your business back in the black for sure."

Nick suddenly realized that Jaymee dangled the roofing business in front of her father like bait. Every time he pushed her too far, she would bring up the subject of getting the business back in the black, and it always had the desired affect. The old man sat and washed down the pills with a glass of milk and obediently started on his meal. Nick wondered what it was all about. The father seemed to have a hold over his daughter, and in a strange way, vice-versa.

"So, will I be able to use the new computer soon?" Jaymee wanted to know.

"As soon as you get everything updated and reconfigured."

She sighed. "That means another month or so."

Nick frowned. "What do you mean?" Transferring programs and files was assembly work, like eating.

"My abilities with a computer don't go beyond turning it on, pointing the mouse, and saving a file," confessed Jaymee with a wry smile. "Anything more difficult usually means reading a manual, deciphering lots of error messages, redoing the same procedure a dozen times, and God knows what else. You'll see. What with all the other chores I've to do, it'll take a month before I get the new computer set up."

She made it so easy, the operative in him mocked him for taking advantage of her. "I can do it for you," Nick offered, calmly reaching for a roll. "I can help you out in the evenings, do anything you want."

Bob grunted at the other end of the table and his watery eyes told him exactly what he thought of that offer. "I'll bet you would do anything she wants," he said. Turning to Jaymee, he added, "You ain't learned a lesson yet, I guess you just ain't as bright as I thought. Help you out in the evenings, do anything you want. You just stick him back to real work and watch that pretty face wilt in the sun."

"He does work in the sun," Jaymee quietly said, but her face was slightly flushed at her father's none-too-subtle accusations. "You don't have to like everyone I hire, Dad, and if you've nothing good to say, why don't you just keep it to yourself?"

"He ain't got much to say to defend himself, does he?" Bob sneered at Nick.

Nick looked across the table, calmly chewing, then swallowing. "What your daughter and I do isn't your business, Mr. Barrows."

"Nick..." Jaymee began.

"Ain't my business?" Bob barked out in sudden wrath. "If I don't keep an eye on her, she won't have any business left at all. The last time she mixed business with pleasure, she near bankrupted me! And sent her ma to an early grave, she did!"

"That's enough," Jaymee cut in, her voice low. Why, why, why did he have to keep bringing it up?

As if her father heard her, he continued, "I've to remind her so she won't forget. She wants to play, let her do what she promised me, let her pay for her mistake first. My daddy taught us to always pay for our mistakes, and she..."

Nick stood up. He'd had enough. "As far as I can tell, you've got the most hard-working daughter around." His voice was no longer that lazy, gravelly drawl. "Let's go for a walk, Jay. I need to work off a sudden indigestion."

There was a cold, dangerous edge to it, and Jaymee shivered at the sound. She stared at his outstretched hand and looked up into calm and steady eyes the color of winter sky. She couldn't read his thoughts as those unfathomable eyes demanded her to do as he said. She placed her hand in his and got up.

Bob continued eating, already forgetting the outburst of a few moments before. "Go for a walk," he repeated. "I'll clean up."

Summer heat blasted them the moment they stepped off the porch into the bright sunlight. The air was thick with humidity and tension. In silence, Jaymee walked toward the lake, heading for the picnic table under the elm oak. The shade beckoned invitingly as the heat beat down on their unprotected heads.

"This used to be my favorite spot," she said, in an attempt to lighten the mood. "I used to sit right here to do my homework. Only the lake kept tempting me, and I always ended up in that small canoe." She sighed, wanting those easy days back.

"You have a nice piece of property here," Nick agreed, as he looked toward the lake.

"It's not mine. It's Dad's," Jaymee corrected. Plucking a small branch of hibiscus off a bush, she pulled out the flowers, plucking the petals off one by one.

"It'll be yours one day."

Her eyes were that muddy color that he knew echoed her mood. "I don't want it. My goal is to move out in two years."

"Why two years?"

"You aren't the only person with stuff to straighten out, Nick." She gazed at the lake with its bright gleaming ripples of gold. "I'm sure you noticed my father and I don't get along too well."

"He isn't exactly there all the time," he agreed. "Drinking will do that to you, though. The violent mood swings, I mean."

Jaymee nodded. "Yes. He's gotten worse the last year but he's a tough old bastard, even after the stroke. He'll be OK when I hand him back his business."

"But why the time table? Why two years?" Nick stretched out his long length next to her body on the grass, leaning back on his hands.

He was so easy to talk to, but she wasn't going to tell her story to this man beside her. She'd already let him in too much. Besides, why would a sad tale of a misguided, trusting young woman interest him? He was only interested in staying long enough to make some money so he could move on. She kept plucking at the spray of hibiscus in her hands.

Nick studied her bent head. She wasn't going to tell. He could see it in the set of her lips, the determined hunch of her small shoulders. She just didn't trust men, especially him, enough to open up and it had to do with whatever happened to the father's business and a certain other man.

"Tell me about Danny."

He spoke so softly, Jaymee was sure she'd imagined it, but those seductive eyes told her that she hadn't misheard. When he looked at her like that, with those long, dark lashes hiding his thoughts, he had a hypnotic effect on her. She couldn't drag her gaze away, even blink. It was a strange sensation, as if he could probe into all her secrets just by staring into her eyes.

"How do you know about Danny?" she demanded, still imprisoned by that strange, searching look.

"I hear his name here and there," Nick told her. She wasn't aware of how much those eyes of hers betrayed. He saw hurt and a deep, dark scar. "Tell me, Jaymee."

"It's history," she said, shrugging. "I'm reluctant to dig up old bones just to satisfy your curiosity. It isn't like you answer my questions about you."

She was a strong woman. Nick already knew it before. Very few people could resist a light probe, the subtle approach he'd been trained in to get information, without revealing a few details. But here was an untrained, unsuspecting woman, the simplest target for a quick exercise in subliminal pressing, retaliating with the ease of an evasive expert. She batted away every attack with a simple defense — change the subject and remove herself as the focus.

Nick had never wanted to dissect a non-target as much as he did this woman. He wanted to know why she was the way she was, what she was thinking, what made her tick; in short, everything. Most of all, he wanted her under him, naked and unafraid, as he explored every inch of her, physically and emotionally. And he was going to do it. He'd take and explore her until she yielded all her secrets to him. He'd give her what she feared most and make it what she wanted most—he'd like to restore in her the power to give herself without fear.

Subtle didn't work. Push harder. "Is he really your fiancé?" he asked, catching her busy hands in one of his.

Startled that he knew so much already, she dropped the wretched bloom. "You're a busybody and persistent as hell."

She tried unsuccessfully to wriggle her captive hands free. "He was my fiancé, OK?"

"Was?"

"Yes! Well, he hadn't really broken off our engagement when he disappeared, but eight years ought to qualify it in the past tense, don't you agree?" She wriggled her hands harder.

"Do you miss him? Do you still want him?"

"No!" She glared at him, disgust in her eyes, as if he'd conjured up something distasteful in her mind.

Nick released her and picked up the mangled spray of hibiscus on her lap. Plucking out a still untouched blossom, he tucked it behind Jaymee's ear.

"Good," he said. And kissed her.

*

Three days and Jaymee still could remember the feel of his lips. She understood that she'd been given an ultimatum that afternoon. He hadn't said anything, but he didn't need words. That kiss said it all.

She forced it out of her mind, as she'd been doing for several days now, as she watched Nick at work. He seemed to be getting the hang of roofing, moving around as if he'd been doing it for years. She now let him shingle the back side of the roofs, where it was usually the easiest, without the complicated roof designs. At the rate he was going, she ruefully noted, she'd have to raise his pay soon, but she had to be careful, or the other two roofers would be grumbling.

She liked watching him at work. The way those smooth muscles rippled as he carried the boxes of nails on his shoulder. The way his lanky frame looked impossibly graceful in that awkward position for a tall man. And even that beautiful, exposed throat moving as he thirstily gulped down cold water from a bottle made her catch her breath. And, he had developed a marvelous golden tan that made those blue-gray eyes glitter even more potently.

Her fingers lifted to her lips. Since he had kissed her, he hadn't attempted to touch her again. When he showed up for a few hours on Sunday, he was reserved and distant, his mind seemingly focused on her computer. She was almost jealous of the damn thing, although she had to admit that watching him at it was a fascinating exercise indeed. His mind seemed to be laid bare in front of her when he was immersed in whatever it was he was doing to her computer, and after sitting by him quietly for a while, she had added one more clue to this mysterious man. Nicholas Langley, despite his easygoing demeanor, had a brilliant mind. She could see it in the intense light burning in his eyes as he "talked" to her computer, in the way he solved one problem after another. What was he doing as a laborer? The question gnawed at her even more since the incident by the lake.

The kiss. God, if that could be called one. She had very little with which to compare the experience, but she felt branded, like he'd marked her somehow. She could still taste him, a hot salty mixture of lust and possessiveness. His lips had been firm, unyielding, and his teeth had deliberately drawn blood where he bit her on her lower lip. Ignoring her startled gasp and struggle, he had sucked on the little wound and licked the blood off with a slow and tantalizing tongue. He'd left her with the strange feeling that she'd signed some sort of blood pact with the devil.

The last few days hadn't lessened the feeling. The silent ultimatum stretched like a live wire between them. She strove to look normal underneath his unruffled watchfulness, but she wasn't fooled. The wolf, she realized, was showing itself. It was there in the glitter in his eyes, whenever she caught him looking at her as she washed the dirt off her body at lunchtime. She felt it every time she stood too close by him. Nick was, and she didn't need him to tell her, as he put it, letting — no, making — her get used to him. Meanwhile, lest she forgot, he deliberately stalked her like a predator about to decide on the moment of attack.

Jaymee shivered in the asphalt-melting heat. Fear and excitement jostled for position. For the first time in eight years, she was unsure of herself. Catching his knowing eyes on her, she decided to do what she did best — change the subject.

"Lunch," she said, unnecessarily, since Dicker and Lucky were already off the roof. She decided that a crowd would lessen the danger of a wolf on the move, and went to eat at Hungry Boys. She should have known that escape was not in her future.

"What's the special today?" she asked Mindy, after gratefully gulping down a glass of ice tea.

Mindy tucked a stray lock of blond hair back in place as she ignored Jaymee, her eyes hungrily moving up and down her companion instead. Nick was the picture of healthy manhood, tall and glowing with his new tan.

"I'm looking at it," Mindy drawled.

Nick gave her a crooked sexy grin as he winked back at the bold waitress. "You're looking good, Min."

Jaymee had known Mindy forever, and her friend didn't know what blushing was. Until now. She stared at the flush of pleasure on her friend's face as she preened, then coyly teased, "Well, you're looking at dessert, my hungry boy."

Jaymee wanted to empty her glass of tea over Nick's head. He was seducing all the female population in the restaurant with that smile, she thought, as she surveyed the avid attention of the three waitresses, the owner's wife, and the three old ladies sitting by their table. It was too bad, she dolefully mourned, that her glass was empty.

Coughing superciliously, she politely chipped in, "I hate to interrupt such a delicious exchange, but there's an extremely hungry woman here."

For a moment, she was tempted to add, "and that man is my dessert," but curbed such catty behavior. Jay Barrows didn't fight over any man.

Mindy sniffed and pulled out a pencil from her apron. "Roast turkey, stuffing, vegetable soup," she recited, glaring at Jaymee. "Is that what you want?"

"Yes," Jaymee answered, glaring back at her friend.

"Nut," muttered the waitress, as she wrote the order down. "You, too, hon?"

"Sounds good," agreed Nick, obviously very amused at something.

"Nut!" Mindy repeated for Jaymee's benefit as she walked off.

"What's wrong with you?" Jaymee called after her, exasperated.

"You could have gourmet, and you opt for meat and potatoes. Nut!" she called back over her shoulder as her generous hips swayed their way back to the kitchen.

"She must be a good friend of yours," Nick commented, breaking open a packet of sugar.

"What, do you want me to give you her phone number?" Jaymee asked, irritated and a little jealous.

"If I wanted it, don't you think I could just ask her?"

That shut her up. She pursed her lips mutinously and snatched up the newspaper left on an empty table nearby and opened it in front of her face.

"It reads better the right side up," her tormentor wryly told her.

Sure enough, just like her world had been lately, the newspaper was upside down. Jaymee obstinately kept the paper that way, glaring fiercely at the reverse picture of a banana. After a few minutes, Mindy came back with soup. She surveyed the scene and arched a penciled brow at Nick, who calmly began on his soup. After putting down the other bowl, she snatched Jaymee's paper from her fingers.

"What now?" Jaymee growled at her unrepentant friend. She was used to Mindy's brand of brash friendship, but today she seemed to be even more intent on getting her cornered.

"Next Saturday," Mindy said, hand on hip.

"I haven't forgotten," Jaymee informed her, "but after today, you can expect cellophane tape for your present."

"Cellophane tape?" Mindy repeated, puzzled.

"Yeah, rolls and rolls of it. Enough to tape your mouth shut until your next birthday," said Jaymee, and stuck her tongue out.

Her friend laughed, a loud husky chuckle. She looked at the quietly eating Nick. "This is what I get from my best friend for inviting her to my birthday bash." A wicked light entered her blue eyes, and she turned to Jaymee, darting a glance at Nick, and added, "On the other hand, cellophane tape could contribute to a nice, sticky situation."

Jaymee rolled her eyes, then mockingly lifted her hands heavenward. Nick laughed at the two of them, enjoying the sight of her at a loss for words. She was smiling fondly at the waitress, even while appearing exasperated with her.

"Happy birthday on Saturday," he said, trying to play peacemaker.

Mindy slapped a palm on her forehead as if it just occurred to her. "You're invited, big guy. My special guest. Let Jaymee bring you along."

Jaymee almost groaned aloud. The last thing she wanted was to go with Nick to a party as a couple. She wouldn't look at him, picking at imaginary lint on her pants instead.

"Love to," Nick said, looking across the table.

"Excellent!" exclaimed Mindy. "Jaymee?"

"What now?" she muttered, picking up a fork.

"Bring more cellophane tape." The sassy waitress didn't wait for a reply as she tucked the empty tray under one arm and trotted off.

"She's something else," Nick commented, still amused.

"A regular stand-up comedienne," agreed Jaymee, still unable to believe that her supposedly best friend had steamrollered her.

"If you don't want me to go, I won't," Nick softly told her.

"If I dare show up without you on her birthday, I might not live to see mine," she informed him, shuddering at all the possible paybacks of which Mindy was capable. From experience, her friend was more than original in the art of revenge.

Nick grinned. "In that case, then it's my duty to take care of my boss. I promise to behave at this…bash, as she called it."

"No one behaves at Mindy's birthday bashes," Jaymee warned. "You're expected to eat her barbecue, drink her beer, dance with the birthday girl, and there's even karaoke, if you're drunk enough." She sighed, gave in, and smiled. "You'll enjoy it. Mindy is a great person."

Buttering his roll, Nick casually said, "Since I won't be able to transfer your files on Saturday, let's do it tonight then. I've a few free hours after work."

"If you want to. I don't want you to feel that you have to."

"No problem. Why let you muddle through when I can do it for you painlessly?"

"Thanks, Nick." She was relieved that he offered to do it. She really wasn't looking forward to reading Windows for Dummies. "You've been a great help."

Nick ignored the twinge of guilt and smiled back winningly. "You've been more help to me than you realize, too." He gave her the buttered roll.

As someone who had been in tighter spots, Nick had learned not to question providence when opportunity arose. He told himself that he wasn't taking advantage of Jaymee, knowing that his feelings for her were complicating the very simple issue of survival. What he was doing had to be done. It was that simple. In return, he helped her out with her computer problems.

Fair enough. So why the unexpected guilt? Because he wanted to be honest with this woman, that's why. When he'd kissed her last Saturday, his savage need had shocked him enough to make him step back to evaluate the whole situation. He accepted the desire for Jaymee, that the attraction he felt was more than any feeling that he'd ever experienced for another woman. He could even deal with the strange possessiveness he had for her. Something about her pulled new emotions from inside him. Maybe it was her innocence. Or, her tightly-reined control. Whatever it was, he realized that her response to him was instinctive, despite of her fears, and that in turn transformed him to some chest-beating primitive. He laughed under his breath at that notion. The woman was driving him crazy, that was what was the matter.

That kiss, he admitted now, made him realize for the first time since he joined his covert agency that he wanted to step out of the shadows and share his own true self with somebody. He wanted Jaymee Barrows to know who he was and to accept him for what he was. He also realized, knowing her abhorrence of deception in his sex, that the longer he deceived her, the more hurt she would be.

Hopefully, some communications would be waiting for him when he checked tonight. The quicker he ended this situation regarding his mission, the better. Then, he glanced at Jaymee, who was obviously enjoying her turkey special now that Mindy had quit baiting her, then, he could fully concentrate on more pressing matters.

# Chapter Five

When Nick showed up at her house later that evening, Jaymee was again not at home, even though the blue truck was parked in the driveway. He sat on the railing of the back porch and watched the sun disappear behind the tall pines across the lake. Where did she go that didn't need her vehicle? Was she with Mindy? He knew now that it wasn't the missing Danny, but that didn't mean she wasn't seeing another man. His frown deepened as he realized that he had taken for granted that she was unattached; she had never said that she didn't have a special someone. After all, it was inconceivable to expect her, or anyone, to be without a partner for eight years.

She appeared suddenly, panting hard, as if she'd been running at full speed. She bent over, hands on knees, breathing hard.

"Sorry," she apologized. "I forgot the time. Got back as fast as I could."

"It's OK," Nick said.

He wanted to ask her where she'd been, but that would only make her wary of him all over again. Right now, mentally, she was where he wanted her to be. She was opening doors that were locked before, and he wanted her to open them herself, for herself. Even if his own personal program was in jeopardy of crashing every time she was within his sexual radar. Even if he had a perpetual discomfort in his pants at night when he thought about her. He smiled, amused at his own thoughts.

Jaymee looked up. His smile made her feel even giddier as she tried to catch her breath. God, he looked good enough to eat. She took in the white cotton shirt and khaki pants, which set off his tan to perfection. The top few buttons were left undone, revealing curling hair. She wanted to bury her nose in that chest and breathe in that warm musky masculine scent that seemed to make her think indecent thoughts. With sudden dismay, she realized that she still hadn't changed from her day at work. Who would get turned on at the sight of her in tarred-up work clothes, still sweaty from the day, so totally unappealing?

Unlocking the back door, she flipped on the light switch, knowing that her father would still be at one of his friends'. She sighed at the pile of dishes in the sink and bent down to pick up scattered newspapers by the kitchen table.

"Sorry, the place is a mess. I should've come home earlier to straighten up."

"Stop apologizing." Nick saw the shadows under her eyes, noticed the quick roll of her shoulders in an attempt to relax. He didn't like her overworking like this. "Look, I can do this without you in the study. If you trust me not to steal your silverware, why don't you go and take a shower or a bath? It'll take me an hour or so to transfer your files and play around with your programs, and that'll give you time for a good soak."

"You don't mind?" A hot soak sounded so good. "I mean, you won't think I'm rude not to..."

"Go," he ordered, giving her a slight push. "If I need you, I'll find you."

Jaymee didn't need more persuasion. A hot soak. As in bubble bath. Heaven. She didn't even look back as she went off.

Nick wistfully looked after her as she went off. That little ass out of her tight lycra pants. The sudden image of Jaymee in a bathtub wasn't going to make the next hour comfortable at all. Ruefully, he looked down at his predicament.

"Down, boyo," he softly muttered, "or I'm going to have to reprogram you."

He decided to get his business done first before transferring Jaymee's files from the old computer to the new. That way, if she joined him after her bath, he'd be finished. Within minutes of connecting, he was in, and he navigated through the high-tech daily changes in the protective links that his agency used to confound the usual breed of hackers. Scanning through, he found what he needed; the right person had recognized his communication.

He printed out the jumbled, coded puzzle, deciphering the message, which read: SITUATION RED. ASSESS. F2F. COORDINATES. He had already expected the warning of danger, but the caution to remain dead, as well as to evaluate the situation was a double warning to be careful. Interesting. He considered for a moment, then relayed another coded encryption. If he had to look out for a "face-to-face," that meant serious trouble. Trust no one.

A triple warning, he amended.  Hesitating, he tried to decide whether to reveal that he didn't escape the boat without first taking care of business, that he had the assignment in his possession.  He'd been in the process of decoding its secrets when he'd sensed something was wrong.  Since his escape, he hadn't had a chance to continue his work without a computer.  He had never turned over an unfinished assignment.  He signed off without adding anything further to the message.

All he could do now was wait.

*

Ahhhhhh.

This was definitely what she needed.  Jaymee sank deeper into the steaming water, blowing bubbles that landed on her nose.  She had washed her hair while waiting for the tub to fill up.  It felt so good to be clean and soft.  She needed to do this more often.

She promised herself that she'd take a few hours off a week for rest, for personal well-being.  Besides, Mindy's party was coming up and she needed to spend a few hours to make herself human again, so she could face all the friends attending the bash.  She smiled, wondering whether she'd remember how to enjoy herself at a party.  She hadn't gone out in a long time, what with her having to stay out later ever since she had to work shorthanded, and on top of that, spending all available time as well as weekends trying to get everything accomplished within her crazy self-imposed schedule.  However, even she had to admit that she couldn't burn the candle at both ends indefinitely.  Her yawn was huge.  Even Superwoman needed to recharge her batteries sometime.  The hypnotic effect of gently lapping water had her half-dreaming as the bubbles popped quietly.

She didn't know how long she floated in the hot water, but the sudden jolt of pain up her left leg shocked her to wakefulness.  She gasped loudly and the violent jerk of her body created a wave that splashed onto her face and into her mouth, causing a fit of coughing as she choked out a scream when she tried to move.

The pain was horrendous.  Hot tears spurted out as she struggled to stand up, but her left leg was totally useless, knotting tighter and tighter until she had to kneel on her right knee for balance.  She leaned out of the tub, her wet hair dripping water all over the tile floor as pain repeatedly pounded up her injured leg. She tried to stand again. And gasped out a few choice words. Someone was pounding at the door. It became more insistent as she held onto the tub's rim.

"Jaymee?" Nick called from the other side of the bathroom door. "I heard you scream. Are you all right?"

Using her elbows, she somehow managed to lift herself up high enough to sit on the side of the tub. "Yes," she choked out, then gasped in agony as the cramp worsened.

The door flew open without warning and Nick's large frame was suddenly in front of her. Squatting down, he held her by the shoulders.

"What's wrong?" he asked brusquely.

Through the haze of pain, she stared at Nick's face, then realized that she was sitting there naked.

"Get out!"

She tried to squirm out of his hold, desperately reaching for the towel hanging nearby. However, the floor was too slippery and she lost her balance. She cried out when she tried put weight on her leg.

Silently, Nick easily gathered her up, one arm under her knees, the other around her shoulders, and carried her out of the bathroom into her bedroom. Jaymee couldn't even protest as she held onto the knotted muscle with both hands. He lay her down on her bed.

"Don't move," he tersely ordered, and disappeared back into the bathroom. He returned with a towel and swore softly at the sight of her trying to pull the tucked bed sheets loose to cover herself.

"You're just going to hurt yourself doing that," he told her, then sat down right beside her naked body.

"Don't!" Jaymee weakly tried to fight off the big fluffy towel rubbing her body. She didn't actually object to the towel. It was the pair of hands rubbing her dry that was cause for alarm. She couldn't believe that she was actually lying on her bed with his hands on her. She'd fantasized about that, without the agony of a cramp. It was too frighteningly like her fantasies, and she struggled more earnestly, understanding with sudden clarity her own danger.

Nick sighed and took the only option left to get her to stop. He stretched his long length on top of her, using his weight to quiet her struggles. Her body felt temptingly soft.

"Be still," he told her softly.

As if she had a choice. Her thigh still throbbing, Jaymee glared up at him, torn between embarrassment and pain. "Get off me, Nick," she said. She might be in pain, but she hadn't lost her sense of self-preservation yet.

"Which leg cramped up?" he asked, ignoring her demand. "You were squirming so much I couldn't see for sure."

"I'm feeling better now," she lied, then gasped aloud when he calmly tested one thigh by putting pressure on it with his knee. It was a lucky guess. "You bastard!"

"You won't tell me."

"I didn't want to!" she yelled.

"Too bad." He got up on one hand, pulling the scrunched up towel across her body. "There, almost decent. Let me see you move your leg."

Did he know what he looked like from her position? Jaymee stared at him as she lay on her bed, naked except for a wet towel on top of her body. He was half-on and half-off her, the front of his shirt and pants wet. A very warm hand lay on her injured thigh. A long moment passed.

"Don't look at me like that, darling," he drawled. "Move your leg, Jaymee."

She tried, and bit down on her lip at the immediate spasm that followed. He nodded, his hand pressing down on the knot.

"A pulled muscle. I'll take care of it."

Looking around, he saw the bottle of body lotion on her bedside table, and leaned across her to get it. Mesmerized, Jaymee watched him pour an indecent amount into those beautiful hands. She swallowed hard as those hands rubbed together.

"You aren't going to do it," she announced, panicking.

"It isn't going to hurt, babe," Nick told her, and two slick hands were kneading down on her thigh, his thumbs pressing and massaging the sore spot.

She cried out something incoherent. Did he say it wouldn't hurt? So why did her body feel like one giant cramp?

"Relax, or I'll have to massage your whole body."

He was teasing her, but the thought of those hands doing similar things to the rest of her made her insides flip somersaults. She eyed him with the keen knowledge of a cornered prey. He had her trapped and the glint in his eye told her that he was very aware of it. Her mind worked feverishly, trying to see a way out. Even if her leg had allowed it, she couldn't jump up and run off with just a towel clutched to her front. She couldn't see herself screaming in maidenly despair; she wouldn't know how. She could just quietly lie there, like an animal playing dead, pretending that his fingers weren't sliding up and down her thigh. She could, if her blood wasn't boiling over from the suggestive up and down motion. His laughter brought her attention back to him.

"What's so funny?" she asked.

"You. You're so transparent, Jaymee darling. Right now you're busy trying to find a safe subject to talk about, as you always do when you panic."

Was she so easy to read? Annoyance replaced embarrassment as she pulled the towel a little higher, then realized that only gave him more view of her thighs. Keep talking, she thought. "What's wrong with that?"

"OK, let's do it your way. We won't talk about my hands on your thigh. Let's talk about your breasts."

Jaymee squeezed her eyes tightly shut, refusing to look any longer into those laughing wolf eyes. That made things worse, since now his roving fingers were all she could feel.

Without her sight, she caught the change in the tone of his voice. "You have beautiful large nipples. Rosy pink, like seashells. I want to...." Jaymee started to tremble and covered her ears with her hands, trying to keep that voice out. She didn't want to see. She didn't want to hear. He wasn't going to get to her. His muffled voice came through her cupped hands. "All right, we'll change the subject."

His hands paused and lifted from her body. Jaymee sighed with relief. Maybe he was done. Maybe...she shrieked as a hot, wet tongue traveled up where the hand was a moment ago. Her eyes flew open, her hands dropped from her ears, and she scooted high up her bed to escape. The hot, wet tongue followed, and the world suddenly exploded into shadows and sound. She kicked at him with her good leg, giving him the opening he wanted, and she found herself under siege as a slow invasion began.

She fought. How she fought. She tried to buck him off and found herself arching into his deepening kiss. She tried to push off with her one free leg and a strong hand held her down, easily gaining more access. The siege was gaining higher ground. She took tufts of his hair in her hands, but just as she was about to yank hard, he found her vulnerable bud. His tongue slid over it, going in lazy circles.

Jaymee forgot to breathe. She forgot about her hands holding his dark hair like reins. An incoming tide of desire overwhelmed everything else. There was, simply, no escape from his tongue. He kissed her intimately, sexually, giving her the same attention she had earlier envied her computer, seeking to get some answers from her as she arched toward helpless surrender.

The long drawn-out kiss from his magical tongue left her gasping his name now. She stood from some unknown height and was unwilling to make that jump. Mindlessly, she undulated against his mouth, desperately trying to tell him to stop. To hurry.

But Nick wasn't in a hurry. He had all he wanted right there, a feast for his senses. All he could think of was the sweet taste of Jaymee Barrows and he wanted to keep on feasting. He felt her uncertainty, her fear of losing control, and he wanted to show her that there was nothing to be afraid of. So he took her slowly, pulling her nearer to the edge without pushing her, savoring her with careful ardor. He finally tasted her increasing need, her urgent hands pulling his hair. She was ready.

Jaymee's head moved from side to side as she edged closer and closer. She was in a dark, sensuous place, with only the feel of that tantalizing tongue guiding her intense longing for release. Each stroke, each lave, was pure dark magic, until...

His fingers. She'd forgotten about those long, elegant fingers.

And suddenly, it was his mouth and fingers. She whimpered when she felt them touching her, opening her. His mouth caught her throbbing desire and his fingers plunged in deep, and Jaymee fell down that cliff of unbearable pleasure, her body clenching and convulsing in a drenching climax, her hands playing with his hair.

She lay helpless, still climaxing, when he lifted his head and kissed his way up her body. With the towel long gone, his lips lingered softly against her belly, her breast, her neck, until he reached her mouth. He kissed her with the hungry need of a man who wanted a woman, a sexual twining of his tongue with hers, slanting his head one way, then another. She could taste herself on his lips, and she shivered when she felt him hard through his pants.

"Look at me." His voice was ragged, husky. Jaymee's breath caught at the piercing need in his eyes, blue outlines around darkened irises. "I want to take you to bed. I want to make you scream under me, holding me, while I'm inside you. I can have you now, but I won't, because I don't want you making excuses about what happened. I meant it when I told you I'll give you time to get used to me, and I intend to keep my word." He smiled that dazzling, crooked smile of his. "That doesn't mean that I won't do it this way every night to pursue my case. I kinda like the idea."

Her cheeks tinted prettily. "Is that what you do?" she challenged softly, her heart rate almost back to normal. "Pleasure your women until they give in?"

That sexy smile widened even more. "Whatever it takes. Wait till tomorrow." He laughed at the look on her face, then shook his head ruefully. "I don't think it'll be good for my health in the long run, though. I'll have a perpetual cramp myself."

Jaymee couldn't help smiling back, a naughty curl of her lips. "I could knead and massage it away."

Nick groaned, laying his forehead against hers. "Tease."

She licked her lips. "Nicholas, I'm afraid."

"Let me have you, Jaymee. Let me take you to all those places you're so afraid of." He kissed her again, and added, "Let me be your lover."

Jaymee sighed. How on earth had she thought she could resist this man? "For how long?" she asked, knowing the answer.

"For as long as I'm around. I'm being honest, Jaymee. I can't promise you more."

How could she argue against a man who was promising her honesty? "I...."

"Shhh. You aren't required to answer me tonight. You're tired and need to sleep." She made a sound of protest when his weight left her body. "Sit up a minute, sweetheart."

She allowed herself to be pulled up to a sitting position. She felt shy about her nakedness and self-consciously pushed tangled curls away from her face, gathering the heavy mass of damp hair in one of her hands. He pulled her hand away.

"No, don't. You don't know how long I've wanted to see your hair loose like this." He splayed his fingers into the curls, arranging them around her bare shoulders. "Where's your brush?"

"I can't use a brush with hair like this. I use a hair pick." She pointed to the dressing table, and he went to retrieve it.

"This one?" He sat back down beside her and then did something no man had ever done to her before. He combed her hair. Jaymee closed her eyes, enjoying the sensuous pull of the comb as he worked on her tangles, running through it repeatedly until her scalp could have moaned in pleasure. She could...get used to this kind of evening. "You have beautiful hair, Jaymee."

"Bothersome," she mumbled, too relaxed to really want to argue. "Unmanageable."

"Beautiful," he told her again, and gently pushed her back against the pillows. "Gypsy hair. Passionate, sexy, arousing."

Jaymee giggled sleepily. "Passionate hair. Arousing hair. A pig with gypsy hair."

"Pig with what?"

She stretched with artless grace, then yawned behind a hand. "As opposed to Red Riding Hood," she explained.

She wasn't making sense at all, but she was too sexy to sit around just for a conversation. Not when other parts of his body wanted to communicate in other, more satisfying, ways.

"Go to sleep, little pig. I'll let myself out," Nick said, thinking he was going to regret this decision for the rest of the night.

"Hmmm. Are you leaving me?"

"I'd better," he replied, wryly looking down at his damp pants. If he stayed, he would definitely not keep his word.

"Yes, Dad will be home soon..."

He kissed her eyelids and they fluttered shut obediently. "Sleep," he ordered.

She smiled, her eyes closed, as she drifted off.

"Jaymee?"

"Hmmm?"

"Where do you go after work? Before you come home?"

She stretched and sighed with pleasure when he tucked the covers over her. "Working," she told him.

"You've another job?" Nick kept his voice light, but anger reared at the thought that she had to work so hard. For what? He wanted to know the whole story. Was she really in such debt?

She must have read his mind, because she answered him so softly he had to dip his head close to her face. "For my future," she said, and fell into a deep slumber, her body satiated for the first time in eight years.

*

A smart Red Riding Hood would take a different route to avoid the Big Bad Wolf, and a smarter little pig would barricade herself inside her house of stone and not come out till the wolf was gone. However, both Red and the pig didn't have a contract to keep, a job to do, and most of all, they didn't dream of being naked with the Big Bad Wolf.

*He had seen her naked.*

Jaymee looked at the reflection of her body in the mirror. It wasn't like she covered herself from head to foot under the Florida sun, she told herself defensively. He had seen what she looked like when she stripped down to a bikini top at lunchtime. Except that he had kissed there. And, there. A slow flush crept down her face, all the way to her toes.

She touched her breasts with renewed curiosity. She didn't look any different from yesterday, but she felt like a new person, someone who had tingling breasts and sensitive skin. Someone who also, she added with sudden humor, seemed to have pet butterflies in her tummy.

Could he really want this body? It was hardly the kind to interest any man. She looked at the strong arms and legs, a fit and trim body toned by her line of work. There was nothing beguiling about muscles and strength. She didn't have Mindy's generous curves and she'd lost the easy comfortable softness of youth. She wished that she could be feminine again, the way men wanted their women, smelling good and with time to take care of her body; she wanted to look good for.... With a brisk shake of her head, she turned away from the mirror. Jay Barrows didn't want to be feminine for anybody. She had roofs to do, debts to pay, and bigger goals to reach.

It was going to be difficult to face him this morning, and more difficult to say no to him. It would be easy to sleep with a man like Nick, but why should she? Why should she, just because he was the most magnificent male to cross her path in eight years, and the only one who had managed to stir her cold, lonely heart since Danny? A brief affair would be disaster. He'd break her heart, even after giving her fair warning. He'd destroy her carefully constructed armor and...and discover that little girl inside. Silly, guileless Jaymee, who loved with such an ambitious, romantic heart. Already, she could feel that vulnerable side of her stirring, responding. That Jaymee, she smiled tightly, wouldn't know how not to love Nick Langley. She would tumble straight into love, and then, what would she do when he left?

Torn apart with anxiety and a need to see him, she drove to work, wondering if she could bear to say no at all, when her body betrayed her at every chance.

*

Nick was used to not sleeping. The Programmer had been trained to withstand any number of punishments that the enemy might use against him. Lack of sleep, synthetic drugs, hypnosis, pain—every operative in his particular unit had a defensive mechanism and the ability to turn their emotions on and off. Some of them had gone so far that they were always off, to make sure nothing interfered with their work.

For the first time in his operative experience, the Programmer, known for his abilities for covert counter-programming of both the electronic and human mind, couldn't control his own emotions. Nick pondered this problem as he drove to work. It was a problem because it—she, he corrected—was becoming more important to him every day. He sighed. He had a new on/off switch and her name was Jaymee, and she'd been eating at him like one of his own subversive programs. And succeeding.

When he reached the job site, Dicker and Lucky were sitting in their truck, smoking. He got out and approached the vehicle.

"What's up?" he asked. They weren't unloading the tools, or getting ready to get on the roof.

"Trouble, man," Dicker said, thumbing at two parked cars on the other side of the road.

Nick looked and saw two men talking by the permit board. "Who are they?"

"That's the builder and the other is one of the city code-inspectors." Dicker flicked cigarette ash out of the window. "The builder won't let us start work, saying that he wanted to talk to Jay."

"And that means trouble?"

"It smells like it," the roofer said.

Just then, Jaymee's blue truck pulled up. Nick watched her frown up at the roof, not seeing any work being done, then looked around searching for them. Her frown deepened when she looked in their direction and caught sight of all the vehicles.

"The boss is going to have a wasted day," prophesied Dicker.

"Shoot, I should have stayed home," Lucky muttered, crushing his cigarette into the ashtray. "It's too damned hot to sit in the truck while they go back and forth about God knows what."

Jaymee's eyes were still on the two other men when she reached them. "What happened?" she quietly asked.

"The builder wants to talk to you, Jay, that's all he told us," Dicker informed her. "Here they come."

"'Morning, Mr. Anderson," Jaymee greeted a burly man. Nick assumed that he was the builder, since the other man was in uniform.

"Hello, Jay." He towered over Jaymee as he stood in front of her. In his fifties, he had the sunburned complexion of an outdoor man, slightly balding with a shaggy mustache peppered with gray. He looked irritated, and Nick stepped closer, standing behind Jaymee. "We have a problem."

Jay could feel Nick's presence, but kept her eyes on the builder. She didn't like this at all. "What's wrong?" she asked.

"John wants to have a random inspection of some of your roofs." Mr. Anderson nodded at the inspector beside him.

"What's wrong?" Jaymee calmly repeated, this time directing her question at the other man.

John wiped the sweat off his forehead with a crisp, white handkerchief. He stood like a military man, a clipboard clutched to his chest, his thin lips a straight line across his narrow face. "We've received a complaint about your roofs," he told her in a clipped, accusing voice, slightly high pitch. "A code violation." He cast her an equally accusing glare.

Jaymee sighed with the impatience of someone waiting for a punch line. "And?" She made a "continue, please," gesture with one hand.

"Beg your pardon?"

"What is the complaint?" Jaymee asked, trying not to be rude. "What code have I violated?"

"Well, someone called in and said you've been undernailing the shingles. Instead of six nailing, you've been telling your men to four-nail, even two-nail. You've also not been properly applying tar in the valleys."

Nick saw the slight stiffening in Jaymee's shoulders, but her voice sounded mildly surprised. "Really?" She folded her arms. "Who filed these complaints?"

"You know we can't reveal that information." The inspector wiped his forehead again, then adjusted a piece of paper on his clipboard. He clicked on his ballpoint pen with an important flourish. "I can't let you or your men start work until I'm sure that everything you've done is up to county code. This is a serious complaint, Miss Barrows, and I'm very thorough with my inspections."

"I'm sure you are," Jaymee said, with a polite smile. "Can you give me a few minutes to rework my men's day before I follow you to whichever roof you want to check?"

"Of course." John noted something down onto his clipboard. "Are you coming with us, Anderson?"

"What for? Either the roofs are done right, or they aren't. My being there won't make any difference. I've other things to do. Call me on the cell phone when you're through, will you, John?" When the inspector walked back to his truck, Mr. Anderson turned to Jaymee. "This is serious, Jay. If you really did that, I want you off my property effective immediately. I can't have the word getting around that Excel Construction cuts corners and violates code ordinances, or some of these zealous inspectors will just give me headaches looking for more violations."

"There aren't any problems with my roofs," Jaymee assured the big man.

"You know how it is, Jay. The more codes they add, the higher our cost. Right now, I don't make much per house as it is. You understand, as a businessman, I'm always listening to bids and deals from other subcontractors."

Nick didn't like the man's implication. He wanted to step between them, to protect her, but of course he couldn't. For the first time, he wished he had the right to do that.

Jaymee heard Mr. Anderson's warning like far-off thunder. "It's your right to compare prices, of course," she murmured politely.

"We'll just have a talk after you get through with John."

"Sure."

Jaymee gave a cold smile, then turned her back to the contractor, effectively dismissing him. "Dicker, go pick up the order at the warehouse and leave the material at my house. Then you and Lucky can meet me there after lunch."

"OK, boss."

Jaymee ignored Mr. Anderson as she headed back to her truck. "Bring your tool belt, Nick."

The burly contractor stared at her retreating back, then looked at Nick. Nick stifled a grin, obeying orders. General Jay, as he usually called her when she acted that particular way, wasn't in the mood to be intimidated, even by the big man who signed her check every week.

When he joined her in the truck, Jaymee finally smiled at him. Starting the vehicle, she turned on the air-conditioning to a full blast before turning the truck around to follow the inspector's. She blew hair out of her eyes.

"The day is shot," she said, with a sigh, "and I haven't even climbed on a roof yet."

He took hold of one of her hands and gave it a quick squeeze. "I assume this is Rich's and Chuck's doing?"

Her smile became a grimace as she nodded. "Petty creatures. I want to punch the lights out of them."

"What if the inspector finds something?"

"He won't." Her voice was confident as she kept her eyes on the inspector's truck, following him through the subdivision. "I went back on every roof those two have done, and made sure there wasn't any undernailing after I caught them. I think they just started doing this stupid stuff recently, when I let them work alone without me."

Nick could imagine her checking everything. Others might have shrugged and hoped not to get caught, but Jaymee was a perfectionist, a detail-meister. "So what would the inspector want you to do?"

She shrugged. "Probably climb onto a roof with him and lift up a couple of shingles here and there to show him the nailing. John has a reputation of being a pain in the butt, if he doesn't like you. And he doesn't like me, so don't be surprised if he wants all kinds of things done." They slowed down in front of a stucco house. "Bingo. One of Rich's and Chuck's houses."

She parked the truck. Nick ran a hand down her back and felt her shiver.

"Want to have some fun with Mr. John Inspector?" he asked, a slight grin forming.

Jaymee would much rather have fun with the man beside her. He had that glint in his eyes again, she noticed, the one that made him look roguish. She watched the inspector step smartly out of his vehicle, brushing his pants with the perfect starched creases. Her eyes narrowed.

"I'm losing money, anyway. Might as well have some fun."

They discreetly slapped a high-five.

The next two hours, as the sun went higher and higher in the sky, Jaymee dallied as long as possible on each roof, calling out to Nick to retrieve tools that somehow managed to slide off the roof. Like he'd warned, the inspector was very thorough on the first roof, but as he became hotter, he cut down on his requests to check the smaller stuff.

"The shingles are stuck down good, aren't they?" Jaymee cheerfully commented as she took her time detaching the one at which the inspector was pointing. Using a flat bar, she finally loosened it enough to flip it up for him to see that there were indeed six nails in that shingle. "Any other area?"

"Over there, by the valley," the inspector said, puffing up the incline.

Nick took the flat bar and imitated Jaymee, but being a novice, he soon poked a big hole through the shingle.

"Ooops." He looked adoringly apologetic at Jaymee, and it was all she could do not to smirk at the schoolboy expression on his face. "Sorry, boss."

Jaymee shook her head. "Go down and get some cement. We'll have to patch it up." She turned to the inspector and said, "He's rather new at this, but he's quite good for a beginner."

"Uh-huh," muttered John, wiping sweat off his flushed face.

"As you know, it's all cemented down at the valley," explained Jaymee, "so it'll take a little longer to peel it back."

"Never mind," the inspector said. "If it's cemented, that's all I need to know. Just patch that up and let's go on to the next roof."

"Oh, sure. Nick, where are you?" Jaymee yelled, standing at the edge of the roof.

"I'm looking for the cement," he called back.

Jaymee rolled her eyes. "It's the blue can in the back of the truck!"

"Oh!"

"He's a little slow," she sweetly told John. "Gosh, it's hot today, isn't it? Must be a hundred degrees up here."

By the third roof, the inspector's crisp, white shirt was plastered against his skinny frame. The pants lost the starched-up look. The man was sweating so profusely, Jaymee gave him a towel to wipe off.

"We should take a break, John," she told him. "Let's do that, and then continue with the other houses. How many more did you want to see? We'd better get on them before the noon sun bakes them up."

John shuddered as if he couldn't bear the thought of staying out in that heat all day. "This is it," he firmly declared, marking down on his clipboard. "Everything looks fine to me, Miss Barrows. The complainant was obviously wrong."

She pulled off her tee-shirt and wiped the perspiration from her body with it. She gave the inspector a brilliant smile and tilted her head back. "Can I get a copy of your inspections? If any other contractors have doubts, I can just show them your forms. That'd really help me out, John." She walked to the flushed-face man and handed him her water bottle from the cooler. "Something to help cool you off."

A few minutes later, she waved jauntily at the departing inspector, then turned to find Nick leaning with folded arms against the tailgate of her truck, his head cocked to one side.

"What?" she asked.

"Come here," he ordered, softly. That schoolboy look was gone. Jaymee slowly approached him, wondering what had brought out that glint in those blue-gray eyes. When she stood in front of him, a long finger slid under her chin to tilt her face up. She stared, squinting against the bright sunlight. "Where did you learn to do that?"

"Do what?"

"Tease a man like that. The poor son of a bitch almost had a heat stroke when you took off that tee-shirt."

A slow, sultry smile spread on her face, making Nick catch his breath. Without her usual guarded expression, she was like sunshine, her face warm and inviting.

"Serves him right," Jaymee said. "I wasn't teasing him, anyhow. I was hot, too, what with your great acting talent in making us suffer through all your mistakes."

They both started chuckling, and the humor grew into full-scale laughter as they remembered the poor inspector toasting in the heat when Nick dropped the hammer off house number one, forgot the inspector's nail-puller on house number two (that had caused them to drive back to retrieve it), and lastly, disappeared for almost fifteen minutes to look for a portable bathroom. All minor, but added to the minutes on each baking roof.

Jaymee found herself in his arms, still laughing helplessly. It felt good to be hugged by a man again, to share funny moments like this. His hands traveled up and down her back, and she laid her cheek on his chest, inhaling the scent of sweat and man.

She was so small, he could drape her over his chest like a pet, Nick observed, as he circled her waist with his hands. So tiny, and yet, so strong. He wanted her so much.

Jaymee could feel him growing hard against her and she rolled her head back. His gaze was hot and untamed, and she could see the tic of his jaw muscle just under his left ear. For the first time in eight years, she didn't feel the usual fear, the need to back away from such blatant invitation. Her spirit was strangely light, as if some burden had been taken off. Boldly, she placed her small hands on his muscular shoulders and braced her weight on them, then she climbed onto the bumper, planting a leg on each side of the tall, lanky man, trapping him between the vee of her legs. His gaze blazed a few degrees higher.

"Do you know, Nick Langley, that you have the longest and sexiest eyelashes on a man that I've ever seen?"

Her face so close to his that he could see the changing green flecks in her eyes. "Is that right?" he drawled, easily balancing her weight against his body. Draped on him like a pet, he repeated silently.

"Mmmhmm. It's terribly unfair what those eyes do to a woman." There was a growing excitement inside Jaymee that made her feel sexy, invincible. Tentatively, she licked his crooked smile with a pink tongue, tasting him. "Delicious," she murmured, and did it again, this time, a lot more boldly. "You're incredibly edible."

He was so hard he could feel his pants' zipper. "I..." He slid his hand behind her neck. "...just found out something that's been puzzling me."

"What's that?" Jaymee nibbled on his lower lip. She felt his thudding heartbeat under her palm.

Nick growled, trying to catch those teasing lips. He applied pressure on her neck. "I couldn't see how you and Mindy could be such good friends, but now I know why," he muttered, pressing her closer.

"Oh?" She resisted a little longer.

"There's a lot more Mindy in you than you let on, Jaymee girl."

"Mmmmmph!" And that was all he allowed her to say as he tugged hard and her teasing mouth fitted against his demanding one. He kissed her with a leisurely thoroughness that zoned out the world, until they both forgot where they were, and how hot it was, until a passing truck honked. Some guys hooted as they drove by.

"Ravish me too, lady!" one yelled.

"Give him a heat stroke, babe!" another suggested with a leer.

Jaymee surfaced, slightly out of breath. "What are you doing to me?" she demanded, still dazed from the kiss. "I'm standing on the bumper, at a job site, letting you kiss me!"

"Umm, excuse me, boss," Nick drawled, his own breath slightly uneven too. "I'm the one being ravished."

He pointedly opened his arms to show how helpless he was under her. His hair was sexily tousled by her roaming hands. His shirt was untucked, almost pulled off his shoulders.

Did she do that? Jaymee jumped off the bumper. She must appear like a desperate woman, tearing at his shirt in bright sunlight!

"That's all I need! Get a reputation for shoddy work, then get another for running around with the help." She pulled on a dry tee-shirt over her bikini. Why was she behaving so strangely? This wasn't her at all, this bold, restless woman. She'd better get back to normal, dependable Jay as quickly as possible. She took a deep breath. "Let's get this meeting with Anderson over with. I've a bad feeling about what he wants."

Nick sighed. He was so aroused, he'd have flipped down the tailgate and had her there, if they weren't out by the road. He couldn't recall a single time when a woman switched from kissing him to business with barely a blink of an eye. He must be losing his touch. He tucked in his shirt. His sanity, obviously, was a lost cause, what with his libido creating havoc every time this woman was around. He watched her behind as she climbed into the truck and grinned. This kind of insanity, he decided, was a lot more fun than the kind with which he usually dealt.

The reminder of his actual life sobered him. Watching Jaymee smooth back those tempting curls, her cheeks still rosy from the sun and his kiss, it occurred to him that there were other things, much, much more enjoyable in the real world than playing hi-tech games with mostly unseen enemies.

\*

When they were on the way to the contractor's office, Nick asked, "Why all this worry over the contractor? The inspector didn't find any violations, so there shouldn't be any problems, right?"

Jaymee's mouth twisted in a grimace. "You don't know this area very well, do you? He's going to ask me to cut my price."

"Can he do that? Didn't you sign a contract with him?"

"Where have you been?" Jaymee gave him a long stare at the stop sign. "Construction down here doesn't work like that. If they want to fire you, they fire you."

"Can't you take them to court?"

Jaymee laughed. She pulled the truck in front of a building with a big sign that said "EXCEL CONSTRUCTION." Leaning over, she pinched Nick. Hard.

"Ow!" He rubbed the spot, frowning.

"Just making sure you aren't dreaming," she smoothly told him with a mischievous smile.

"I'm going to paddle your ass for that!" Nick promised, still looking at the mark.

"Poor baby. I'm going to add this to that list about clues to not being a construction man," she teased.

"What's wrong with going to court?" Nick demanded, when they were walking toward the office. "Broken contracts are litigable, according to tort law."

Jaymee stopped dead in her tracks and burst out into such hard laughter, she had to sit down under a decorative palm planted in the parking lot. As he continued to frown down at her, she went off into another round of chuckles. She held up a hand, asking for his help to get back on her feet. When he did, she wiped away tears with the heel of her hands, then cleaned them on her tee-shirt.

"I'm not laughing at you, not really," she said, in between gasps. "You know, the last time I heard talk like that, I was taking a college business law course."

Nick arched a questioning brow. "College, huh?"

Jaymee copied the gesture, lifting her brow in answer. "Yeah, except none of those things work like that. Small businesses like mine don't have the money or the time to go chasing after contracts and small claims, Nick. We're too busy trying to keep the business going. By the time you pay off the lawyer, you're probably worse off, so why bother?" She started toward the building again. "Come on, I'll show you how it is in real life, Mr. Programmer."

The off-handed nom de guerre almost made him trip. Jaymee didn't notice the sharp look he gave her, already skipping up the steps to the office. She called over her shoulder, "Hurry up. I want to get back home to see what trouble Dicker and Lucky are in now. They're still on the clock."

He grinned. The woman was cocky, confident, and damned arrogant when it came to her business. He couldn't wait to see the softer side again, when he finally got her into his bed.

\*

"You don't seem disappointed about losing the subdivision," Nick commented later, as they drove back to where his jeep was still parked.

Jaymee shrugged. She was devastated, but that didn't matter now. "That's how it goes."

"Why didn't you come down in price as Anderson wanted?"

The competition, according to the builder was offering two dollars less per square for material and labor, and he wanted Jaymee to match or beat that price. A square was approximately a hundred square foot, and Nick calculated that dropping two dollars for a forty-squared roof would probably eat up the little profit she'd make per job. He'd stood there and admired the way she'd refused to back down and give in, choosing instead to tell Anderson that he should hire that other company, if they could give him the same quality of work at a lower price.

"My price is very fair as it is, and he knows it," Jaymee scoffed. "The competition's Gregg's Roofing, and I know Gregg's. They're a huge operation, with high overhead, and I know they can't stay with this lower price without losing money."

"So, either Gregg's will raise the price later, or Anderson's merely gambling on the fact that you might swallow the two dollars," Nick concluded. There wasn't much difference between price wars and covert wars, he surmised. Mostly a game of chicken.

"Yeah. Even if I'd been crazy enough to give that price, I have no guarantee that next month he won't find another competitor with another lower price offer. How much cheaper can I go before I cut my losses?"

"So you just walk away and find another subdivision?"

"I have other builders that need roofers. Don't worry, you still have a job, Nick. Here we are." She stopped the truck behind his fire engine red jeep.

Nick took her averted chin between his thumb and finger and gently tugged on it till she reluctantly looked at him. Her eyes were that dark, murky color again, the swirl of emotions tightly hidden in their depths. She was more upset than she let on, he realized, remembering the constant pressure of some debt that she owed.

Running his thumb across her obstinate lower lip, he asked, "After work, in the evening, what other job do you have?" At her look of surprise, he added, "You mentioned something like that last night, remember?"

Did she? She couldn't remember a thing about last night except...except.... She felt the telltale heat suffusing her face again. Her wandering thoughts brought out an answering heat in his eyes, and she hastily stammered, changing the subject to anything, anything, but that, "It's nothing, really."

Nick wouldn't let her chin go. "You said that about your cramp last night too," he told her in the same quiet voice. "You worked till your body gave out on you, Jaymee. Why?" His voice went lower, to a gravelly growl. "I want to be with you tonight."

A slow burn started at those direct words, an unfamiliar aching that pulsed inside her. Jaymee swallowed hard, trying to compose herself. "I...I have stuff to do."

"You're a non-stop working machine, but unless you tell me what job you do after work, I'm going to stay and tire you out." He leaned so close she could smell that intoxicating masculine scent that seemed to drive away all her common sense. "Babe, there are shadows under your eyes at night. You could barely stay awake when I worked with your files, and yet you still go about vacuuming and housekeeping. Now I find out that you actually work somewhere else in the evenings. No wonder you're always tired. No wonder your leg cramped up."

He made her sound so horribly ugly. Shadows under her eyes. Tired-looking. She must be so boring. When did she become like that? Jaymee impatiently pushed away her self-pity. She made a last resort to defend herself. "I like to work."

"Not till you drop," he countered, but he didn't sound accusing or mocking. "Look, I'm not criticizing you. I know how strong a person you are, but lean a little, damn it."

"On whom? My dad?" she shot back, one corner of her mouth lifted in disgust.

"On me." Nick's hand slid from her chin to her shoulder and he pulled her even closer. "For now. You're an amazing woman, Jaymee, but give yourself a break."

Amazing? Strong? She stared back in confusion. Did he just praise her?

"Your eyes say you don't believe me," he remarked, when she didn't say anything.

"It's difficult to jump from being told you're tired-looking and owl-eyed to you're amazing and strong in less than a minute," she pointed out.

Nick grinned. "Women," he complained. "They always zero in on the wrong things first."

Jaymee's eyes were green and suspicious. "And how many women have you been telling that they're strong and amazing?"

He gave the query a long enough consideration to see her small eyes narrow into warning slits. She looked like a cat about to pounce, he thought, amusement rising. This new switch was unexpected; he hadn't realized that he could make her jealous.

"Not any that looked tired or owl-eyed," he finally drawled out, then kissed her on the lips hard before she could respond. "I think it's safer for me to be in my Jeep now. I'll be a good worker, but you're going to talk to me after work—" He opened the door, and added, "—boss."

*

Not that there was much work to do for the rest of the day. "The day just isn't meant to be," she said to no one in particular, as she stood in her driveway staring at the looming dark clouds descending like angry warlords.

"Where do you want us to meet tomorrow, Jay?" Dicker asked from under a tree in her front yard.

"Do we have any job, seeing that Excel's fired you?" Lucky wanted to know, scratching the back of his neck with a twig.

Jaymee didn't correct the wrong assumption, that she was fired. Still looking at the ominous sky, she said, "I'll line up a few jobs. We were supposed to do a roof this Friday for another builder, but I'll see whether it's ready for us tomorrow. Meet me here in the morning."

The two men moved toward Dicker's truck. "Who did Excel get to replace us, do you know, boss?" Dicker asked.

Jaymee shrugged. "I think it's Gregg's, but I don't really know."

"Say, that's where Chuck and Rich said they were working now," Lucky commented.

"Mighty good timing, if you ask me," observed Dicker, as he closed the big toolbox mounted behind his truck. "See you in the morning, boss. Bye, Nick."

Nick nodded as he adjusted the hood that protected his Jeep from the elements. "Yeah. See you, Dicker."

Jaymee watched him for a moment. "Need help?"

"No, I'm almost done."

"I'm going inside for a late lunch. Hungry?"

He gave her a look that sent her scrambling toward the back of the house with his laughter following her. How did he do that? She nervously rubbed her hands on her pants. One look, and she felt like a tar kettle on fire. Where were her well-practiced rebuffs? A few weeks ago, she'd have squashed such blatant come-ons like a gnat, and the poor man would have left her alone after that. But of course, Nick was a humongous gnat, and she laughed at her silliness. Another thing—where did this silliness come from?

Big plops of rain came down just as she climbed up onto the back porch. She waited for a minute or two, but he didn't turn the corner.

"Nick?" she called over the rush of wind that usually signaled the beginning of a Florida summer storm. It was suddenly dark outside, all sunlight curtained off by rain-swollen clouds.

"Get inside, Jaymee. I'll be there," she heard him answer. Satisfied, she went into the kitchen to prepare a quick snack.

Finishing his task, Nick glanced around the front yard, ignoring the fast falling rain. He had an uneasy feeling that he was being watched, and he scanned the terrain carefully. With the wind picking up, he couldn't really see anything among the moving clumps of trees in the acreage. Big sheets of rain descended suddenly, ferociously, and he hurried to the back of the house. Too late, he was instantly drenched to the skin.

Jaymee took one look at him and shook her head. "What were you doing out there?" She put away the bread and screwed the cap back on the jar of mayonnaise. "Guess I'll get you a towel first, and something dry to wear."

She disappeared in the direction of her bedroom. Opportunity knocking, he quoted his favorite saying under his breath, and promptly followed her.

Jaymee had a suspicious inkling that she was walking into a trap of her own making. He didn't make a sound as he casually walked behind her, past the sofa in the living room, round the corner, past the spare bedroom. Her room at the back of the house was down a long corridor and it usually only took a minute from kitchen to bedroom door. Today it appeared to last forever as she trotted down seemingly narrowing walls.

She stopped outside, turned around and firmly said, "You can't come in here. I'll get the towel and a shirt."

"I've been in there before," he reminded her and came closer.

Was that thunder from outside or was that her heart? "Nicholas...you're not making this easy," she breathed out.

Nick gently reached behind her and opened the bedroom door. "Easy is laying shingles in the summer. Easy is working till you drop." He backed her into her own room, drops of water trickling onto her dry clothes. "Handling me should be a piece of cake, Jaymee."

Despite the precariousness of her situation, she couldn't resist a small smile. "So you compare yourself to a job for me to handle?"

"Don't you take care of every detail in your work?"

His drenched shirt contoured the muscles of his chest and stomach. His long hair, dripping wet and blown by the wind, looked like a mane. She could see the tic under his ear again, the sudden flair of his nostrils, the tightly-drawn passion on the plains of his face.

"Yes," she answered.

"Don't you make sure everything is perfect when it comes to your work?"

She couldn't deny her obsession for getting things right. "I...try."

"Don't you remember everything there's to know about every one of your roofs? The color, the square footage, down to the day you were on it?"

She stared into those blue-gray eyes, drawn by their seductive power. "Yes," she said again.

Nick's eyes became intensely, fiercely demanding. "That's how I want you to handle me, Jaymee. As easily as you handle your perfect roofs."

He didn't have to tell her that her time was up. He'd waited and patiently let her get used to him, as he had so arrogantly told her. It must be magic. He'd brought out the Jaymee she'd desperately tried to hide and now, he summoned her like a pagan witch calling for a spirit under his power. The rain outside drummed on the roof and danced against the windowpanes, like some incantation that rendered her powerless to this man. His foot kicked back, and the door behind him clicked shut.

# Chapter Six

The bedroom was darkened by the storm outside, and Jaymee couldn't see Nick's face. In the shadows, his words coursed through her veins like warm brandy, and she felt hot and out of breath, like she'd been running fast. Except that she couldn't run any more. She realized that he'd stalked her all this time, allowing her to move away only because he wanted to.

Now, with her bed behind her, the door shut, the rain a steady rhythm outside, and no job to finish, there was nowhere she could hide, no work for her to use as an excuse. With small, jerky movements, she backed away. Nick's hand snaked out and held her arm, pulling her inexorably closer.

"Easy," he repeated softly, as if she was a nervous mare. "Easy, sweet Jaymee. We'll do it slow and easy."

"You're all wet," she said belligerently.

Of course he was all wet. She was going to get him a towel and that was what got her into this situation. Her mind fought for control over the internal storm muddling through her system, as she allowed herself to be backed all the way into her bathroom.

"Dry me," he murmured in that soft, gravelly tone of voice. The look in his eyes made her gut clenched. She swallowed.

Without thinking, she automatically pulled the towel hanging on a hook, then stupidly stared at the wet clothes on him. Her eyes followed the heaving motions of his chest, moving up to study with fascination the droplets of water that were still running down his strong neck, and still higher, all the way to the wet lock of dark hair that curled over his forehead.

"I can't," she whispered.

"You have to take off my clothes first," he whispered back. "Take care of me, Jaymee."

She opened her mouth but words wouldn't come. Instead, she pushed the toilet seat down and gestured at it. He sat, opening his long legs and pulling her between his thighs. She gave him a desperate look, mutely begging him to release her, but he only took the towel from her and then placed her hands on him, near the waistband of his jeans.

The glitter in his eyes seemed to pull at her. He had a power over her like no other man.

Jaymee found herself pulling the wet shirt out of his pants, tugging it as he helped her by lifting those muscular arms. Picking up the towel from his lap, she slowly rubbed his chest with it, one hand following the path of the towel. It was strangely empowering as she moved over him, taking her own time at it, exploring every part of him that had fascinated her. He was cool to the touch, and she pulled the towel languorously over his chest, then down those abs that she was sure didn't come from roofing work, her finger scraping over the little "outie" belly button. The feel of his skin—the texture, the softness of his body hair, the ridges in the abdominal muscles—mesmerized her. Had she ever felt a man's body like this before? All power and promise and patience. For her. Just for her.

It was exciting to feel a man's passion, and she reveled at his barely suppressed desire under her exploring hands. It moved like an electric current everywhere she caressed. Over the taut shoulders. Slowly down the broad back. And up the flat of his belly over his broad chest.

Nick kicked off his shoes and stood up, waiting. Her teeth biting down on her lower lip, Jaymee reached cautiously for the top button of his jeans, and his belly sucked in as she released it. Her fingers hesitated over the zipper. She stared with intrigued rapture as the bulge under the restricting material grew, daring her to touch it. He still didn't say a word, just stood there, but she could hear his deep and harsh breathing.

For her.

She touched him, and heard a groan, but her eyes were riveted to that part of him that was pulsating under her hand. It felt impossibly huge, hidden from her, and she wanted to see him. Slowly, tentatively, she pulled at the zipper. He helped her with it, and she soon found out why.

Nick Langley wasn't wearing any underwear. He was all male glory under those jeans and his erection sprang into her waiting hands. She gasped at its heat—a fierce, powerful arousal that called out to her, demanded her.

Nick's eyes closed for a moment as he checked the immediate painful need to thrust into those small hands. Sweet baby Jesus, but the woman didn't know the torture she was giving. With a smothered groan, he sat back down on the toilet seat. It was either that, or push her against some wall and go at her like a mad, lusting bull.

Instead he sat still, letting her take charge. Her hands were heavenly soft and wildly exciting. She touched him like a man wanted to be touched, with teasing gentleness mixed with a tinge of sadistic torture. At least, that was how he viewed it, as those hands moved down his hard length and cupped his softness, running her fingernails with unexpected mischief back to the tip where it was most sensitive. He growled, unable to bear it any more.

Startled, she looked up, a dreamy expression on her face. "You wanted me to take care of all the details," she said, still stroking him.

He felt himself hardened even more at her words. "You're doing an excellent job," he told her, the harshness in the tone of his voice bringing a smile to her face.

He watched her pull at his jeans and he kicked them off. He wanted her naked and reached for her, but she surprised him by kneeling down between the vee of his thighs. All muscles tensed. It was all he could do not to growl again when she leaned down and tentatively tasted him.

That did it. No more.

Nick dragged her onto his lap. She sat willingly astride him, intimately pushing against his engorged need that was begging for release.

"Do you know what you're doing to me?"

He removed the pins and barette in her hair, scattering them onto the tile floor. The heavy tresses flowed down in ringlets, just the way he wanted it.

"My big, bad wolf," she whispered. "Not nice. Not safe."

He'd warned her about that in the study. "And definitely never easy," he admitted, and with one fluid motion, ripped her old tee-shirt to rags.

Her small eyes grew positively huge as he impatiently pulled at her bra, snapping the material in half. He was still in control—barely. His turn to taste.

Jaymee gasped as he sucked at her nipple. His mouth felt shockingly hot, in contrast to the coolness of his skin. The pleasure zinged through her body. Wanting more, she rocked back, giving him more access, even as she pushed down against the rock-hard length burning so intimately against her. To know a man would want her so—the scent of clean male flesh, the feel of his heartbeat under her hand—was the most erotic sensation she had ever known. She whimpered at the sensuous assault of his mouth and tongue, and dug her nails into his shoulders.

In response, he wrapped her legs tightly around his waist and stood up, and she clung on as he strode back into the bedroom. Standing at the foot of her queen-size bed, she felt his hands grope the back of her Lycra pants and easily rip that apart too. Her body trembled with shock at the barely contained violence of his actions. He lowered them both onto the bed, and she lay there passively, staring up into the dark shadows of his face.

His head lowered and she closed her eyes. His kiss was hard and possessive. His tongue danced across hers and demanded response until she became lost in a vortex of desire and need. Licking her lips, he ran his tongue down her neck, over her breast, stopping on one rosy nipple, then traveled down her torso to dip into her belly button. She arched helplessly and heard the front of her pants ripped to shreds as well. His roving tongue went lower, over skimpy panties, and tasted the soft, silky flesh between her thigh and her waiting, aroused sex, and she moved restlessly, letting him get rid of what was left of her pants from each leg.

"I'm going to eat you," Nick promised, from between her legs and bit down on the soft flesh of her inner thigh. A soft wail erupted from her as he started to nibble the vulnerable flesh. His hand on her tummy held her down and nudging the panties aside, he began to do exactly as he promised. Unlike the night before, he wasn't teasing or patient; this time, he was all conquering male, intent on taking what was his. Her breathing came out in gasps as she tried valiantly to hold onto some sort of control.

Shifting position, he put two hands on her last piece of protection and with a savage hiss, tore her wispy string bikini away like pieces of paper. A moment later, his weight was on her, and he held her face still between his large hands. Staring deeply into her eyes, he began to push inside her. He nudged her thighs higher, demanding more.

Control slipped away like the outgoing tide. Jaymee whimpered. He felt hard and immensely huge against her vulnerable flesh, and every one of her feminine muscles bucked inside with panic at the unfamiliar siege. Unfamiliar, because it had been eight, long years. Her muscles, taught to resist, fought to stop the invasion, tightening and pushing back.

"Relax, baby," Nick said, sounding strained. "Let me in."

But her body seemed to have a mind of its own, and was determined to forbid entry. He inched in, and despite her readiness, she groaned at the discomfort. A niggling doubt arose. Maybe there was something wrong with her. Maybe she just wasn't good at this and was going to embarrass herself. Panicking, she started to push and fight him off.

Nick felt her growing alarm and looked down at her, her eyes so tightly shut, little drops of tears squeezed out at the corners. He immediately stopped pushing, kissing her eyes until she opened them again. He could feel every tremor of her body. His own was trembling too, desperate to have her. He'd never wanted—needed—a woman more in his life, and determined not to frighten her, he fought for every ounce of control that was left in him.

"Look at me, Jaymee."

Her eyes brimmed with tears and her lips trembled. "I c...can't do it, Nick. You're too...big."

Nick just smiled tenderly down at her and told her, "Yes, you can, darling. I forgot to go slow and easy, that's all."

Fiercely clamping down on his raging desire, he rained soft kisses on her face, until she started responding. He searched for a distraction and found her ear.

Jaymee jerked when his tongue slipped into that erogenous shell and helpless gurgled as it wickedly explored. All the blood in her brain seemed to disappear. She tried to squirm away, but it insistently plunged in and out until she melted into the pillows, moaning softly, incoherently. In the helpless throes of that clever tongue, her body let its guard down, and with one decisive thrust, Nick pushed inside her, filling her all the way. She gasped at the fullness of his possession. He pushed her thighs higher still and sank even deeper inside her.

Nick fought for control. God, she was tight, holding him as possessively as he wanted to take her. If he moved, it'd be all over. A roaring need blanketed everything else, and he groaned at the sheer agony of needing to thrust and yet not daring.

Jaymee couldn't breathe, gasping for air, as his hard length continued to fill and stretch her. The discomfort disappeared as her body adjusted and accommodated to his size. Every nerve sang with anticipation. Why wasn't he moving? She needed him.

"Please," she moaned. "Please, pleasepleaseplease..."

Nick moved out, then slid back in. They both moaned in unison.

He moved slowly at first, carefully, as if he were afraid to hurt her. The pleasure from the tortuous slide of his thick length inside her was beyond anything she'd ever experienced. And each time he plunged deeply, she didn't want him to leave her, and he returned, steady and sure, to take her even higher. She arched up, wanting more.

Wet and hot. Nick closed his eyes at the feel of her womanly softness. Home and paradise. Every stroke was bliss and agony, and with every thrust, he wanted to go deeper into the woman. Bury so deep, his thoughts would just fixate on this feeling of being taken and giving himself. So deep, like this. And this. Take this. He didn't think he'd ever get deep enough.

There was taste and texture, as flesh slapped into flesh, as tongue tangled with tongue. Mindless pleasure built until each glide of his flesh was a mini orgasm, and she couldn't see or hear anything but their beating hearts echoing each other. And then the world simply tilted off its axis and the universe was bright with exploding stars.

They shuddered against each other, still mating with tongue and flesh and soul, speaking a universal language as they strained and pressed again and again. At last, a warm, sweet darkness overtook their frenzied dance. Minutes, or forever— they couldn't tell—went by. The rain still pattered on the rooftop. The room was dark and musky. In the shadows, still joined, they stared at each other, afraid that if they moved, the magic spell might be broken.

Jaymee searched for words, but none came. Never had she given herself like this to a man, so totally that her body felt like it was no longer hers, her mind in a stupor from the experience. Whatever she'd felt before for Danny was some silly myth, compared to this churning maelstrom. Her heart rejoiced, but her mind mourned, because she knew that she'd fallen in love. She loved him, and he'd told her he was leaving.

Nick stared down at the passionate woman under him. Did he think he could switch her on and off, give her what she wanted and needed, and somehow avoid any long-lasting effect on himself? He'd known from the very first that she was different, that his feelings for her were more complex than mere attraction. What they just shared proved it—she belonged with him. He belonged with her, damn it. And there was nothing he could do to make it last. It was simply not possible. He couldn't see her away from her business, plucked from her responsibilities that she took so seriously.

Jaymee stirred under him. "I think I died," she said, awe in her voice.

He smiled down at her. "Am I too heavy?" He shifted.

"No," she immediately protested. "Don't. Not yet."

He understood. Like him, she didn't want to disconnect yet. He was, to his amazement, still semi-aroused. Not possible, after that mind-blowing orgasm that had had him pounding into her like a wild animal, but the hard evidence was undeniable. He surged back in, and they both sighed with pleasure.

"I can keep going till the storm stops," he offered.

Jaymee smiled in the darkness. "I don't think it will ever abate," she told him.

Her honesty touched him. She was a woman who didn't play coy or hard to get. She had resisted out of fear, and once she had discovered that the fear was nothing, she'd given herself wholly, taking back ecstasy in equal measure. He loved her lack of pretense. He loved her passion, which she'd hidden behind her work.

He inhaled sharply. Did he just say he loved?

"Do you still want lunch?" she asked, her shyness interrupting the sudden earth-shattering disclosure.

"Hmmm?" he asked, still grappling with the truth.

"Food," she repeated. "Sustenance." Her stomach rumbled helpfully.

Nick laughed. "Woman, you're bad for my ego. I kiss you, and you talk business with a contractor. I make love to you, and all you want afterwards is food."

He pulled out of her, and she contracted, still reluctant about letting him go.

"I'm just fueling you up, that's all. Can't have you running on empty." She laughed when he bit her shoulder menacingly.

"Later," he promised, "but only after you tell me about your other job."

Jaymee sighed. She'd forgotten about that memory of his. "See here," she said, as she rolled off the bed, "there must be a fair exchange. I'll tell you my secret, if you tell me yours."

Leaning over the night table, she turned the light on, and they both blinked at the sudden brightness. She did it on purpose, wanting to look at him.

Nick lounged on his side lazily, watching her as she stood up. She was damned distracting, and she knew it, using her nakedness to try to get information from him. He grinned. If he didn't know her, he'd have suspected her of being the enemy. His grin widened as she picked up the little rag pieces of what was left of her clothing, dangling it in front of her with bemusement, like she couldn't believe those were once her clothes. So, the woman wanted to barter, did she? He wondered what she would say if he told her the truth.

"Every one of them?" He kept his voice light.

Jaymee heard the challenge. She had been around men long enough to recognize a retreating male when she saw one. Unaware of how she looked, she put her hands on her hips. "Scared? I'm not going to beg you to stay, Nicholas Langley."

She was magnificent, her hair thick and unruly, teasing her breasts, which peeked temptingly at him between the dark auburn curls. In the lit room, her eyes glowed deep green. He wanted to give her everything that she wanted, and more, but since he couldn't, he would give her honesty, or as close to it as he could.

"Secrets can be dangerous," he warned.

Jaymee just smiled, climbing back into bed. She wrapped her arms around his neck. "I don't need to know your secrets to see that you're dangerous to me, Nick. I know you're going to leave me, and I know it'll be soon. Just let me at least know why, even if you have to lie."

"I've never lied to you." Withheld information, perhaps, but never lied. However, he'd deceived her, and he knew she hated deception, above all else.

"You don't trust me," she stated, her eyes downcast.

"No," he denied. "It's not that. We'll eat, wait out the storm, and we'll talk. With our clothes on." He cupped her breast. "If we stay in this bed any longer, we won't be talking for a long time."

He put her hand back on his aroused state. Jaymee blushed. She still wasn't used to this kind of intimacy. Looking down, she unconsciously licked her lips and heard him groan. She looked questioningly at him.

"Don't, darling," he said, amusement and exasperation in his voice. "That look ought to be banned for indecency."

"I beg your pardon," she said, huffily.

"Lustful. Simply sinfully indecent." He kissed her long and thoroughly, then reluctantly got off her. "I need some dry clothes, after the way you tore mine off."

Jaymee stared at him incredulously. "Why you—" He was already walking away, and she got up and went after him. "Tore your clothes off you! Of all the twisted, chauvinistic—"

His laughter drowned out her accusations as she beat on his back all the way to the bathroom.

*

Nick liked her company. The release of their pent-up tension put them at ease. They were relaxed and talking comfortably. She was surprisingly well-informed about current affairs, and her interests covered a variety of subjects that had nothing to do with construction and business. They conversed like old lovers, sometimes touching, sometimes kissing, in between jokes and discussion.

The mood remained light and companionable as they ate and waited for the rain to stop, until Jaymee's father returned some time later. He scowled at the sight of them lounging on the sofa.

Nick studied him for a few seconds. For once the old guy wasn't drunk.

"You lost the Excel contract," Bob said, not even stopping to greet either of them.

Jaymee sipped her coffee, not moving from the curled up position against Nick's hard frame. "Word gets around fast," she observed, as she stirred the hot liquid with a spoon, "or did you just get your gossip straight from your good friends Chuck and Rich?"

"They tell me the inspector's got a complaint about you," Bob accused. He came closer and stood behind an armchair. His face was red with anger, as he glared down at them. "You were cheating on the job, they said, and got caught."

Nick put down his cup on the coffee table and sat up straighter. Jaymee didn't even stir, sliding comfortably against his arm as he shifted positions. He couldn't get over how cool she always was when it came to handling her father.

"Is that so?" Bob continued his tirade against his daughter. "Did you ask them to undernail the shingles?"

"If I told you that I didn't, would you believe me?" she quietly countered.

"Excel fired you. Obviously, you did something wrong. Look at you, sitting on your butt on a work day. I wouldn't have done anything like that in the old days, but since you took over, everything's gone wrong."

Jaymee was used to these accusations, but she wasn't going to allow her father to spoil today. Not today. Without answering, she drained the rest of the coffee, took Nick's cup from the table, and got up to go to the kitchen, leaving her father alone with Nick.

That didn't stop Bob at all. Without bothering to lower his voice, he turned on Nick. "It's you, isn't it? She's got her mind on you and not on what she's supposed to do. Instead of taking care of the business, she's sitting here and telling the men to cut corners."

"She has never told us to undernail or cut corners," Nick said quietly.

"How would you know?" the old man sneered. "You just hang around her, and probably couldn't tell a nail from a staple."

Nick stood up, towering over the other man. "I know that your daughter would never do anything that's dishonest. I can tell that you just like to stand around and point a finger at everything, yet you don't bother to help her at all. Why don't you stop tossing down that alcohol and see the world clearly for once?"

"I can see all right. I can see she lost a good account and Gregg's got it. It's clear she doesn't care that such bad news gets across town quickly."

Nick wanted to shake him hard. If he didn't know how frail the old man's health was, he'd do more than that. He took a step forward. "If the alcohol hasn't killed off all your brain cells yet, why don't you ask around town whom Chuck and Rich work for these days? How come they know about the undernailing, if they didn't do it?"

He watched as Bob frowned with sudden confusion.

"Let it go, Nick," said Jaymee from the kitchen doorway. "The rain's stopped. Let's take the walk I promised you." She sent her father a hard glance, and said to him, "Either you want me to run the business my way, or you don't. I've been keeping my part of the bargain, Dad. You keep yours."

Bob snorted and turned to sit down on the sofa. Picking up the television remote, he pressed the 'ON' button. "The good Lord knows I'm going to die before I get my money," he said, changing channels.

"Oh, you'll get your money," Jaymee promised softly. "Every damn penny of it."

She took Nick's hand and led him out the back door. Once outside, she set off at a brisk pace, going deeper into the woods on one side of the property.

The trail was muddy and slippery from the rain, but she was surefooted, as if she had used it many times. Nick followed, looking around now and then. When the silence continued, he put a hand on her stiff shoulder and stopped her.

"Don't let him do this to you anymore," he said, turning her around to face him. He stroked the lines around her mouth, thumbing her lower lip gently. Her eyes were glittering from unshed tears. "If I hear another one of his accusations, I'm going to bash his face in, your father or not."

"Oh, Nick!" Jaymee had to smile, even though she was still angry. "You don't even know why my dad is the way he is."

"I don't give a fig. He has no right to say those things when he doesn't even know what you do. I'm tired of standing by while he batters you like you're some punching bag. He's nothing but a frustrated drunk. I don't know why he's so bitter, but drinking isn't the way to solve any problems. And certainly," he looked down at her possessively, adding, "not by treating my woman like dirt."

Jaymee stared. She wasn't used to having someone else defend her, fight her battles for her. It was confusing and...thrilling. Not knowing what to say, she latched on to the one important phrase. "Your...woman?"

Nick's gaze was steady. "You have a problem with that?"

"Yes!" she said, then turned away. "You can't say that to a woman, then leave her!"

"What if I have no choice?"

She could understand that. She'd had no choice for eight years. She sighed. "You told me that you aren't a criminal."

"I'm not."

She started off on the trail again, looking over her shoulder. "Come on. I'm going to show you my secret and then you're going to tell me yours, and it'd better be as good a story as mine, or I'll...I'll fire you!"

Unexpected amusement rose in him. The woman could run circles around him and tie him in knots with the speed she changed subjects. Part of the reason why he was so attracted to her was precisely the way she could delve into things without asking questions. By changing topics and circling around, she always managed to get what she wanted. A true businesswoman, he grudgingly admitted, and a worthy evasive expert, even if she didn't know it. Curious about this secret of hers, and wanting to know all he could about her, he didn't say anything any more, following her deeper into the woods.

"We're now on the neighboring property," Jaymee told him, about twenty minutes later. "It isn't as big as my dad's and it's pretty overgrown. Once we get out of these woods, you still won't see much because of the huge bushes and tall weeds."

Pine trees and sabal palms rustled in the wind as they made their way. "Did you run back home to meet me from here the other day?" Nick asked, recalling how she was out of breath.

"Yes. It's usually an easy jog when it's dry, and the shade keeps out the heat." She pointed ahead. "There it is."

'It' was a two-storied weather-beaten ranch house sitting forlornly on a neglected lot. Overgrown bushes grew over cracked cement paths and long branches criss-crossed too closely to the house. It was obviously in need of work, judging from the peeling paint, rotten overhangs, to the dirty, cracked window panes. Nick tested his weight on each of the front wooden steps before walking onto the porch.

"Don't worry, the wood is fine there," assured Jaymee. "It's rotten in the back porch, though."

Taking out a key from her pocket, she opened the surprisingly large door. Once inside, Nick noticed that the house had been swept and cleaned out. It was in various stages of remodeling. The carpet had been stripped from the floor, revealing old terraso tiles. Tools were scattered all over, as well as cleaners and polish.

"What do you think?" she asked, standing in the middle of the mayhem.

He looked around, dumbfounded. "This is your other job?" Would the woman ever cease to surprise him?

"Uh-huh. I'm working on the floor now. They carpeted over these tiles, can you believe it? It's in pretty good shape, so I'm going to clean it up. Then I'm going to take out the old trim and replace it with something fancy." She kicked at the connecting doors between the rooms. "The doors are next, although I kind of like them. They are the old heavy oak, not the cheap hollow junk they sell at the House Depot these days."

Jaymee knew that she was babbling, but she couldn't help it. This had been her secret for such a long time, and now that she had someone with her, she wanted to show off. She was very proud of all her work, even though she still had a long way to go.

The glow of pride radiating from her did funny things to Nick's insides. "Do you plan to live here?" he asked, wondering why that would be a secret.

"No, of course not."

"You said that it had something to do with your future."

"Remind me not to talk to you when I'm about to fall asleep, OK?" she said crossly, and sat down on a small stool.

Nick grinned crookedly. "That's the only time, it seems, that you can be cajoled to answer my questions. Either that, or it's because you liked what I did to you before." He loved making her blush, still couldn't get over such shyness at her age. Joining her on the floor, he stretched out his long legs, leaning against the wall. "OK. I see a big house in need of major work. I know that you work here in the evenings. You don't plan to live in it, so being the businesswoman that I know you are, I assume that you're going to sell it and make some kind of profit." He blinked, suddenly understanding. "Money for that debt about which I keep hearing? Money for your future?"

Jaymee unwrapped a stick of gum and popped it into her mouth, studying him thoughtfully as she chewed. "A detective, right? It's Nick Sherlock Holmes Langley, isn't it?"

He shook his head and didn't offer any clue. Instead, he took one of her hands and laced his fingers through hers. Bringing it to his mouth, he kissed her knuckles one by one. Feeling her heart beating faster again, she told him, "Oh no, you don't. Don't even try distracting me."

"Why do you work so hard, Jaymee?" His breath was warm against her skin. "Tell me about the debt. How much do you owe, and why?"

Jaymee stared at their intertwined hands. He didn't know how hard those questions were to answer. They would bring back painful memories. She was afraid of the usual accompanying pain and loneliness.

His grip tightened. "Trust me," he said.

She jerked away sharply. "Don't say that! He said that too. Those were his exact words that got me here."

God, it had started, the awful torrent of memories pushed into her consciousness, and as always, she felt helpless against the onslaught of those hateful emotions—shame, guilt, hopelessness.

But Nick just prodded on, wanting to know everything. "Who? Your old boyfriend, Danny?" When she refused to answer, he pulled at the hand he held until she reluctantly fell into his lap. He held her close and although he was gentle, the tone of his voice was that of someone who was used to giving orders. "You'd better not even try to compare me with that guy. Do you think about him when I kiss you? When I make love to you?" The thought of that made him angry as hell.

Jaymee was startled at the notion. "Of course not! I haven't thought of Danny like that in years."

That calmed him down a little. "But he's still playing you like a puppet, isn't he?"

"What do you mean?" It was difficult to concentrate when he was so close. She breathed in his scent and she wanted to kiss him again.

"Jaymee, baby, much as it pleases me that you haven't had another lover after that scumbag, it also tells me why you've been rejecting men for so many years." Her head jerked back and he calmly met her glare. "Danny was a huge mistake. Not only did he betray your trust, but he also used you and stole more than money. And worse, you had no one to turn to, what with your father blaming you and losing your mother. You're afraid of being hurt again, so you hide behind your work. You continue letting your father bully you..."

"Stop right there," she cut in. She poked a finger at his chest. "You have no right to judge me. You don't know anything about me."

She jumped off his lap and walked to look out of a dingy window. Staring unseeing at the dirt streaks across the panes, she took a deep breath, then exhaled. She needed to gather her scattered thoughts, if she were to tell him about Danny. She wanted to tell a clear story, to explain why she was the way she was. It dawned on her that she needed to face her past, not run from it all every time it's mentioned. Why not now, when she stood there in the place that represented a new life to her, with the man who already dominated her thoughts more than any past love?

"Have you ever seen a path so strewn with flowers, so lit up by stars, that made you so sure that you couldn't possibly get lost on it, because it could only lead to paradise?"

The words tumbled out haltingly, and her voice sounded far away, cool and flat, at war with the beautiful image she evoked. Nick wanted to walk to her, but found himself caught by the need to hear more. He knew without a doubt that this very private woman had decided to show him herself at her most vulnerable, and he felt humbled by her trust. She didn't know it, of course, but she was essentially giving the Programmer the switch to her operating system. He could stop her because he didn't like her vulnerable to him, but he kept quiet. He would deal with the guilt later. The need to understand her overtook everything else.

"I guess I was a hopeless romantic," Jaymee continued, in the same faraway voice. "I was so sure of myself back then, and Danny was..." Her shoulders slumped. "...well, Danny turned out to be a snake in my paradise. We met at college, and Mom and Dad were captivated by him. He was suave, handsome, smart, and talked passionately about making it big. Dad sang his praises to me, and I didn't need much encouragement. He was Mr. Perfect, you know? I was a roofer's daughter and had no idea about life.

"My dad loved talking to him. Danny had such great plans, telling my dad that he could expand his business if he'd only invest in roofing materials, keep them in a rented warehouse, and stock the roofs himself. Labor didn't make enough profit, he said, but materials, now that's where big money could be made. He drew plans and showed Dad five-year projections of how much his company could grow, even bigger than Gregg's Roofing, the biggest company in town."

Jaymee stopped, unable to go on. The hard part was next. She was a different person now—tougher, stronger, wiser—yet she felt like some creature that lived in a shell about to be exposed to danger. Suddenly, she felt Nick's presence behind her, his warmth comforting and reassuring. His hands were gentle on her shoulders, massaging the tense muscles.

"Continue," he encouraged. "Were his calculations wrong?"

Jaymee laughed bitterly. "Oh no, that wasn't it. I backed up his projections, showing my dad all the calculations from my business classes." She blinked hard several times. "See, Dad, I had proudly said, Danny was right. Most large companies made their money from materials because they could buy wholesale and sell at retail. Blahblahblahblah. Macro economics. Business theories. My dad loved it. Meanwhile, Danny and I got engaged and the plan grew out of sight. Dad was suddenly seeing himself bigger than Gregg's, no longer working in the sun, just living off the company run by his son-in-law."

She leaned back, her head against his chest. Nick's arms crossed in front of her, holding her securely. She listened to the steady thud of his heartbeat. It felt like home. "Dad gave Danny down payment for shingles and to set up the warehouse. Then Danny suggested buying a highlift so we could stock the roofs." A soft sigh escaped her. "Dad borrowed heavily against the business and the new house he'd just built for Mom."

Nick had seen enough greed and evil in his profession to know that the conclusion of this tale was the kind that destroyed lives. "He gave cash to Danny," he said grimly.

It never failed to hurt. No matter how many years had gone by, the pain would still be there, waiting. Jaymee choked down a lump in her throat. "Yes."

"No materials. No highlift." Nick felt her pain, understood how difficult it was for her to face that kind of failure. He could only imagine the young woman she had been when she lost everything—her love, her security, her pride.

"Yes," she repeated. She tried to move out of the circle of his arms, but he wouldn't let her. After a brief struggle, she gave up and let his warm embrace seep through the cold mantle that always settled on her whenever she thought about Danny and what he did. "He...didn't come back from out of town. Never answered my calls. Dad had a stroke not long after. Mom...well, Mom had always been weak, and the idea of losing her house....She loved her house. It was her everything, sitting in that back porch and watching the sun set. Dad blamed me for her death. The drinking started then."

"This is the same house you live in now?" Nick wanted to kill the long-gone Danny for the havoc he'd wrought on Jaymee and her family.

Jaymee clenched her hands into fists. "Mom had insurance and...do you know why Dad hates me? She willed it to me, and instead of using the money to pay off his company's debts, I paid off the house instead, so that Mom will always have it. Does it make sense? She can sit on that porch in spirit, as long as she wants to."

"Yes." But he could guess the showdown between father and daughter over that.

"It didn't to my father. We could always move, he said, but the business wasn't going to survive in the red. The debt was mine, because I had to show off my fancy college education, bring home a no-good college swindler. I was nothing but a..."

"No," Nick interrupted. "I don't want to hear you belittle yourself."

"But it's true." Jaymee looked down at her clenched hands, and willed them to open.

"No, you're just repeating Bob's words. Don't ever, ever make your father's accusations your own, Jaymee."

But she had. She knew she had. She saw nothing but her own stupidity that had destroyed her future eight years ago, how with misguided trust, her dreams had turned to ashes. She couldn't move on with her life, not with her father penniless and her mother dying. Nick turned her slowly to face him and she didn't resist, knowing that he couldn't see the turmoil inside her.

Nick shook his head. That cool, unruffled look was exactly the same face she put on whenever her father started on a tangent. She thought she could hide from him, but she didn't know about her eyes, so dark they were almost black, and he wished he knew how to make the green come back.

He was filled with rage against the old man and his crazy accusations, against that bastard who had broken her heart and forced her to bury herself like that. He was a man used to getting his own way, usually in charge of counterattacks. This new feeling, of being unable to help, rankled. He was a fucking man of action, all right. He, who was so good at covert action, but so helpless when it came to normal activities. His job had always been to fix problems, but they were technical ones, the kind over which nations killed each other. This was different. How could he fix a broken pride? A ruined optimism?

He didn't need her to finish her story. It didn't surprise him anymore how well he understood her. Jaymee had essentially taken over her dad's business to pay off those debts because she'd accepted her father's foolishness as her own. He was so angry he was trembling. She had worked for eight years, essentially paying off a huge debt that was her father's. He knew how hard she must have worked, taking over a business at that young age and trying to make ends meet, at the same time dealing with her own mother's death and a father's bitterness. No wonder she had retreated from emotional entanglements and turned into a working machine. It was her way to block out pain, her own on/off switch.

Nick kissed her forehead, breathing in her unique fragrance. This was his woman, and he'd find a way to make life a little better for her before he left. He'd replace the painful past and give her something good to remember for the future.

## Chapter Seven

This was the first time Jaymee had talked about what happened eight years ago. Not even Mindy knew the whole story. It wasn't as difficult as she had thought, or maybe it was just because it was Nick and not somebody else. She looked at him closely, and was relieved not to find pity in his eyes. She didn't think she could handle his pitying her.

"How much was the business in the red?" Nick interrupted the silence.

"Once the house was paid off with the insurance money, the business was left with liens of a little over a hundred thousand dollars," Jaymee replied flatly. "I couldn't risk Dad having another stroke, so I made him a deal."

"You negotiated your future for his business," Nick told her. "You felt so guilty that you condemned yourself into hard labor."

Surprise fleeted momentarily into the dull bleakness in her eyes. "I've never looked at it that way before," she admitted.

"Of course not. You were too busy accepting the blame and taking on your dad's responsibilities."

"I am to blame." Her voice was soft, despairing. If not for her naïve trust, she wouldn't have brought Danny home, nor encouraged her father to let Danny meddle with his business.

"No, Jaymee," Nick said quietly, and stepped back from her a little so she could look up at him without getting a crick in her neck. "I want you to listen at me. From now on, you'll only hear my words when you think about this. You—are—not—to—be—blamed. Your father was the businessman, damn it, not you. You were a college student, not someone savvy in business dealings. Your father got conned by greed and a smart-mouthed charmer."

"So was I," Jaymee pointed out, jerking her chin up. "I was just as stupid as Dad, and I bought into Danny's stories just as much as he did."

Nick shook her hard. "Will you let that damn guilt go? You were in love with a bastard. That was your mistake, and for your information, darling, it's a very common one. It's a mistake you could learn from, with consequences you could live with. Believe me, there are some mistakes that have more dire results."

Like walking into a trap. Like the needless deaths of innocent people. He pulled her back into his arms. He didn't want to let her go, ever. But what he wanted didn't matter compared to the kind of life his job demanded. He didn't need to think it over to know a single mistake could haunt him for the rest of his life. He sighed, focusing back on Jaymee. "Look, sweetheart. I'll grant you that you paid a higher price for that mistake than most others, but place the blame in the right places, woman. Your father's business sense wasn't quite straight if he gave cash to someone he hadn't checked out, son-in-law-to-be, or not."

When did she grow to need his arms around her? "There you go again, Nick," Jaymee mumbled into his chest. When did standing in his embrace become natural?

"What?"

"Checked out," she repeated his words. "You're talking like a detective again."

How could he not be crazy about her? She never missed a thing he said. "Does nothing escape you?" he teased, lightening the mood.

"Details are important in roofing," she retorted. "One mistake, and you might fall off. One mistake, and you're in the hole for one hundred thou."

"I'm not a mistake." He solemnly gazed down at her, and was privately relieved to see a little green returning into her eyes.

"Not yet." Jaymee calmly returned his glare.

"Are you comparing me with Danny again?" His voice was cutting, threatening.

"You aren't like Danny," she denied, shaking her head, "but you can hurt me like he did, maybe more. You don't tell me about yourself; nor did he. I've a feeling that you'll take away something very precious to me, and there'll be nothing of you left when you're gone."

Not if he could help it. He'd never hurt her. He'd leave her something. Looking around the room, he picked out the things that needed done. Maybe he'd even tell her something about Killian Nicholas Langley, just a little of the truth.

"As long as I'm around, I'll help you with this project," he offered.

"This house?"

"Yes. I'm a very good carpenter, didn't I tell you that? I'll repair all that rotten wood and do the heavier work."

"Why would you want to help me?" She asked, puzzled. No one had ever offered to help her in anything before. What she had, she'd achieved on her own.

He didn't answer. Instead, he asked, "Tell me something, how much does your company still owe your lienors?"

Jaymee cocked her head. Nick's choice of words often struck her as someone at ease in the world of law. She was getting more confused about him by the minute. She decided to test him. "About twenty thousand, give or take a few."

"Once you sell this house, is the profit going to pay off that lien?"

She laughed and broke away from him, giving the room a sweeping glance. "This place was barely habitable when I got it, Nick. It belonged to the owner's grand-uncle or something, and she couldn't sell it in its condition. It was, however, perfect for someone like me, with all those liens and bad credit. I made her a deal."

"A land contract?" Nick guessed.

She was right. Electronics, now lien laws and property contracts. Interesting. Turning her back to him, Jaymee hid her triumphant smile. She pretended to pick up some tools. "Yes, the easiest contract between two parties. She lives in New York and was relieved to not have to worry about property taxes as well as get the place back into order."

"Contract written out by a lawyer, I hope?" He couldn't help it. He knew she would see to all the important details, but there was a need in him to make sure she'd be protected.

Jaymee smiled at him. "You'll be insisting next to check out the contract yourself," she teased. The serious look he gave her told her that he was actually going to ask that, and she shook her head. "Nick, I can take care of myself."

"I know that," Nick ruefully conceded, running a hand through his hair. She followed the movement, and wished to do that too, remembering how soft it was. "Still...." He shrugged, unable to explain.

"It's not terminal, but definitely difficult to cure," Jaymee agreed.

"What are you talking about?"

Two dimples appeared and disappeared as her amusement grew. "Macho-sitis," she told him, trying to keep a straight face. "A kind of male itch to take over."

Nick laughed. "Imp." He helped her put away the tools scattered around. "OK, I'll back off the contract thing for now. Tell me about your big profit margin."

"There isn't going to be one," she told him. "I've invested all my own spare change into this house and when it's done and sold, I'll be lucky to clear ten thousand, max., Nick."

He frowned. "So much work, so little profit. Is it worth it?"

It wasn't a logical undertaking at all, as far as he could see. There were easier ways to make twenty grand.

Jaymee could read his mind. "It isn't what you think. This project isn't for the roofing business. This is for me, for my future, remember?" She reminded him of her words the night before.

"I don't get it."

She waved her arms dramatically. "The roofing business is doing fine. I use most of its annual profit to pay off the liens—sometimes ten thousand, sometimes fifteen in a good year. Excel Construction was the big fish. It would have cleared all the remaining debt in a year and a half. That is," she amended a little bitterly, "if I hadn't had to let it go." She picked up a broom and leaned it against the wall. "No, this house is for myself."

"Is that what you meant when you said that it's for your future?" Nick asked, getting more curious by the second.

She nodded, excitement creeping into her voice. "Yes. See, I don't want to be a roofer forever, and once the liens are paid off, my bargain with Dad is to sell his business and give him the retirement money he lost in one lump sum. I wouldn't owe him anything any more." She ran a finger along the wall and looked at the dirt on it. "I've lost my college education and don't have the finances to return to school, so I decided to remain in construction, only this time it would be in remodeling. The license and state exam cost about three to four thousand dollars. The rest of the profit goes into start-up costs for my new business, as well as moving expenses when I leave Dad's house."

Nick was sure she had every detail down pat in that brain, determinedly following each step toward her goal. He admired her tenacity, her independence. "I like the plan," he said.

Walking with slow deliberation around the room, he saw a way to leave her something of himself. By helping her with this house as long as he was here, the profit she made would have part of him as a memory. And by giving himself to her this way, he'd play an important part toward her future too. He'd be with her that way, as a good and happy memory, and he would know, wherever he may be, that she was happy and secure in a future he'd helped provide. Yes, he was determined to give her that, at least.

Jaymee wondered about the thoughtful light in those slate-gray eyes. She felt empty, depleted of every emotion, but it wasn't a bad feeling. Talking about her bottled-up plans and memories had been strangely cathartic. It wasn't the past she was afraid of. It was the future without the big, silent man with her.

For eight years, her goal had been simple enough: she had meticulously planned out her life in the safest and most logical way. Having been burned once, the safest course was to avoid emotional entanglements and consciously or unconsciously, she'd steered clear of anything that remotely jeopardized her organized, working world. That is, until this man came along and showed her what she had been missing.

He was a stranger and yet, he wasn't. She seemed to have known him forever. No. Don't even go there, Jaymee. Forever wasn't possible with Nick, as he'd as much warned her. But she wanted forever. What was she to do?

She'd do what she knew best. Change the subject and carry on. "I think that's enough of the Jaymee Barrow's 'This Is Your Life' show," she said, giving him a quick smile. She took the chewing gum out of her mouth and wrapped it up in a piece of tissue before throwing it into a nearby trash can. "Now you know where I am in the evenings."

Nick grinned back. She didn't know how that particular mystery had kept him awake the past few nights. He headed toward the stairway on one side of the room. "You've done a lot by yourself," he noted. "Come on, show me the rest of the place. We'll make a list of things that need work."

Jaymee wrinkled her nose. Taking over seemed to be second nature to Nick. Already, he was telling her what to do about her own project! "I have a list already," she told him.

"Good, then I'll make one for myself," he said, mockery in his eyes. "I know you view your last eight years like it's a prison term, babe, but you've to realize that you've done nothing wrong. It's Danny who committed the crime, your father who got conned out of his money, not you. Stop punishing yourself."

She didn't know whether to be angry or amazed. "And what do you think my problem is then, Dr. Langley?" she asked, crossing her arms. "Since, of course, you're saying that the missing hundred thousand dollars is just a figment of my imagination."

Good. There was some color back in her cheeks, a returning combative sparkle in her eyes. "Do you want my professional or personal opinion?" he countered, and not waiting for her reply, went on tour of the house for himself.

She made an exasperated sound and followed him into the kitchen. "Both, of course," she said to the broad back, then stuck her tongue out.

"Cabinet tops need replacing. Sink too." He looked in the pantry and nodded in approval. "Nice and roomy." He grinned at the snort coming from behind him. He did enjoy riling her so. Turning around, he continued, "Professionally, I think you could reach your goal, but you're going to need help with the heavier work. Yours truly is volunteering, so why not just accept it gracefully? Gratefully, even."

"Gratefully?" He was making her more and more irritated.

"Yeah." They walked out of the kitchen and Nick strolled into the back room. "I like the archways," he said approvingly. "What's this room? Sitting room? Study?"

She chose to ignore his observations. "Gratefully?" she repeated through clenched teeth.

He let out an exaggerated sigh. "Yeah, showing me your gratitude will earn you points," he said drolly. "You know, I like this room. You must too, since you sleep here."

"How did you...?" Jaymee pursed her lips when he sat on the huge sofa bed at the end of the window and lifting up various articles of clothing, dangled her underwear from a hooked finger. "Give me those!"

She tried to snatch the cotton and lace triangles from him, but he kept them out of reach. Laughing, he lounged back, his head against the sofa pillow lying on the armrest.

"Great sofa. I could actually stretch my legs all the way." Another thought made him frown. "This place is very isolated. I don't think I like the idea of you alone in this house. Don't do it any more."

That did it. Jaymee launched on top of him, forgetting that her weight was meaningless to his muscled strength. "Listen, you overbearing, arrogant man," she said, ignoring the crooked grin forming on his lips. "I'll do as I like, sleep where I want. Nobody tells me what to do, much less where to go to bed at night."

"Exactly," Nick agreed in a deceptively mild voice. She was so mad she didn't notice his own leg curling over hers, effectively trapping her against him. "That's why you need someone like me to knock some sense into you. Someone could come out to this deserted place and here you are, all alone. Stupid, dangerous idea."

Jaymee glared down at him. "This house is locked. I have electricity, so it's not like it's dark and deserted. What's the difference between sleeping here, or at the house, alone? Any man can do it and no one will say a thing, but the moment a woman does it, hah! It's suddenly soooo dangerous!"

She scowled when he waved her underwear at her again. She stretched out over his body, trying to reach them. Too late, she realized his trick, as his other arm went around her waist, arranging her until she lay across him, thigh to thigh, chest to chest. She was suddenly aware of another part of him, nudging into her. Her eyes widened as she realized her predicament.

Nick's smile was devilish. "Exactly," he said again, curling his other leg over hers, locking her limbs with effective ease. He deliberately nudged against her again. "You can sleep wherever you want, Jaymee, as long as it's with me."

There must be something wrong with her. She wanted him again. It was as if some dam had broken, and now there was no holding back the torrent of emotions held in check for so long. How could a musty-smelling, cluttered old house suddenly become so charged with sexual energy? She could feel his male heat, pushing hard and insistent, through his jeans.

"You said we're supposed to talk," she reminded him huskily.

"Later." His hand went under her shirt. "Listen, it's raining again."

"So?"

"So, we aren't going to work anywhere for the rest of the day, are we?"

"I told you, the day's shot."

"Hmm. All that unused energy surely needs an outlet. And that's the doctor's personal opinion."

Her whole insides shook. How was it possible that he could make her weak from mere words? Determinedly, she mounted one last defensive battle. She was in control of the situation still, wasn't she? They were going to talk, no matter what, she vowed.

Using the age-old female excuse, she said, "I'm too tired."

An empty house. A bed. A desirable woman. And a whole night ahead. Nick Langley couldn't have executed a better program. He wanted this woman more than ever, now that he knew her story. She had the softness that drove him crazy, and the toughness that challenged him to keep taking her over and over, just to make her grow soft for him.

He wanted her. Now.

Slowly, deliberately, he showed her those lacey panties again, and watched her eyes widen as he moved them closer to his lips. With devilish purpose he kissed the crotch of the little triangle, feeling her immediate reaction as the corresponding part of her body pushed against him in shock. He almost groaned from the pleasure. His murmur was low, promising. "I know a way to wake you up."

Jaymee could only squeak. Did she vow that they would talk first? Later, she amended.

\*

Much, much later, and after expending energy in the most satisfying way, Jaymee lay on her side, resting her head on one hand as she studied the sleeping man beside her. Her lover, she told herself. She wasn't sure whether to laugh or cry. She was supposed to be using her head. She was a sensible and wary woman, keeping out of trouble for her very valued peace of mind. Where was that common sense now? All but gone, stolen by this man with his clever hands and determined seduction. She grimaced. How, she asked as she looked at his gloriously nude form, was she supposed to resist that?

Nick lay asleep on his back, one arm flung over his eyes to block out the dim light from the old lamp by the sofa bed. His other hand was on her thigh, fingers possessively splayed over the soft inner flesh. His naked body, as she knew now, was warrior-hard, with the supple muscles that suggested training. She made a mental addition of this new clue to his mystery, wondering whether she would ever know, or whether he would just disappear from her life without her ever finding out.

Just like some tall, dark stranger in a Western novel. Don't forget handsome, she added with silent wryness, taking in those long, incredible eyelashes that cast shadows on the masculine plains of his face. He looked relaxed, and thoroughly sated. She flushed at that thought.

She wanted to trace her finger around those sensuous lips that hadn't left a spot on her body untouched. Moving lower, she admired the broad chest with its diamond-shaped sprinkling of hair that arrowed down a flat stomach. She lingered even lower. Talk about insatiable. That part of him was asleep too.

A small, intimate smile touched her lips. She couldn't believe the things she'd done with this male body. Perhaps she'd imagined it. However, one glance around the room and the wreck they'd made of it, testified to the hours of pleasure in which they had indulged recently. There were items of clothing strewn everywhere. She squinted. Was that her bra in the corner? His jeans were tossed in a bunch right across the room. There were sofa pillows all over the place. She vaguely remembered him placing one of them under her hips and her face flushed pink as she recalled the incredible pleasure that particular position had brought, as he pushed deep into her again and again.

It still scared her, the way he could make her forget about everything else but him. He was a demanding lover, making sure every part of her responded to his touch as he described in sexy detail what he was going to do. How he could talk when she was a mass of moaning sensations, she would never understand, and that was what was so unsettling and frightening about him. He seemed so in control all the time, and a part of her resented that, wanting him to be as wild as he drove her.

His muscles rippled gently as he stirred. The hand on her thigh caressed her, his long fingers teasing slightly before letting go to slide lazily up his tanned stomach to scratch his chest with sleepy satisfaction.

Jaymee reluctantly sat up, sweeping the tangled curtain of hair from her face. Her body felt sore in unfamiliar places. Fingers curled around her wrist.

"Where do you think you're going?" Nick's voice was a husky drawl.

She glanced back at him. His eyes were still shut. "Bathroom," she told him. "I wonder what time it is."

He grunted and turned over onto his front, giving her a tempting view of his tush. "It's about Oh-four-hundred hours. Come back to bed soon."

This was weird. She was used to falling asleep here some nights, but never had imagined that she would be traipsing around the place naked, with an obviously equally-naked man asleep in one of the rooms. And who could tell time like that? She checked the little clock in the kitchen area. Four fifteen. Oh-four-hundred hours. Who the hell talked like that during the wee hours of the morning?

He was still in exactly the same position when she returned, and she wanted to run her hand up and down those muscular flanks and ravish those sexy buns. She fought against her naughty urges and looked around for her clothes instead.

"Aren't you hungry?" she asked, finding a shoe under the sofa bed.

"Nope."

"I have some crackers and cheese somewhere."

"Ugh." He held out a hand. "Come here."

When she placed her hand in his, he pulled her back into bed, turning on his side to make room for her. "Nick!" she protested. "I have to get up."

"For what? It's four in the morning."

"Four thirty," she corrected. "I thought I would get up and get some stuff done. I didn't do a thing today. Yesterday, I mean."

"So what are you going to do at this Godforsaken hour, little workaholic?" he asked, amusement lacing his sleepy voice. "Mow the grass? Lay a couple of squares of shingles in the dark? Maybe wash your truck?"

Jaymee chuckled at his ludicrous suggestions and ran a teasing hand up his chest. "Sarcastic beast," she pleasantly chided, pulling his chest hair hard enough to get him to grunt. "Some of us have paperwork to do. Besides, I wake up around six, anyway. This will give me a head start."

Nick groaned, finally opening his eyes. As usual, she managed to amuse and exasperate at the same time. "Only a workaholic will see being awake at four in the morning as a head start." He bent his head close to hers. "There are other, more interesting, things to do at this time of the morning."

He kissed her with a slow thoroughness, tasting the mouthwash she'd used in the bathroom. He pressed against her.

"Nicholas..." she began, when his hand slid between her legs, but her voice trailed away.

"I don't know about you, Jaymee girl," he whispered, as he explored her silky secrets, "but I can't seem to get enough of you. Each time gets better and better."

She appeared to agree. Blindly, she reached for him.

"What about the paperwork?" he teased, as she undulated wildly against him.

"Stuff the paperwork!" she fiercely announced, and bit his chest.

*

They walked back to her house early enough for a quick bath, a change of clothing and breakfast. While Jaymee made coffee and scrambled some eggs, Nick disappeared into the study. A moment later, she heard the unmistakable beeping noises of the computer and printer.

"Is the new computer set up for my business files?" she asked loudly, over the sizzle of bacon.

"Yeah. I'll show you later."

"What are you doing now?"

"Checking on something."

Jaymee shrugged, going back to preparing the meal. Having a computer as a rival was better than another woman, she supposed. Besides, she was too hungry to care.

In the study, Nick frowned at the screen. No communications. It had only been a few days since he gave out his location, but he'd hoped for an affirmation of some sort. Something just didn't feel right. He would have to make a decision soon, if…

"Breakfast!"

He turned off the machine and went back into the kitchen. His mouth watered at the smell of bacon and eggs. Jaymee poured him a cup of coffee, then sat down next to him. Her small eyes were bright were laughter as she looked at him.

"You owe me a load of laundry, at the rate you use up all my favorite tee-shirts," she said, giving him that delightful chuckle that he loved to hear.

Nick looked down, then grinned. He had just pulled the first shirt out of her dresser and put it on in the dark. It was another one of her crazy tee-shirts. This one said: 'She Must Be Obeyed.'

"I'm a browbeaten man," he told her, showing the proper humble demeanor, then spoiled it by promptly taking a big, noisy bite of toast.

They bantered back and forth, until Bob came downstairs. Nick was surprised again. The old geezer was sober and actually looked alert.

He looked at the two of them at the table, then groused, "I hope he didn't spend the night here. It's still my house."

"No, he didn't," assured Jaymee briskly, and got up to get an extra cup. "Coffee, Dad?"

Bob grunted and sat down next to Nick. Slowly chewing on his breakfast, Nick nodded at him. "Good morning, Mr. Barrows."

"Either you're darned early for work, or you stayed here overnight," Bob accused, eyeing them with suspicion, as Jaymee quietly set a plate in front of him, along with his coffee. "Which is it?"

"Neither," Jaymee replied, while Nick finished chewing his food.

"Don't tell me he ain't been with you all night, with that shirt of yours on him," her father went on, nodding towards Nick.

"She didn't tell you that now, did she?" drawled Nick, buttering another piece of toast.

"I don't get it. She ain't got nothing left for the likes of you to want. Let me make it clear, boy. I ain't going to mortgage the house to back another money-making scheme, you hear?"

The morning's cheerfulness escaped the big kitchen like a slow leaky balloon, leaving an uneasy, tense silence. Jaymee didn't say a word, just returned to her seat, and began eating her bacon and eggs like nothing was wrong.

"More coffee?" she asked Nick, holding up the pot.

Nick pushed the cup closer to her, and without taking his eyes off Jaymee, said in a pleasant voice, "There's plenty of her to want, Mr. Barrows. You're just too blind to see it." He smiled when Jaymee's startled eyes darted up to meet his.

"Listen to him, Jaymee girl," Bob sneered. "He's as smooth a talker as that other one. Only this one doesn't know that you're up to your eyeballs in debt, and there ain't nothing left for him to steal."

"Dad, maybe he likes me," Jaymee lightly suggested, returning Nick's smile. She took a nibble of the bacon, still looking at his handsome face.

Bob gave a short laugh. "Haven't you learned? They don't like you for yourself, they see the business, the money they can get from you! Even I learned that. And at your age, you ain't going to catch a young stud's eye that easily, Jaymee girl. Why, your ma…"

Nick cut in. This time, the tone of his voice was no longer pleasant. "I suggest that you shut up, old man. Either that, or get back into your booze, so I'd at least have an excuse not to punch the daylights out of you."

"Nick…" warned Jaymee, hesitantly, shaking her head. This wasn't going to do any good. She used to argue with her father when he started to act like this. Now she just walked away. After all, what was there to say to a man who suddenly lost his business, wife and health all in a year? "Just eat and let's go. I'm used to it."

"No." He was inflexible. His blue-gray eyes, no longer lazy and amused, glittered as he looked at Bob Barrows. It was time to put an end to this. He studied the old man's quickened breathing, the light sheen of sweat on his forehead. No better time than when he was still clear-headed.

Jaymee couldn't see Nick's expression, but he must have conveyed a strong message to her father, who surprised her by dropping his gaze. Her father, who never backed down, actually looked nervous. She shivered slightly when Nick spoke up again. His voice sounded so cold and lethal, so unlike that warm gravelly drawl that she was used to.

"There's a certain type of man who takes advantage of young girls, isn't there," he said to Bob, "the kind that steals their innocence and betrays their trust? You know it, don't you, old man, being a father and all? You saw how your daughter was tricked. And there's another type of man, who shirks responsibilities, preferring to blame everyone else but himself. You know that too, don't you, Barrows?" Being polite, Nick thought, was a waste of time with this man.

Bob slammed his hand on the table, spilling coffee. Jaymee stood up to get a cloth, but was stopped by Nick's hand. She silently pleaded for him to stop, but he was still staring at her father.

"Don't let him talk to me like that, Jaymee!"

Jaymee licked her dry lips. In spite of how her father hurt her feelings, she still was concerned for his health. Besides, she would rather not have a family confrontation in front of others. "Nick..."

"No." Again, he refused her plea, his eyes burning her with their intensity. "I told you yesterday not to let him put you down again. If you won't do it, I guess I'll just have to be the one to make the point clear."

"I can take care of myself," Jaymee told him, although the look in his eyes was intimidating. She wasn't used to anyone taking her side. From experience, when others heard about what happened, they commiserated with her father, not her, and of course, excused his drunkenness and behavior. She tugged at Nick's hand holding hers.

He merely ignored her, turning his attention back to Bob. "Let's talk about type of daughters now, shall we? There's the type who can't wait to leave home to start her own life, isn't there, Barrows, the one that has a family of her own? And, there's the type of daughter who doesn't strand her father with a mountain of debts, choosing instead, to help him back on his feet. Great daughter, don't you agree, old man?"

The fingers handcuffing her wrist were as implacable as the man. Jaymee didn't know what to say. She had always chosen to just walk away when her father's words began to hurt, retreating back to work. There were always reasons to excuse her father's anger towards her. She had made them all, and accepted each accusation without retaliating. She now realized that by not defending herself, she'd made her father worse. It'd never bothered her before, until this man—her lover—took exception to her father's treatment of her.

"Nick, he's on medication," she said quietly.

"If he can't stand to hear the truth, there's always booze," Nick scornfully said. "Deaf and blind. Nice way to live."

"You don't know what she did!" Bob's face was livid with resentment. He looked shocked, unused to being put down by anybody. "I lost everything because of her! Everything!"

"What did she do? Took over your dead business and brought it back to life again? Paid off a house that would have been lost? What exactly have you lost, Bob Barrows? What's missing but your pride?"

Bob just stared back, stunned. He looked like a bundle of shingles just hit him on the head. Nick calmly finished his cup of coffee and stood up, still holding Jaymee's hand. Picking up another piece of toast, he walked to the door, with Jaymee in tow.

With a last glance at the silent man at the table, he added, "You just think about it, Barrows. What material things have you lost these last eight years that you don't have now? And who made sure that you didn't lose them? That fancy college education wasn't such a waste, was it?"

Nick stepped onto the porch and turned to Jaymee, who stood staring up at him with mute amazement. A light smile touched the corners of his lips. "There's no way I'm going to allow my woman to be treated like that. Now, where are we going to work today, boss?"

## Chapter Eight

Jaymee sat in the garage of the new house, sipping a bottle of cola, during a break from work. Oh boy. She was in much, much more trouble than possible. Nick had taken her truck to get some ceramic tiles to fix a leak later this evening, when it would be cooler. It had been barely an hour and she was already missing him. She massaged the back of her neck, frowning. She sighed. Definitely, absolutely in trouble. She was in love with Nick Langley.

It had warmed her insides to see him defending her so fiercely that morning. No man had ever done that for her. It made her feel special that she meant something to this man. But...she still wasn't sure how to deal with him. She'd been so sure that he was merely amusing himself, yet he did these things that confounded her. He was protective. And tender. And caring. She sighed again. The qualities that were so darn attractive.

There were so many things about him she didn't know although she was piecing the puzzle together little by little. First, he was definitely not on the run. He didn't strike her as someone who was constantly looking over his shoulder. Second, underneath that potent charm was the alertness of a hunter. After witnessing this morning's episode with her father, she hadn't a doubt that Nick could take down anyone who was on the wrong side of him. Lastly, he was some kind of electronic expert who spoke legal and political terms with the ease of one educated in related fields. He watched; he played with electronics; he was in top physical condition. She smiled wryly at the last observation. Oh yes, she was very sure about the last fact. If she didn't know how her imagination tended to be colorful where this man was concerned, she'd make him out to be some sort of military guy, like the Green Beret, or something. She'd read somewhere that the Green Berets were electronic experts, could speak several languages, and trained like a machine. Oh yeah, right, Jaymee girl, she mocked, as she took another sip of her cola. Didn't the same article showed some Green Berets carrying big, wicked-looking Bowie knives? She tried imagining Nick with a green beret and a Bowie knife. Cute. And she was going bonkers.

"I heard old Mindy is having her annual bash tomorrow, boss, is that right?" Dicker broke into her reverie.

"Hmmm? Oh. Yes. Are you going?"

"Maybe. If I'm not fishing or something."

"Mindy makes the best barbecue, man. I'm going," Lucky chimed in.

"Yeah, and if I go, I'll have to shop for a birthday present," Dicker grumbled, wrinkling his nose. "I ain't no good with women's things, man."

"I would guess the same things your old lady likes, Dicker," Lucky said, rubbing his beard.

"What, you mean Mindy wants me to paint the fence and buy her some lottery tickets?"

Jaymee laughed, shaking her head. "Now, Dicker, I'm sure you didn't buy Rosy lottery tickets for her birthday!"

Dicker scratched his neck, looking sheepish. "Sure I did. Ten dollars worth. She was mighty happy coz she won a hundred bucks."

"Man, you don't have not one romantical bone in your body." Lucky puffed out his chest. "I'm going to buy Mindy one of those sweet-smelling perfumes, what is it called — Possession."

Dicker and Jaymee laughed at the misnamed product. "You mean, Obsession, Lucky," Jaymee said.

Grinning back at them good-naturedly, Lucky shrugged. "Obsession, Possession, bah! I can name them perfumes way better."

"And what are you gonna call your perfume?" Dicker wanted to know. "Fish-ion? Shingles?"

They all chuckled. "Roofing Cement Potion," suggested Jaymee, still laughing.

"Or just plain Sweat," Dicker bantered.

Lucky assumed a thoughtful air as he continued scratching his beard. "Nah, not sexy enough. I'll name my perfume Lucky Charms. Yeah, just like me."

They all hooted, and that was how Nick found them, laughing uproariously in the garage. One of his dark brows arched up. "Not laughing at some of my mistakes, I hope," he said, putting down a can of roofing cement.

"That's it! That's it! Nick's Mistake!" Lucky thumped an empty box and laughed so hard he fell off the cement block on which he was sitting. He managed to gasp out, "Oh, that would be some foul-smelling perfume."

"We've somehow gotten around to naming Lucky's new perfume that he was going to give Mindy tomorrow," Jaymee explained to the mildly amused and perplexed Nick, smiling up at him. "So far, our top contestants are Roofing Cement Potion, Sweat, and Lucky Charms. Besides Nick's Mistake, of course." She didn't hide her laughter, as she added, "Not that we're making fun of your work, Nick."

All three of them went off again. Nick grinned, not minding being the butt of their jokes. It'd been a long time since he was made fun of that way, not since his days training with the army Rangers. Besides, he liked listening to Jaymee's laugh. She didn't do it enough.

"Nick is smart, man, he can name a perfume for a woman," Dicker said, when they stopped for breath. "Unlike Luck-man's Possession."

"Sure he can," agreed Lucky, his gap-toothed smile cheeky. "Remember he knows them big words that got Up-Chuck all flustered."

"Now that's what I would name my perfume for my old lady," cracked Dicker. "All-Flustered. Perfect. What would you name your perfume, Langley?"

Jaymee chewed on her lower lip while the other two men turned expectant eyes at Nick. She knew that it hadn't escaped their notice that Nick was wearing her tee-shirt that morning. She didn't care whether there would be gossip. Enough with living with the fear that people would continually bring up Danny. She'd never felt so alive, so comfortable. Looking at the tall man who had changed her outlook so much, she couldn't even remember much about her old feelings for Danny.

There was simply no comparison.

She was also glad that he was getting along with her workers. Dicker and Lucky now included him in their daily chats, and she liked the way Nick mixed with them so easily. Right now, his eyes were half-closed as he considered Dicker's question about naming, of all things, a perfume. It struck her that he just wasn't the type of man who would sit around a bunch of guys playing name games. Again she had the odd feeling that he was hiding something.

"I don't know. You guys have chosen all the good ones," he joked. Leaning over, he picked up Jaymee's cola and finished it off. She stared at him in fascination. Wiping his lips with the back of his hand, he continued, "I supposed Smartass is out of the question? Or, Scary Screamer? Or Maniac?"

The other men chuckled, as if sharing some in-joke. Jaymee rolled her eyes, then stuck her tongue out at Nick. She would bide her time to punish smart-mouthiness. She was the boss, after all.

*

"Don't feel so smart now, do you, Mr. Big Words?" Jaymee mocked Nick later that day. She had left Dicker and Lucky at the job, taking him with her to fix the leak in the tile roof. At the moment, she stood with perfect balance, each foot planted on a ceramic tile, hands on her hips. She looked smugly at Nick, feeling slightly avenged for the knowing chuckles her men had given when he named his perfume. Tease her, would he? Well, let's see how he felt being at the other end.

Nick concentrated on first making sure that he didn't slip. The ceramic tiles weren't slippery, but because of their inverted 'S' shape, his big feet couldn't fit on the dented part of the tile, like Jaymee's did, and so he had to put his weight awkwardly its the rounded curve.

Crrrunch.

A crack line appeared under his foot. Wincing, he put his other foot down. Aanother crunching sound.

Normally, Jaymee would have given any employee the proper tongue-lashing, but the sight of the big man gingerly trying to walk toward her was almost worth the money she was going to lose, at the rate he was breaking the tiles. She just stood there, a big grin on her face.

"I'm going to take all the damage out of your paycheck tonight, if you don't stop breaking them," she warned sternly, but her mischievous smile gave her away.

"It's like walking on eggs," muttered Nick, when he reached her.

"You're lucky I had you pick up those extra tiles this afternoon, or we'd have some missing pieces, what with those big feet of yours!"

Nick grinned. "OK, so I made it up here. Now what?"

Jaymee cocked her head. "Ever made love on a ceramic tile roof before?"

He groaned. "No, and I'm not going to start now." He watched Jaymee turn around and nimbly walk up a few rows higher. Her butt was at eye level. He groaned again. "OK, we'll do it."

"Not if you can't catch me," she teased, squatting down and loosening one of the tiles. She pulled a few out of the way, and said, "Here, you can stand more comfortably on the fern strips below the tiles."

Nick did as she suggested.

Jaymee pointed to the material exposed by the tiles. "That is called base sheet, and it's thicker than felt paper. It's meant to protect the roof, in case water gets under the tile."

"Obviously, it doesn't work, because the roof is leaking," observed Nick.

"Usually it's because there is a hole somewhere that the previous roofer didn't patch up, or they didn't use base sheet, opting for lower grade material instead, and it rotted away because of the water. Sometimes they didn't layer it properly." She tapped on a water stain where she had taken out a tile. "There, see? That's a clue, dear Mr. Watson."

"How does water get under the tile, Sherlock?" Nick asked, squatting carefully down beside her.

Jaymee shrugged. "Cracked tiles, holes in the lead boot, could be a number of things. That's why this 'underlayment' is very important. Finding leaks on tile roofs can be tricky, since water stains showing on the ceiling inside the house don't usually match the spot on the roof. That's because water moves differently when it travels under the tiles, like underground caverns, you know?"

"And these fern strips act like diverters, shooting the water in different directions, right?" Nick traced the water stain pattern above the little strips of wood that supported the tiles.

"Right. So, we have to follow this water stain, take off the tiles as we go, and tada!" Jaymee gestured dramatically.

"The leak!" Nick finished for her.

"Elementary, my dear Watson!"

By the time they were done, it was almost six o'clock. Nick enjoyed the new lesson. Searching for leaks on roofs wasn't that different from the other kind of leaks that he specialized in, he supposed. Look for the source and eliminate. In a general perspective, life in the outside world could be just as exciting. Then he remembered what was left of his beloved boat. And not so dangerous.

"So when can I add 'leak expert' as part of my construction man resume?" he quipped, as he loaded the truck with broken tiles.

Jaymee couldn't resist it. Putting on her best Chinese accent, she parodied a line from a famous TV show. "When you can walk on tile and leave no crack, my son, then you are leak expert. Until then, I am still master."

Nick grinned as he watched her throw her head back and laughed. She was getting feistier by the day. And suddenly, he wanted her again. She stopped in mid-laugh.

"Let's get something to eat," he said, his voice low and full of dark promise. "Then I'll show you who your master is, little Red Grasshopper."

Jaymee made a face at him. By now she'd learned to recognize that blatant male look. "What bad puns you have, Mr. Wolf."

For the first time in eight years, she couldn't wait to get home. After paying Dicker and Lucky, they prepared a simple meal together. Dinner was the way Jaymee had always imagined romance to be — on the back porch, with the view of the setting sun and the shadows and golden lights of the lake in the distance, and her lover feeding her cold meat and wine. They kissed and joked, drawing out the evening into night.

"Tomorrow, I'll help you with that old house," Nick said, lazily twirling her curls with his forefinger. The sunset was bright, making her hair a fiery halo. He remembered it against him, the way it caressed down his chest when she trailed kisses down his body. He shifted position.

Jaymee snuggled deeper into his lap. "You're a hungry monster," she murmured, absolutely aware of his discomfort.

"Wolf," he corrected. "Let's get to bed, so we can have your head start tomorrow."

She chuckled. "I'm sure you want to just rest, so we can work on the remodeling," she mocked.

"Of course. You don't have to do a thing, just lie there," he promised, and gently nudged her off his lap.

They were making their way to the old house, kissing and teasing each other, when Nick suddenly pulled her to a stop. He looked around sharply, his eyes alert. Puzzled, Jaymee followed his eyes, but there was nothing but trees and shadows.

"What is it?"

"Shhh." Nick hadn't been able to shake off that 'being watched' feeling for a few days now. This time, he was sure. Putting Jaymee behind his body, he carefully looked for signs.

Jaymee stared at the appearance of a knife in Nick's hand. A huge, ugly thing, with serrated edges. A Bowie knife. Where had he hidden that thing?

A voice suddenly came out from among the shadows — disembodied, hushed, deadly. It made her blood run cold. "I was beginning to wonder whether you'd lost all your training."

Jaymee gasped, looking around. She couldn't see anything. Suddenly, out of nowhere, there was a swishing noise, and something streaked past. Nick cursed and grabbed his arm. She turned and gaped in horror.

It was the strangest feeling, as if she were watching everything from far away. But this was real; she knew it was unbelievably real. That was real blood oozing out between Nick's fingers where he was clutching his bicep.

# Chapter Nine

The evening sun was spotty among the trees and bushes, making it impossible to discern between shadows and shapes. Jaymee looked around, trying to calm her overworking imagination. Right now, even the trees looked gothic and menacing.

She glanced back Nick, who had instinctively pulled her closer. He wasn't paying attention to her right now, his gaze darting around and searching for their unseen assailant. The deadly expression on his face made her catch her breath.

There was a whooshing sound from her left, and he immediately pulled her out of the way. The thing, whatever it was, flew by her at tremendous speed, so close that she felt the little breeze it made. She was too shocked to make a sound.

"Better," the disembodied voice continued, dark and sinister in the stillness. "I think I'll go for the jugular next."

"Come out, damn it!" Nick challenged.

Jaymee could only stare in muted horror as a shadow jumped in front of him and started attacking. Nick pushed her from him with one hand while his other blocked a chop. She watched with disbelief as the two men fought, both strangely silent through their exertions. They moved in some kind of stylized exercise, although the grunts of pain when their punches and kicks connected told her that the fight was quite real. Their assailant had his back to her. He wasn't as tall as Nick, but was obviously as strong and capable, as he countered Nick's blows with swift retaliation. She found herself gripping her throat in horror when one of his kicks connected and Nick cursed, grabbing at his wound, before he ducked low. The Bowie knife fell on the ground.

There must be something that she could do! Wildly searching the ground around her, she picked up a sturdy looking branch. Without further thinking, she charged at the stranger with the branch high and aimed at his head. Either she missed, or he moved, she didn't know—she had her eyes closed—and the momentum of her forceful blow brought her right in the middle of the action and she landed on her knees. Frightened out of her mind, she hurled the branch in her hand at the attacker, then whatever she could grab—rocks, twigs, dirt, whatever. Someone's arm encircled hers to her body and lifted her off her feet. Screaming, she kicked out in panic, trying to escape, her loosened hair flying around her shaking head like a whip.

"Stop it! Damn it, Jaymee! Stop!"

It took a few frenzied minutes before it sunk in that it was Nick who had imprisoned her in his arms, and that the attacker was standing in front of them. He just stood there, watching, his hands relaxed by his sides. Jaymee ceased her struggles and stared back, her breath coming out in short gasps.

"Damn it," Nick said in a low voice, "what the hell did you do that for? You could have met with me later."

It took a second or two before Jaymee registered that he wasn't talking to her, but to the stranger. She went limp with astonishment. He knew their attacker? Why, then, did this man try to hurt him?

"How?" asked the stranger. He was very soft-spoken, as if he seldom raised his voice. There was a hint of mockery in it now. "I didn't know you'd grown a Siamese twin for company. It's been almost three days, and I still haven't seen you actually alone yet."

Nick gently put Jaymee on her feet. Turning her around, he studied her dirt-streaked face, making sure that she was unharmed. He lifted a few curls plastered against her cheek. "Are you all right, sweetheart?"

She nodded, still trying to grasp what was happening. "Your arm! He...he shot you or something!"

Rage filled her at the thought of his being injured, and she was about to whirl around to confront the enemy again when Nick gathered her into his arms. He looked down at her tenderly, a small smile forming on his lips.

"It's OK," he assured her, reading her mind, knowing her fiery temper by now. "He didn't really hurt me. He was playing around."

Jaymee looked up and followed his gaze as he looked over her head at the other man, who lifted an insolent brow in answer. She frowned, more than a little confused.

"Playing around?" She touched Nick's injured arm, checking the wound that had stopped bleeding. There was a vertical slice across the flesh, but it didn't look very deep. "This is playing around?"

Her voice was slightly higher than usual. She showed him the blood on her fingers.

Nick sighed. This wasn't going to be easy. "Jaymee..." he began.

But Jaymee wasn't in the mood to be placated. She turned around to face this man who was "playing around." The first thing that caught her attention was his strange eyes, set off by the tanned face. They were very light, the color of chipped ice, as they glittered out of his face. Her mouth gaped as realization dawned.

"Why, you're related!"

He had Nick's eyes, the same shape, down to the long eyelashes, although there was no blue in them as he returned her stare with the same familiar watchfulness that Nick had. The deadly coldness in them made her shiver, in spite of the humidity of the evening. Wolf eyes. And this one was a killer wolf. He was shorter, but had the same slanted shoulders, the same whipcord leanness. His face was rugged, with chiseled features. She realized that he looked so menacing because there was simply no expression on his hard face. But those eyes. And those long, long lashes.

Nick stroked her tensed back. "Yes, this is my cousin, Jed."

The man didn't attempt to shake her hand or acknowledge her in any way. Instead, he turned his attention back to Nick.

"I got tired of waiting. After checking her out, I calculated no risk in exposing myself when she's with you."

"You didn't answer my message. I couldn't know for sure whether you'd reach me so soon," Nick explained.

Jed nodded. "Too dangerous. I need to talk to you face-to-face." The corner of his lips lifted in a mere trace of mockery. "I'm sorry to have to interrupt your plans. I'll try to make this quick."

Nick squeezed Jaymee's shoulder lightly, then walked over to his cousin. She continued staring, absorbing the meaning of "checked her out" and "too dangerous." She watched the two men lock arms in salute.

"Long time, cousin. Hoo-yah, Airborne."

"Hoo-yah. All-the-way," Jed greeted back softly. "We thought you didn't jump out of the boat in time."

Nick shrugged. "It was close." He stepped back, then moved toward a clump of trees. "Were you standing here when you tried to scare me, you son of a bitch?"

"No, I was at six-o'clock."

He frowned. "Funny, I thought I saw a shadow here first." A wry smile suddenly curved his lips, and he gave a loud sigh. He called out, loud and mocking, "If I find worms in my hair this time, I'm going to turn you over my knee!"

The rustling of leaves above Nick caught Jaymee's attention, and her eyes widened even more when someone popped out from the low branches, hanging upside-down. A woman—she noted, growing ever more amazed—because of the two pigtails hanging down.

"So if they're spiders, I'm OK, right, Cousin Kill?"

Not a woman, Jaymee realized, but a teenager. With green hair.

Nick reached up and tugged at the green pigtails. The owner deliberately tumbled down and he caught her in his arms without missing a step. "You've grown, little trouble," he said to the bundle he held.

"Little Trouble" wrapped her arms around Nick's neck and gave him an affectionate smack on the lips. Jaymee felt a tug of jealousy. "Not so little. I'm a grown woman, Kill!"

"One with green hair. How interesting," drawled Nick. He set her down and looked at Jaymee again, his arm around the younger girls' shoulders. He gave her a searching look, but couldn't gauge her mood. "This is my second cousin, Jaymee."

"Little Trouble," chirped the girl with an impish grin, giving a small wave.

Jaymee liked her immediately. She had an engaging smile and the face of a doll.

"Grace," Nick said, pulling a pigtail. "Her hair is usually a very normal brown."

Grace, Jaymee assumed, must be Jed's child, although with her green hair and dark brown eyes, she didn't share any family resemblance to the two men. She was actually very exotic looking. She must also have a foreign mother, judging from the almond-shaped eyes and high cheekbones. She was about her height, with a slim body, a lively face, and especially bold eyes.

"Hello," she greeted back.

"Sorry we startled you, Miss Barrows. Jed didn't mean it, honest."

Jed? She called her father Jed? This was giving Jaymee a headache. And how did this girl know her name? With a helpless shrug, she glanced back at Nick. He was studying her, that watchful look back in his slate-gray eyes. With his dirty tee-shirt, his black hair dampened by sweat, and dried blood staining his arm, he looked intimidating. Letting go of Grace, he walked back toward her.

His voice was soft and persuasive. "Look, I know you're confused and have questions, but I can't talk now. I need to have a private chat with Jed. Why don't you run back home first and clean up? I'll join you later."

Jaymee cocked her head to one side as she regarded Nick for a moment. Soft and persuasive wasn't going to save Nick Langley from telling her exactly what was going on. He wasn't going to sidetrack her with that killer charm this time. She was getting profoundly tired of making wild guesses.

"I can do that, cousin Kill," she acquiesced, but her eyes spoke volumes. "Have your relatives eaten dinner? Maybe they would like a bite to eat?"

Nick glanced over his shoulder at Jed. He saw the questions in Jaymee's eyes, and knew the night of hot wild sex he'd planned wasn't going to happen. Another painful thing he could blame on his dear cousin, and, for whom, he added, he had a few questions too. Like, why was Grace with him? It was the first time he'd seen his cousin bring his daughter anywhere while on a mission. Something definitely wasn't right.

"A drink will be nice, but no need for food, thank you," Jed replied for Nick. "May Grace go with you, Miss Barrows? I promise to get her off your hands as soon as possible."

"Of course," Jaymee said, and smiled at the teenager. "Ready?"

"Yeah."

"She isn't allowed anything but water," Jed said.

"Don't you trust me, Daddy Dearest?" Grace mocked, suddenly sounding very grown up. Her calling Jed 'dad' confirmed Jaymee's suspicion of their relationship, but her demeanor was hardly daughter-like, as she stood there, laughter in her eyes. So different from that cold, expressionless man she was addressing.

"I just wanted to make sure Miss Barrows doesn't tempt you with orange juice," he replied calmly.

Grace groaned, as if in pain. Then she pouted.

Jaymee frowned, puzzled. "She can't drink anything but water? Do you have a special diet, Grace?"

The young girl sighed dramatically. "No," she answered in a doleful voice. "I'm in training." Realizing Jaymee's incomprehension, she continued, "I can't eat for two days, you see, and I'm addicted to OJ. See you later, Jed."

Moving down the path Jaymee and Nick had earlier taken, Grace turned to look back at the two men, with a cheeky smile and the two green pigtails that made her look like an imp. "Oh, by the way, how much do you want me to tell her when she questions me, Nick?"

Her voice was innocent enough, but Jaymee noted the very adult mockery in those dark eyes. She seemed to be taking a lot of delight in riling her cousin.

"Enough to live up to your name, trouble," answered Nick wryly.

Grace chuckled and skipped out of sight. Jaymee threw Nick a troubled gaze before following the younger girl, backtracking to her house.

Nick plowed his fingers through his damp hair. "What was with that fucking dramatic entrance? You scared the hell out of her."

Jed calmly brushed dirt off his clothes. "She's quite brave, attacking me like that." He gave that ghost of a smile again. "Protecting her big, strong lover."

Nick considered Jed more as his brother than cousin. They had grown up together—Jed on the streets in Dublin and he, in a farm house, not far. His parents were very poor, but his cousin had it worse, showing up now and then at their door with bruises left by his stepfather. He loved his cousin, but the son of a bitch was proud and refused any help of any kind. One day, he'd just disappeared and they'd all thought him dead. One never knew with Dublin. Gang warfare, crime, poverty, and political assassinations were tough on a kid living on the streets.

A few years later, Jed had suddenly reappeared—a very different Jed, in uniform—and had invited Nick to get out of Ireland, like he did. Nick went. He had then served with him in the same Ranger platoon.

It was Jed who had recruited him into COMCEN's Virus Program, as part of the nine-member unit, a team of evasive experts trained in various ways to destroy. Nick's expertise was in the electronic area, in breaking codes and eliminating enemy plans by planting counter-programs within their computer, missile, and satellite systems. Jed had similar training, but his job was deadlier. He assimilated information when there was no way to steal into the system electronically, and he was, simply put, an assassin. Jed was one of the few people Nick knew whose switch was always off.

"Gracie mentioned she's in training," he said, a slight frown forming. "Why are you doing that?"

Grace was sixteen or seventeen—he could never remember—but being that she barely saw her father between assignments, the fact that she was in training with him now was significant.

Jed didn't answer immediately. Walking behind a bush, he pulled out two backpacks. In a voice devoid of emotion, he said, "They cancelled Diamond's wife."

Nick inhaled sharply, shocked. "Emma is dead?" he repeated the information slowly. He couldn't believe it. Emma was part of an independent agency called GEM. An old girlfriend, in fact. Good friends afterwards, he was the one who had introduced her, code-named Emerald, to Diamond, joking that they would make the perfect engagement ring. They had hit it off immediately and he had been glad for them. Anger struggled with rising grief. "Not…like my accident?"

Jed slung one backpack on. "There was nothing we could do. Diamond and I were standing on the beach."

"Explosives," breathed out Nick. His hand fisted. He cursed once. Twice. But it didn't ease the pain of losing a friend. "How's Diamond taking it?"

"He's AWOL at the moment. There was also a bomb planted in Winter's farmhouse. They're targeting family members."

Realization dawned. "That's why you have Gracie with you."

Jed nodded. "I left a message at Command saying that I won't be back till they find me. That should give me enough time to train Grace. I connect through to check up on activities now and then, and caught your message. That's why we're here so soon. Grace and I were in the vicinity, since I wanted to train her in jungle heat for a while."

"Does this mean that the killers know all our identities?" Nick asked. Things were worse than he'd suspected. He had thought that only he was the target, not the entire unit.

"No way of knowing, but they're looking for the few of us from that last assignment. Command sent out trackers to neutralize the situation. It'll take some time."

"That's why you left me the message to stay dead. You didn't want the enemy to know I was still alive."

"Not until you were aware of the situation," Jed agreed, throwing the other backpack at Nick.

They made their way slowly toward Jaymee's house. Jed kept quiet, giving Nick time to absorb and process the information.

Nick ran through the events that had led up to the last meeting. He mentally skipped past the knowledge that his friends were dead. Not now. Later.

A few minutes later, he said, "They think they'd gotten rid of me, but they aren't sure whether the others have my information. Someone betrayed us because they knew our rendezvous point."

"That means they are after four of us, me included," Jed said without any inflection in his tone. "I suspected as much. Now you know why I want Grace with me, prepared to defend herself if needed."

Nick nodded. Grace was probably the only person in the world Jed loved. There was no closer relationship he knew than Jed's and Grace's, and certainly none stranger. They were more equal friends than they were the usual father-daughter bonding. Grace had known about her father's "different" lifestyle since she could talk, and had basically grown up without a parent, living with her maternal grandmother in Ohio. Nick loved her, but sometimes she was too mature in her observations even for him.

Jed interrupted his thoughts. "Do you have it?"

Nick understood his reference. "Yes."

"Where is it?"

"I haven't broken the code yet."

"We have to do it and give the code to Command. That's the only way to neutralize them, destroy their satellites."

"Yes," Nick agreed. "I'm close. I'll hook it up tonight and you can take a look. We'll decide on the course of action."

"What about your other plans with Miss Barrows?" Again, that very light mockery seeped back into Jed's voice.

Nick sighed. "I'm going to have to make some deft explanations."

"Lie," Jed suggested.

"She hates lies, and sees right through them."

Jed arched an eyebrow. "It's part of the job, Nick. Evasion is our unit's core work," he reminded him smoothly.

"She's not an assignment, Jed," said Nick, in a low and furious voice.

"She'll be your weak link, and then they will come after her."

"Not going to let that happen."

They broke out from the woods, walking into the well-kept back yard of the house.

Jed's light eyes glittered in the setting darkness. "Don't make my mistake."

Nick didn't say anything, although he knew what Jed meant. Jed never spoke about his wife to anyone else, not even his daughter. Grace had grown up thinking her mother had died a natural death.

Staring up into the lit windows of the ranch house, with that back porch that he had grown to like, Nick remembered the vision of Jaymee and her children. He recalled his silent promise to leave her with good memories and a hopeful future. There wasn't much time left, now that Jed had shown up. There was a mission he had to accomplish, and once it was over, he was going to have to leave Jaymee. He had to, for her safety. There was no way he was going to put her in danger and lose her. Like Diamond lost his wife. His lips set into a tight straight line as he made his way toward the lit house. His companion didn't utter a word, his silver eyes hooded and thoughtful.

*

Back at her house, Jaymee brought out some washcloths, knowing that she would probably need some for the two men that were coming behind them. The initial fright when she first met this strange father-daughter team had disappeared, especially since the younger girl was a normal, talkative teenager. Granted, she looked weird with that green hair and she did come up with some very adult observations now and then, but she found Grace a very smart and interesting young lady.

In fact, she felt startlingly calm about the whole thing. In the back of her mind, she knew that she was just going through the motions, that in reality, she wanted to scream and pound on something in frustration. Instinct told her that she was going to lose Nick—was that even his real name?—very soon. She breathed in deeply. She would stay calm. No sense in being angry over what she'd warned herself all along.

Pushing away her troubled thoughts, she studied the younger girl as she cleaned up at the sink. With that green hair and exotic features, she looked extremely alien in Jaymee's very normal kitchen. Small boned and doll-like, her skin shone like fine porcelain, rosy with the bloom of youth. Now that they were in a brightly-lit room, she could see where the girl resembled her father. She had the same mouth, the lower lip full and generous, except that she tended to keep hers in the typical sulky teenage pout. It made her look very grown-up. And on her chin was a tiny dimple that she had noticed on her father's, not as deep a cleft, but still emphasizing her mouth like an exclamation point.

When Grace was done, Jaymee offered her another glass of water. She went to sit at the kitchen table, meeting her scrutiny with knowing eyes, as if she had been aware of being watched. Her brown eyes sparkled with a boldness that was beyond her years, which from a quick guess, was either fifteen or sixteen. She took several greedy swallows of water, reminding Jaymee of the earlier conversation in the woods.

"Tell me about your training," she said, wetting a washcloth for herself. "Are you sure you can't take anything but water?"

"Don't even show me any OJ," Grace said, then rolled her eyes before smiling cheekily. "Jed is drying me out. I'm doing survivalist training, a more sophisticated way of calling dieting to near-death."

"Sounds horrible," Jaymee remarked casually.

"It is horrible. You should hear my tummy after two days without food."

"What?" Jaymee put down her cloth, shocked. There was simply no reason to put a young girl through that. Maybe they were just too poor? "You're going to eat right now."

However, Grace just shook her head emphatically. "Don't worry, I'm fine."

"I'll be the judge of that." Jaymee was outraged. That cousin of Nick's must be insane. "You don't have any extra pounds to lose, Grace." She walked to the refrigerator. "Come on, don't be proud. What would you like to eat? Chicken? A hamburger? Salad?"

Grace leaned back in her chair, her eyes clear and solemn. "Thank you for caring," she said, suddenly very polite, "but my dad and I have a program to follow. We'll eat tomorrow, don't worry. Maybe he'll even let me have some juice." She tempered her refusal with a smile.

Jaymee shook her head in exasperation. "This is getting more confusing by the minute," she said to no one in particular. "Tell me something, Grace, why did your father hurt Nick?"

The girl shrugged, playing with the rim of her glass. "He was too slow."

"What?"

"Jed would never hurt Killi…Nick intentionally, Miss Barrows. Nick was...ah...not paying attention."

"That doesn't explain anything!" Jaymee exclaimed. "People don't go around hurling missiles at their cousins to see whether they're paying attention!"

People didn't go around with green hair either, but here was one person doing that. In fact, people didn't go around pretending to be construction workers when they were electronic experts either, and she knew of someone like that too. All in all, she decided that she was seeing too many people who weren't what they seemed and she was getting heartily tired of it.

Grace just gave her a wink, then examined her fingernails, which were also bright green. "I'll leave Nick to explain that one," she told her, humor in her dark eyes.

Jaymee looked at Grace across the room, not at all sure how to handle a fifteen year-old going on twenty. "OK, tell me this. What were you two doing on my property?"

"We traced Nick's instructions to here, but couldn't get him alone," Grace explained. "I guess Jed decided that he didn't want to wait another night outside the other house. Too many mosquitoes in your woods, Miss Barrows."

"Jaymee," Jaymee said absently, still trying to untangle the knot of information in her brain. "What do you mean, traced Nick to here? Didn't you know where he was all along?"

Grace stretched her back sinuously, reminding Jaymee of a lazy kitten. Twirling the end of one of her pigtails with a finger, she sat considering an answer for a few moments. Finally, she replied carefully, "Nick hasn't told you anything at all, has he?"

It was humiliating to admit such a thing, especially to a cocky teenager. She refused to feel angry or hurt, emotions she associated with the opposite sex, emotions she hadn't allowed herself to feel for a long time now. She had no one but herself to blame, since she had known all along that Nick was hiding something from her.

Stiffly, she acknowledged, "He told me he wasn't running away from the law."

"Oh, he certainly isn't a criminal." Grace looked in the direction of the door. "In fact, I hear them coming right now. I'm sure he'll answer everything you want to know."

"Right," muttered Jaymee under her breath, walking over to refill the girl's empty glass. "Like his real name, for starters. Didn't you call him some other name?"

The younger girl grinned. "It's easy, Jaymee. With men like my cousin, you just got to ask the right questions." She leaned confidentially over the table, a very female smile on her lips, and added, "I'll teach you how to handle an evasive expert, if you like."

Jaymee stared at her. Evasive expert. He'd used just that term the other day, damn his soul. Was there anything he said to her that wasn't part of a game?

"Oh joy," she enthused in a flat voice.

*

Nick didn't like Jaymee in her present mood at all. He sensed the change in her the moment he stepped into the kitchen with Jed. She was standing at the sink, washing the last of the dirt off her hands and arms, her hair tied back in a ponytail. She glanced up, caught his stare, then looked away. He especially didn't like the look in her eyes. They were that murky color again as she gazed at him like he was some strange insect. He had expected anger, anticipated a heated argument, not this cool and withdrawn woman. He didn't like it. It infuriated him that she closed him off so easily.

After laying down the backpack, he walked in measured steps towards her, as she continued cleaning her hands with calm absorption. He wanted to grab her by the shoulders, make her pay attention to him.

"Sorry to crowd up your kitchen," he said instead, although he knew that he needed to apologize for more than that.

Strange how very familiar he had become to her, standing there by her sink. In her house. Yet, she really didn't know him at all. "No big deal," she told him, dropping a clean, wet cloth into his hand. Averting her eyes, she turned to the other man. "Want a drink, Jed?"

"Please, thanks," Jed answered, putting down his backpack. He looked at his daughter. "How many glasses?"

Grace showed him two fingers. Nick, unable to catch Jaymee's gaze, joined his niece at the table. He gave her an affectionate smile as he wiped away the blood and dirt.

"Why the green hair, trouble?"

Grace shrugged. "It seemed a good idea at the time."

"You should have seen her date," Jed said. He accepted the glass of water and washcloth from Jaymee. "Thanks, Miss Barrows. He had purple hair."

Laughing, Grace defended her date. "I thought he looked cute."

"So your dad punished you by making you train with him, huh?" Nick teased, ruffling her green hair.

Grace wrinkled her nose. "Nah, I was going to drop him, anyhow."

"Why, didn't you like the poor boy?" mocked Nick. "Or, did daddy scare him?"

"I don't scare her dates. I reason with them," Jed said, leaning against the counter.

Grace looked at Jaymee and rolled her eyes. "He reasoned by standing threateningly outside on the porch and not saying a word to poor Tommy. Pfffft!" She stretched, again reminding Jaymee of a sleepy kitten. "Oh well, it saved me from hurting his feelings that night."

"Why?" Jaymee asked, intrigued. Her own dating experience had been sadly lacking, and certainly never would have encompassed a purple-haired date.

"His hair color clashed with mine," Grace explained with such dead seriousness that the adults in the room burst out in laughter.

Well, two of them, anyway, Jaymee corrected. Jed merely smiled, if that slight tug of those lips could be called a smile. "We can't have that," she agreed.

"I'm staying at the beachside. You can bunk there, if you like," Nick told Jed.

"A bed? A shower?" Grace chipped in, grinning. "Wow, what's that?"

Jaymee frowned. This was going too far. She usually disliked prying into other people's business because she resented it when others did it to her, but the idea of a young girl being forced to live without food, bed and shower was too difficult to accept. Didn't she need to go to school, or something? She must help this child. She looked at Jed.

"Where were you two staying when you were waiting to get Nick alone?"

"I'm sure you know that we were trespassing on your property, Miss Barrows." Jed's light eyes met hers squarely.

"Please call me Jaymee," she said. "I don't understand this training business Grace has been telling me about. You can't do that to a growing girl, not allowing her to eat for two days! It's unhealthy, to say the least. And what's this about no shower or bed?"

Jed shot Nick a glance, which the latter answered with a crooked grin. "It's called survival training for a reason," he told her, in his soft-spoken manner.

"Training for what?" retorted Jaymee. The man had to see that he couldn't starve his daughter. "Armageddon? I'm taking her to an outdoor birthday party tomorrow, and she'll be eating and drinking."

She stared back challengingly at the dark and brooding man, very aware of Nick's watchful gaze on her. She was still afraid of this cousin of his. There was something very elemental about him that made her extremely uncomfortable when he stood too near. But Grace brought out inexplicably motherly instincts in her, and she felt the girl needed a woman's hand. There was something wild about her.

Grace laid her head against Nick's shoulder and purred out, "I like her. She's yelling at Dad."

"Better him than me," murmured back Nick amiably. He hid his frustration as he willed Jaymee to meet his eyes, something she had steadfastly avoided since he and Jed came in. "She does have a temper, Jed."

"We've witnessed it first hand, when she yelled on the roof," Jed told him. He placed the empty glass on the counter and straightened up. "Grace is supposed to eat tomorrow, anyway, so I won't argue. She can go with you."

"You can come along too," Jaymee invited.

"No, thank you. I don't attend parties."

"Free food, Dad. Come on," coaxed Grace. "You can torture me later."

"You go ahead."

Nick stood up. "Come on then. I'll take you to my place." Tossing Jed the keys to his Jeep, he added, "I assume you know which vehicle outside is mine. I'll join you in a few."

Jed nodded. "Grab the backpack, Grace."

His daughter obediently did as she was told, and the two of them went outside after greeting Jaymee goodnight.

Nick studied Jaymee as she gathered up the empty glasses and dirty washcloths. She was banging the glasses a lot louder than needed, although the blank expression on her face betrayed nothing. He felt his own anger surging as she gave him the silent treatment. Oh no, she wasn't going to withdraw the same way she did every time her father bothered her. He wouldn't allow it. A few swift strides and he was behind her at the sink and without warning, he turned the water off.

Jaymee calmly wrung the washcloths dry. She fought the urge to lean back against his hard body, to feel his arms around her again. "So, where did you learn how to move like that?" she casually asked, flapping the wet cloths.

Nick reached over and pulled the cloths out of her hand before turning her around. "It won't work, you know."

"What won't work?"

"I won't let you withdraw from me, Jaymee. You can try your polite sarcasm on someone else, like your father. Look at me, damn it!" He forced her chin up. "I know I owe you some answers, but I've to go with Jed right now. Will you be up late tonight?"

That did get her to look at him. "You're presumptuous. Maybe I don't want you to come back tonight," she said.

"Where do you suppose I'm going to sleep, with Jed and Grace in my little efficiency?" He caressed her back, felt the involuntary response. "What, are you a use-em-leave-em kind of woman?"

"You aren't getting off this time, Nick or Kill, or whoever you are," Jaymee warned, glaring at him now. "You've put me off with kisses long enough. I want to know."

His crooked smile only made her madder. She balled her hand and jabbed it into his flat tummy. She couldn't really draw her elbow back enough to land the hard blow she had in mind, but the grunt it elicited gave her a certain amount of satisfaction.

"What was that for?" he asked, rubbing where she hit.

"I thought that was the standard greeting from your family and friends. They attack you without warning," Jaymee sweetly told him. "I was assured by Grace that you usually jump out of the way fast enough, that this time you weren't paying attention."

"I was distracted," Nick agreed. He continued his caress. "Let me come back over tonight, Jaymee."

"I need time alone. I want to think things over." Not that it would help, since she couldn't make heads or tails about this man, except that she'd fallen in love with him. "Besides, I need to do some paperwork tonight."

Pride made her bite down on the questions churning inside her. If he wouldn't tell her, she wouldn't ask. She would never ask anything from a man again.

"I want to be with you, you know that," Nick said, his eyes glittering with suppressed emotion. "Why do you think I've been spending virtually every moment with you?"

Jaymee let out a sigh. "I don't know," she replied, suddenly tired. "I do know, yet I don't know. I want to know, and I don't want to know."

She drew a tentative finger down the front of his tee-shirt. He grabbed her finger and lifted it to his lips, feathering a kiss on the tip, then lightly biting it. She closed her eyes at the feel of his tongue and his teeth.

"All right." She gave in. "I'll leave the back door unlocked. I'll probably be up in the study."

"No, lock the door," Nick ordered. "Give me a spare key."

It rankled that he expected her to trust him so absolutely. Such male arrogance. "And if I don't?"

But Nick had been on Programmer mode since Jed had pulled that stunt on them in the woods. Even as he fumed over Jaymee's sudden coolness, the trained part of him was calmly assessing his options. He needed her to give in, and knew which switch to pull to get her to give in to him. Although another part of him recoiled at the thought of taking advantage of her, he blocked it off. He was the Programmer, and manipulation was what he did best. Later, he would study this unnatural reluctance when it came to Jaymee, but right now, he acted by instinct.

He smiled, and watched the sudden wary look in her eyes. Amazing how she was always aware that something was wrong, even though she never knew what he was up to. It was easy to reassume the role of lover, before Jed's unexpected interruption. All he had to do was think of her in his arms. Naked. And doing... He gave an inward sigh. Bad idea. He leaned closer, wishing he had more time.

"If you don't give me a spare key," he cajoled, "I'll huff and puff till your house falls down, and then you're going to be sorry, because I'd probably eat you." He caught the beginning of a hint of humor on her tempting lips, and felt relieved. "Give me the key, sweetheart, and a nice kiss before I go."

Jaymee could never resist him when he smiled like that. The horrid thing was, she knew that he did it on purpose too, that he was being exactly what she'd known him to be. By acting like the bad boy she'd accused him of, he sweet-talked with words, seducing her to do exactly what he wanted. She just couldn't resist that smile.

She faked a glare as she allowed herself to be led from the sink area. Pulling out a drawer, she found the spare key and dropped it into his open hand. She continued glaring at him when he pointed at his lips with a long, index finger. Putting both hands against his hard chest, she stood on tiptoes, and when his head came down, she gave him the merest wisp of a kiss, then gave him a slight push.

He grinned. "It's Killian Nicholas Langley, so I haven't been lying. Lock up behind me."

He turned and disappeared out into the night. Jaymee stared at the door for along moment, then turned the lock. She felt as empty as the house.

# Chapter Ten

Balance the checkbook. Update the payroll. Write down the week's mileage. Check the inventory. Jaymee went through her routine, finding comfort in the familiar. This was what she had deliberately made her life, and boring as it may be, it offered a sense of security, a sense of control. When Danny had left them in chaos, she'd come up with a plan. Simplify. Cut out everything and just simplify. It was an escape and a solution. It helped her to stay sane when her mother's health worsened and her father went to the hospital, fallen by a stroke. It gave her a sense of direction when she was lost under a pile of credit lawyer mail, demanding payments.

Numbers and planning. The step-by-step climb back to some semblance of control had counted on these details, and Jaymee found out that the more she simplified things, the more she got things done.

However, somewhere along the line, she had also decided to ignore her emotional needs. Emotions fed chaos, she reasoned, and thus, she'd simplified her life one step further— stay away from relationships.

The first few years after Danny went by in a blur. She buried her pain under a mountain of responsibilities, and by the time she surfaced, she'd retreated inside, hiding behind work. There were times when she was lonely, but it was used to forge another brick into her wall of resistance.

Jaymee liked living inside her little self-contained area. Life was simple. And safe.

So, why did she venture out of her nice, safe haven? Neither nice nor safe. She managed a small smile as she plugged numbers and signed checks. Nick—Killian—had warned her that he was neither, and she'd still plunged unheedingly into a relationship with him. She took a long swallow from her drink, staring at the columns on the screen.

The problem was, the parts she knew of the man on her mind wouldn't add up like her balance sheets. He could charm and seduce like the best of them, all right, but she had also seen the side of him that was edgy and powerful. Tonight, there had been something dark and frightening in his eyes when he thought they were being ambushed.

And what ordinary person got ambushed, for God's sake? She speared her hair in disbelief as the possibilities of what that incident meant played havoc with her imagination.

The sound of the back door caught her attention, and she heard her father's familiar walk. "Jaymee girl?" he called out.

"I'm in here."

Bob opened the study door and looked into the room before walking in. "Alone?" he asked.

Jaymee waited a beat for the usual deprecatory remarks that followed, but none came. Looking at her father, she was surprised to find him clear-eyed.

"Yes," she answered, studying him.

Bob glanced at the computer and the papers on the desk. "Have you found more work to replace the Hidden Hills subdivision?"

Jaymee shook her head. "I haven't been looking around. Several builders have some work for me, so I'm not too worried."

"Yes, but a subdivision is steady work. It's a shame that we lost the account."

We? Did she hear right? It had been forever since her father included himself in the business. "That's true," she agreed. "Is there anything you needed, Dad?"

Bob picked up a bill from the pile, looked at it, then put it back. "I just wondered how the inspection had affected our business, that's all. Builders don't take kindly to undernailing. I'm worried that word might get around."

Her father was behaving very strangely. Something was different, the way he spoke, the way he looked at her. Pushing her chair away from the table, she stood up.

"Nothing to worry about," she said. "I had the inspector give me copies of his findings. Whoever sent in the complaint didn't know that I had gone back to check the roofs."

She left out Chuck's and Rich's names. Bob surprised her by bringing them up himself.

"You went back because you knew about Chuck and Rich all along."

Jaymee shrugged, wondering where her father was trying to trip her up. "I had my suspicions."

"And you made sure those roofs were done right after firing them, didn't you? You've always taken care of everything, haven't you?"

"Why the sudden interest, Dad?"

He fidgeted with the papers again, drawing a slight frown from Jaymee. "Everything's in order, right?" he continued in that half-stating, half-questioning tone of voice. "All caught up."

"Dad?" She wondered whether he was really as sober as he appeared.

"That computer makes all the paperwork so much easier, doesn't it?" he went on, still fidgeting with the bills.

Jaymee studied her father a few seconds. "Paperwork is still paperwork," she said slowly. "I'm really behind filing these bills away."

Bob cleared his throat. "Is it still the same system?"

She nodded, too stunned for a moment to say anything. Finally, she said, "There's a pile of bills in the shoebox that needs sorting."

Her father avoided meeting her eyes. "Good. Well, good night. I suppose you'll be at Mindy's party tomorrow."

"Yes. Good night."

She remained where she was as her father closed the door behind him. She couldn't recall the last time her father hadn't been caustic or drunk while talking to him. Tonight, he was neither.

She was tired. It had been a very long day and a nap sounded a lot more tempting than house chores. She dimmed the lights and lay down on the sofa. If Nick didn't show up by midnight, she would go to bed. Closing her eyes, she let out a long sigh. She didn't even know where he stayed. Details, she needed details.

\*

Nick checked the time as he made his way to the back of Jaymee's house. She had left the porch light on for him. He paused for a second before inserting the key into the lock and turned. Such a familiar act, turning a key and walking into a house in the dark. Familiar and intimate. He smiled humorlessly.

Things hadn't quite gone the way he'd wanted this evening. Jed's sudden appearance not only changed his plans, but also sped up his intention to slowly reveal himself to Jaymee. There was no hope for that now, knowing how her mind worked. Not after she'd witnessed that little display in the woods. Jed had done it deliberately, of course. Jed, who never stopped pushing anyone to his limit, who constantly tested everyone around him. Nick's lips curled up resolutely. He'd be damned if he allowed his cousin to test Jaymee or toy with her in one of his usual mind games. Not this time, cuz.

Light shone from beneath the study door and he quietly opened it. The computer was still on, but Jaymee was curled up on the couch, her face hidden against the back pillows. Closing the door, he lay down the book bag he'd brought along, and went to sit on the floor by the sofa. He heard her soft, even breathing, and didn't have the heart to wake her. She didn't sleep enough as it was.

He glanced back at the computer. He'd shown Jed how far along he'd gotten before he was alerted that there was an explosive aboard his boat. After debriefing him, Jed had agreed that they needed to break the code before he could surface again. If the program fell into the wrong hands now, the loss of lives thus far would be a waste. Most of all, they needed to get the ones who were responsible for his near-demise, as well as their friends' deaths. Their enemies weren't stopping there, that was certain, and Jed wasn't going to wait around for them to dig and find out about Grace. Nick could understand his determination, especially now that he knew about Emma's death. Reaching out, he wrapped a long ringlet of Jaymee's hair around his finger. He didn't think he could bear it if she was hurt because of the nature of his job.

He took out a flash drive from the side pocket of the book bag. Jed's programs were nowhere near the capacity of what his specially-designed software could do, but since his precious belongings were at the bottom of the ocean, he would have to make do. It would take some time, with some serious rewriting, to get these programs ready the way he wanted them. Might as well get started while she slept.

*

Jaymee heard him at work even before she was truly awake. With her eyes still closed, she could see with her mind's eye the expression on his face as he concentrated on the screen, his mouth occasionally quirking as he thought out a problem, his fingers moving knowledgeably on the keyboard.

She opened one eye. The room was in darkness, except for the illumination from the computer screen casting a silver gray glow over the man in her chair. He typed. Her computer flashed back answers to his commands. He typed some more.

She doubted that she'd understand anything on the screen even if she were close enough to make out the lines. His familiar profile, silhouetted in the shadows, projected a mind in its element. He worked efficiently, communicating with that damn machine as if it hadn't given her fits for months. She wrinkled her nose then gave in and smiled wryly. A man in deep thought was a very potent draw to a woman like her. Slowly, she sat up.

Nick didn't turn around. "Don't turn the light on," he said, his fingers continuing their dance on the keyboard. "Come here, babe."

It didn't even surprise her any more, the way he knew that she had awakened. She rose, pushing away the sofa pillow, rubbing sleep from her face, and went to stand behind him. She was right. Nothing on that screen was comprehensible, as rows and rows of what she usually termed computer garbage flashed and disappeared. She wanted to touch him, but didn't. At the moment, he had become a stranger.

He clicked the mouse, and after a series of beeps, her usual normal MENU popped back on the screen. Then, he whirled the office chair around to face her.

"Did you have a good sleep?"

She wished that she could see his face, wondering why he'd turned off the lights. "Yes, I did. Is it very late?"

"Around midnight."

She angled her head. "Not zero hundred hours?" she asked softly. When his hand reached up to touch her, she took a step back from him. "No. You aren't going to divert me tonight with your evasive tactics, Nick."

"I see you've been getting information."

"Grace unintentionally let me know."

His laughter was lightly mocking. "Wrong, sweetheart. Jed's daughter never slips information unintentionally."

Jaymee frowned. "You mean, she wanted me to know?"

Nick settled back into the chair and sighed. "Grace is her father's daughter," he explained. "She likes to test people. She obviously liked you enough to give your unasked questions some answers."

"Not all my unasked questions. She wouldn't tell me what it is that you do." She gestured at her computer. "What it is that you were doing just now."

In the darkness, his voice was enigmatic, with none of his soft drawl. "Tell me. What is it you think that I do—was doing just now?"

He wasn't fooling her this time. Glibly, she told him, "Certainly not my taxes. And you're doing it again, making me go round and round while you sit there all detached. It's pissing me off big time."

There was a smile in his voice. "You haven't done so badly, Jaymee. In fact, you're closer to the truth than you think."

She didn't want to guess, didn't want to be toyed with, any more. Glaring at the dark plains that were his features, she lashed out, "I know what my truth is, but what's pissing me off is your deliberate ways to avoid telling the truth to me. Oh yes, let's kiss Jaymee and distract her when she gets too close. Let's bounce her on the bed if she asks too many questions." She fought back hot tears. "You used me, Nick. Or Killian, whoever you are. You were playing with my mind all along, knowing my secrets, taking me down this far and no further. Well, no more, damn you! I'm not going to let you push my buttons, you...you...."

She wanted to call him a hurtful name, but couldn't even think of any. Her heart ached too much.

Nick could see light reflecting from the tears in her eyes. His own feelings were a jumble of anger and regret. She was right, and there wasn't a thing he could do to ease her pain. Even as he wanted to comfort her, the trained part of him was analyzing her and the situation, always in absolute control. How was he to explain that he depended on that detachment to survive?

Her anger was justified, and he couldn't bear to see her in pain. Yet he couldn't deny a single one of her accusations.

He'd taken and hadn't given back, and he knew, for her, honesty was the most important thing in her life.

"Jaymee..." he began.

"No," she interrupted. She took a deep breath and said in a clear, even voice, "I won't be accused of emotional blackmail. You feel sorry for me now, so you're going to throw out a few crumbs. You can keep your stupid secrets. I told you that I grew up among men, and I understand more than you think...Nick. Placate the crying female. Stroke and pet her. Bah!" She made to turn away.

"Don't. Don't turn away from me."

If he had shouted back, Jaymee would have walked away, just the same way she always did when her father went into one of his tirades. But Nick's words were commandingly quiet, threaded with steel. She stood there, watching, as he stood up and loomed over her in the shadows. She could feel tension emanating from him and once again she was frustrated by the darkness in the room.

He read her mind. "Do you know why I won't let you turn on the light?" he asked as he drew closer.

There was something very dangerous about this dark, faceless Nick, and Jaymee backed away, shaking her head. This was silly. She would not be intimidated. Forcing herself to stand still, she waited as he closed the few steps between them, until he was barely a few inches away.

"Do you feel the difference, Jaymee?" His hands snaked out, gathering her into his arms. His voice was just as dark and dangerous, and she could hear her heart begin to beat faster. "Do you feel this darkness that blankets us? Full of unspoken emotions. Danger, even. And then there's the sunshine you work in, the hot and bright light in which you happily oversee every detail of your roofs. Up there, the sky's always open, the breeze hits you in between blasts of heat, and you feel it and you marvel at how a breeze could make you feel so damn great. And if you see any storm clouds coming, you cover up the roof as best you could." He sighed, and continued, "You can't see where you're going in the darkness, Jaymee. You have to rely on instinct, on manipulating every obstacle to your advantage, so you don't trip over the unexpected. How do I make you understand? Maybe I can show you the difference"

His hands dropped away from her and this time it was he who stood back. The tension between them beat in unison with her heartbeat. Jaymee was very conscious of his anger, his frustration, his desire for her, as they stood facing each other. She had an odd feeling that she had just unleashed the real Nick Langley.

*

Jaymee shivered. She had wanted this, to unmask the mystery of her lover. This dangerous, shadowy figure was still Nick, yet…she sensed that she was seeing him for the very first time. Here, in shadows, was the wolf she had always called him, without his disguise. She swallowed. Okay, maybe she should call him Killian right now.

Standing inches away, he didn't attempt to touch her, but she was more aware than ever before of the idling power that he always held back. Somehow, she'd been aware of this side of him, and had resented his self-control enough to constantly try to uncover his disguise. Now she wasn't so sure whether that was such a great idea. She realized that he was waiting for an answer.

Slowly, she reached out and placed both hands on his chest. His heart beat strongly under her palms. She slid them upwards, tracing the outline of his broad shoulders, and brought them down his biceps, feeling his unyielding strength as she massaged the muscles of his forearms. Moving closer, she brushed her body against his as she moved her hands back up his thighs, his sides, and pectorals, to link them behind his neck. She massaged his neck lightly and laid her cheek against his chest. Hot and musky. And totally male.

He may finally have revealed himself, but he was holding on to his control, as was his nature. She understood him better than he thought. He was trying to tell her that his world was this maelstrom of darkness, the complete opposite to hers.

Not so opposite.

"There are risks in all aspects of life," she said, carefully keeping her voice steady. It was difficult when she could feel his hunger for her vibrating like a live wire between them. Taking one of his limp hands, she placed it over her heart, and closed her eyes briefly to savor the feel of his touch. "I've been avoiding risks for eight years, until you came along. I came out of my own kind of darkness for you, darling."

Her words, so softly spoken, acted as a grenade, blasting the granite restrain, and releasing the undercurrent of emotions that he was holding in check. Jaymee felt a shot of hot breath. Caught a whiff of his scent. Then his lips were on hers, hard, bruising, possessive, as his tongue pushed inside her mouth. One hand tangled into her hair and pulled, making her gasp, opening her mouth wider for his taking.

Deliberately, he straightened up, and with his other hand against the small of her back, he forced her to follow him, until she stood on tiptoes as he continued kissing her, devouring her. She could only cling blindly, as he ignored her lack of height, arching her and pulling on her hair. Her feet dangled helplessly as she held on to her only support, the sheer dominance of his body purposely showing her his power. And it was she who had unleashed it.

This was the Nick she had often glimpsed when he was into her computer, totally absorbed in some program, absolutely in control of the situation. And there was nothing she could hide from him as she clung to him, depending on him not to let go, not to destroy her.

Vaguely, she felt him drag her pants down, along with her panties, and her helplessness multiplied a hundred-fold when his hand slid between her legs from behind and touched her. His tongue and fingers moved in rhythm until she went into a frenzy, kicking her pants off in her need to open her legs for more of his touch. Her whimpers against his mouth went unheeded as he continued his slow assault until, lost in the throes of desire, she could no longer hold onto him, her hands losing strength, as he brought her closer to climax.

It was an utterly devastating sensation, this sense of falling, as she gave up trying to hang on, and her whole weight sagged against his body. His hand was twined tightly in her hair, his other hand deeply imbedded in her. The more she slid down, the deeper she let his fingers inside her.

She cried out, half in fear of falling and half in shock at the unbearable tension coiling itself tighter and tighter till she thought she would explode. She could weigh ten pounds instead of her hundred and fifteen, the ease with which he held her, stimulating that most sensitive part of her with his fingers. She moaned, garbled protests in between pleas, every one of which was muffled by his mouth, as he walked toward the sofa behind her. Each movement rocked her, slid her up and down his knowing fingers, and she was completely in his power, to do as he pleased.

When he released her lips, she found herself being lowered into a half-sitting position on the soft seat of the sofa, and she moaned at the loss of the feel of his hard body. She opened her eyes at the sound of his zipper and tried to focus on the dark form before her.

Hands went under each of her knees, pulling her forward off the sofa until she was almost falling off again, and helplessly opened, she could only hold on to the wedge between the back sofa pillow and the seat as he thrust into her.

With one stroke, he invaded her soul.

Each time he pulled out, he took her a little further off the sofa, deliberately creating that defenseless, falling sensation. He let her know that she depended on him. That he was the master controller.

Deeper, harder. And he opened her wider as he pulled out.

Jaymee couldn't breathe, couldn't think. She could only feel the raw power of the man taking her. She moaned, the burning need for a release taking hold.

"Don't scream, or I'll stop." His voice was rough.

And fingers touched her where they were connected and an incoherent cry rose from her lips, only to become a wail when he did exactly what he warned her he would do.

He stopped.

"No…!"

"You have to be quiet." He touched her again.

"Yes," she moaned back. Anything. Just...don't...stop.

"I won't. No screaming."

She didn't know that she had spoken aloud. She felt her legs being moved even higher, against his shoulders, and he was so deep, that every stroke was a statement of possession.

"I don't like it when you turn away from me like that, baby. It makes me want to turn you around and do this. Make you want me as much as I want you."

His fingers came back to torture her as she bit down to stop from crying out loud. She was so close.

"Not yet," he told her, and took his fingers away.

There was nothing she could do. She discovered that she was utterly powerless. She didn't want him to stop. Even if she wanted to, she couldn't push him away, in her position. And he was still stroking into her, slow and hard, nudging her inside until she whimpered at every thrust.

His breathing was faster now, but he was still ruthlessly in control of her body, as he started to play with her eager flesh again, rubbing as he pushed, teasing with the rhythm of his body. She followed his lead, letting him take her closer to release. But he seemed determine to prolong the torture.

"Please, darling," she finally pleaded, her voice breathless, after the third time he denied her.

"Don't turn away from me again," he told her, his voice raspy and thick. "You drive me crazy when you do that. Crazy. Crazy." He leaned forward, going even deeper. She gasped. "Don't scream, baby."

Engulfed in sensations, she couldn't answer him. The darkness shimmered with flashes of light. A heady heaviness built into a crescendo from her gut, and she tried to control it, fearing that he would stop again, just to torture her. If she could just keep it quiet, he wouldn't know, and she would get what she wanted so desperately. Her head rolled back, her body arched, and she bit down on her lower lip as she tried not to clench down on him, or he would know.

He seemed to know anyway, slowing down until she felt like dying, each thrust in making her moan, each stroke out a silken torture. She didn't think she was even breathing any more. A part of her understood that he was punishing her for trying to walk away. He was making a statement, showing her no mercy at all this time.

"Now." He choked out her name and slammed into her, one hand on her mouth, the other pressing down hard where she was wet and needy.

Maybe she did scream. She couldn't tell. Darkness swallowed her as pleasure exploded behind her eyelids, and she plunged into an endless free fall that went on and on. She held on to the only thing that mattered.

Nick. He was her everything.

*

Darling. It was the first time that Jaymee had ever called him an endearment. Nick wanted her to say it over and over. She was the sunshine in his shadowy world, and he wanted her, needed to take her, completely. When she'd started to turn away, something inside him snapped, but he'd hung on to his control, trying hard not to pull her into his arms. Until she called him darling. And dared him by touching him.

He gave in to his desire. He needed to take her the way a male took a mate, staking a claim. He wanted her so desperately, it angered him, because he couldn't stop this need to have her. She wanted truth. She wanted to know how much he really wanted her. So he took her the way the Programmer was best—with unswerving concentration, obliterating any defenses that stood in the way, and achieving total understanding of every part of the thought process.

Except that Jaymee took him along with her. She wasn't one of the problems in the programs he tackled, nor was she another assignment whose mind he sought to probe. She gave him everything without his asking, offering him more than he dared take. And the more he possessed her, the more she owned him, because he wanted, needed, her softness.

This delicious oblivion with a woman was something new. She made him think of no one else. And he dared not take all that she offered, not with this new danger, of close ones being taken out one by one. He trusted her, but he couldn't put her at risk, as Jed's daughter was. As his friend, Emma, had been, and for which she had paid the ultimate price. Not Jaymee. Not ever.

She stirred under him. "Are you all right?" he asked, unsure whether he had been too rough, knowing very well how much loss of control frightened her. He moved, positioning her more comfortably back onto the sofa.

Jaymee wrapped her arms around Nick's waist. "You may do this all night, but you're still not going to get out of answering my questions."

Her voice sounded husky. She felt weak as a newborn baby. What was it about this man that made her give in to him like that?

Nick looked down at her and then swallowed the urge to laugh out loud. His body shook with silent amusement. Did he think he ever could anticipate her every move? She had managed to provoke him at every turn, surprise him with every twist of this relationship. And her bullish determination only made him want her more. He'd never met a woman so intent on getting what she wanted once she set her mind to it, be it settling a hundred-thousand dollar debt, or getting to the bottom of a mystery. Details, it seemed, were her forte. He almost wished he could get Command to recruit her, so he could get her into his world.

Tired of his silence and his amusement, Jaymee dug her nails into his back. "Well?"

"You won't succeed if you tire a man out with wild sex, sweetheart."

He was back, that lazy, indolent Nick with the mocking drawl, propped over her satiated body, looking down at her through the darkness. "Wild sex part of your evasive tactics?" she asked sweetly.

"Invasive," he countered with devilish mockery.

Jaymee was glad he couldn't see her blush. His invasion had been a thorough victory. "Invade all you want," she invited, her voice low, "but don't evade me."

He was quiet for a moment. "I do work for the government," he finally admitted.

Relief flowed through her. He was letting her in, a little. "I gather that." She kissed his chin, his jawline. "I had visions of CIA and FBI, and all those agencies with acronyms."

"It isn't that simple. We are linked to them, in a way."

"You mean, you do their dirty work," Jaymee said dryly. "I do read the newspapers, you know."

He sighed, resigned to the fact that it wouldn't be an easy task to hide anything from her. "That's all I can tell you," he told her.

He hadn't denied her guess. She smiled in the dark, suddenly liking his inability to see her. This was the way it had to be then. She would take what he would give. "What, no acronym?" she teased. "None of those fancy-schmancy Soldier of Fortune names like Delta Force, Night Hawk, or something macho sounding?"

Nick smothered another laugh. It was her talent, this ability to make him relax his guard. He growled when her teeth nipped a sensitive spot on his neck. He relented. "It's CCC," he murmured, "short for Covert-Subversive Command Center. They call us COS Commandos when they're being nice."

"Oooh, macho," Jaymee whispered into his ear, then blew into it. He nipped up her neck till he found her ear and returned the favor. She shivered at the sensual flicks of his tongue. "I gather Jed is also one of these commandos? Or am I forbidden to ask?"

"He showed himself to you. It means that he likes you, Jaymee." Nick nuzzled deeper into her neck. "Yes, he is one of my unit."

"Unit?"

"Yes. There are different units trained for different jobs, just like any company."

"And Grace is being trained for a job in this company? She mentioned being in training."

Nick sighed again. "Sometimes I wish you'd miss or forget something, sweetheart."

He could only admire her skill, even as he saw right through her. She was attempting to get more information about him by changing the subject and focusing on his cousin and Grace. Like he'd known from the beginning, Jaymee was a worthy opponent.

"If he didn't want me to know, Grace wouldn't have mentioned it," Jaymee pointed out with cheeky logic. "Maybe they were both testing me, to see whether I would remember."

She was reminding him of what he'd said earlier, that his cousins liked to put people through some kind of test. Nick chuckled, reluctantly easing off her so he could sit up. He had better weigh his words carefully. At the rate her mind was working, he'd be telling her everything while she seduced him with that delightful body.

"You're an incorrigible imp," he accused, becoming more somber. "OK. He's training her because of what happened to certain members in our unit. My...boat was rigged with an explosive."

Jaymee jerked up. "What?" She hadn't expected that.

"You wanted the truth," Nick gently reminded her.

She swallowed. "I do." She repeated the words firmly. "I do. I want to know what you do, so when you leave me, I'll understand."

That was why he couldn't resist her. She never beat around the bush. He could waste time diverting her again and again, and each time, she'd find a way to get her answers. That was how she was, and he wouldn't have her any other way.

"I was on assignment, and I escaped." He kept it as simple as he could. "They still think they got to me, and now they are after the others who were on the same assignment. Because we're evasive experts, Jed thinks their easiest targets are our families. My friend's wife was recently killed, and that's why you see Jed training Grace, so she can take care of herself in case something happens to him."

"Evasive expert," Jaymee muttered. "That's really a job description, like construction worker?"

"Nothing I can state on a resume," said Nick, a grin forming. "We have lots of fancy names like that." Like trackers, he silently added. Mind probes. Assimilators. All living in darkness and shadow.

"It isn't so bad," she consoled, a trace of mockery creeping into her voice. "I've to explain what a leak expert is." She moved restlessly against him. "All right, Nick, you don't need to tell me any more. Your truth is as close to my idea of it as it can ever be. I just wanted you to tell me without fudging around."

Nick realized that had always been all she'd ever asked of him—to tell her the truth, not of what he did, but of what he was. And having gotten that from him, she was content not to need further details.

"I'm sorry that I couldn't tell you before," he told her.

"I can only imagine the kind of life it must be, to always be afraid of people betraying you." Jaymee touched his face. She wanted him to know that she understood and accepted what he was. "To have to be careful all the time."

Visions of an exploding boat filled her mind, and she shivered. That was a close call. She might have never met him, if he hadn't been able to….

Nick felt her shiver and understood her fear. What was second nature to him was unfathomable to normal people, and he sought to comfort Jaymee. "It isn't so bad. I get to play with lots of neat toys." He kept his voice light, soothing her with slow caresses. After all, the Programmer did have fun dismantling some of the world's most sophisticated satellite systems. "Besides, it isn't that different from your job."

Jaymee laughed in astonishment. "Right. I have relatives zinging weapons at me while I nail shingles."

"You have your back stabbers, Chuck and Rich," he pointed out, "and you have to be careful all the time while you're on the job. One misstep, and you might fall and break your neck. A careless backward step, and you might fall through a skylight hole."

"Nicholas Killian Langley, you aren't seriously trying to convince me that what we both do is equal?" She didn't know whether to laugh or get angry with him. Here she was, worried about his safety, fearing for his life, and he mocked her with comparisons of the dangerous aspects of roofing.

Nick was only too happy to get her to laugh again. "You even have a gun," he pointed out, "and the bad guys all know you as Jay the Boss. Pretty dandy nickname."

They both laughed.

"I don't know what to do with you," Jaymee chided in between chuckles. "You're never serious when you're supposed to be."

Nick shrugged, smiling. Getting up from the couch, he pulled her up with him. He slipped her hand into his unzipped jeans. "I can show you what you can do with me in your bed," he invited naughtily.

"I'm going to have to deduct room and board from your pay," she teased.

"What?"

"Yup. Also, the torn shirt and pants. The hairpins you keep throwing away. And…two dirty tee-shirts. At least. Let's see, that leaves…why, you owe me money on your next paycheck!"

"Oh, yeah?"

She should have heeded the tone of his voice, but she was busy putting her pants back on. As soon as she straightened up, she found herself lifted over his shoulder. As he made his way out of the study and to her room with unerring ease, he told her softly, "I'm going to pay you back my way, sweetheart, with compound interest for any extra charges, of course."

When Nick finally allowed her to curl up and fall asleep on top of him, she'd tallied up an exorbitant account of extra charges.

## Chapter Eleven

Saturday. Jaymee mentally ticked off each day, hoping it wouldn't be the last day that Nick—it took too much effort to call him Killian in private and Nick when they were around the others—spent with her. It wasn't difficult to conclude that, with the appearance of his cousin, part of his "unit," Nick needn't stay with her much longer. They would be gone soon, off to straighten out whatever they were straightening out. A heavy feeling settled in her stomach whenever she imagined Nick dying in that explosion about which he'd told her. He led such a different life from hers. He'd seen so much, done so much, and all she'd ever done was dreamed. She wondered what he saw in her that made him want her so.

Not because of this mop, that was for certain, she grimaced wryly, as she pulled the wide-toothed pick through her hair. Securing it into one thick braid, she considered whether to put any make-up on, then frowned. Why bother? She would sweat it all off in an hour, and Nick would still see her the way she always was—sweaty and untidy. Not this evening, she vowed. This evening, she would show him that Jaymee Barrows could look presentable.

"Got a tee-shirt?" His crooked smile was bland, his eyes innocent.

Jaymee met his gaze in the mirror. She still couldn't get over him walking around her half-naked, in her room. She watched him sauntered toward her dressing table, still wet from the shower, a towel wrapped casually around his waist. "I thought you brought a change of clothes in that little bag," she said to the moving image.

"That's for later. I need something to work in."

"I think you're just sleeping with me for my tee-shirts," she said, wrinkling her nose at his reflection.

Nick played with her thick braid of hair. The urge to mess up her work and just watch the strands curl out rebelliously tempted him, as it always did. He was fascinated by its softness and rebellious nature; in fact, he was fascinated with the whole package standing in front of him.

"No, sweetheart, I prefer you without them on," he teased.

Color warmed her cheeks as she recalled the night before. She flicked at his outreaching fingers. "Don't mess up my braid up," she warned lightly.

"I don't know why you always tie it up. I'm just going to loosen it later." He bent down to kiss her exposed neck, nibbling lightly. "Well, there's at least something I like when you do it."

Jaymee shrugged her shoulder to nudge him off. "Nick, didn't you tell me that you were a good carpenter?"

"Besides being so good in bed, you mean?" He was in a great mood today, having gotten his planned night after all.

"Big head," she said good-naturedly.

"Big appetite," he came back, a sexy smile on his lips. "You were insatiable."

She stuck her tongue out at him. "You're a big liar too," she accused.

"Oh, are you telling me that you we didn't finish up a whole box of…"

Jaymee felt the heat on her cheeks again. "About the carpenter skills…" she hastily cut in. "Are you really going to help me out?"

Nick pulled her up and turned her to face him. "Still shy?" She looked adorable when she blushed and he enjoyed teasing her so. He could always tell when she was thinking about their intimate moments. The green flecks in her eyes heated up to an intense glow that made him hot all over. Like now. He sighed. "OK, I'll earn my keep. Give me a shirt, some breakfast, and I'll get to work…boss."

He was really as good a carpenter as he'd boasted to be, Jaymee thought later, as she admired the muscles playing on Nick's bare back. He was leaning over the saw while cutting the two-by-fours to be used to repair the rotten back porch. She had been working inside the house, and decided to take a break at half-past ten, to see what he was up to.

Jed and Grace showed up at that moment, coming up the overgrown unpaved driveway. Jaymee wondered how they managed to get there. Jed had taken time to shave and Grace looked less like a wild child, even with that green hair.

She studied Nick's cousin. That man's likeness to Nick was even more pronounced without the heavy stubble he had. He had a leaner face, with a stubborn looking cleft under his generous lower lip. His hair had the same unruly lock, like Nick, except it was a dark polished bronze color. His mouth was harder-looking too, unlike Nick's lazy quirk, some might even described it cruel-looking, with lines bracketing both sides, emphasizing the deep indentation below. Same thickly lashed eyes, except that they were so cold. He was a good-looking man in a rugged sort of way, if he would just smile more. And if his strange, light eyes wouldn't stare with such deadly intensity at their target. There was something very ruthless about Nick's cousin, and she still wasn't certain how to talk to him whenever they were together. She had a feeling those odd little pauses between them were somehow deliberate. They sure made her feel awkward and uncomfortable.

Grace's personality, on the other hand, was like Nick's. She was warm and funny, and obviously adored her father and older cousin, paying rapt attention to everything they said. Jaymee pursed her lips, her usual cynicism questioning the wisdom of that. The teenager definitely needed some female advice regarding men. She wondered how a little girl grew up without a mother, to whom Grace turned when she needed guidance. Perhaps that was why she had this strange adult attitude, even calling her own father by his name. Jaymee couldn't imagine calling her father "Bob." She gazed at Jed again, watching him with a touch of disapproval. He didn't treat his daughter like one at all, asking her opinions about things her own father would never dream of discussing with her at that age. She shook her head—what a strange twosome.

The two men talked quietly in between measuring and sawing and hammering. Jaymee couldn't quite make out their conversation over the din, as she showed Grace how to pry the trim boards from the walls. "You don't need to be too careful," she said, as she gathered the pieces into a pile. "I'm replacing them with new trim."

Grace proved surprisingly proficient with a hammer. "This is cool, Jay," she said, as she used the catspaw to pull the nails out. "Are you going to put some fancy moldings? Perhaps up around the ceiling too? That would look like those antique mansions that I see on TV."

Jaymee smiled. "That's a good suggestion. Maybe you ought to study architecture or designing when you go to college."

"I'm going to do something that lets me travel all over the world," the teenager declared, as she pounded down the protruding nails. "There's so much out there to see, you know?"

Jaymee's smile turned wistful. The excitement of youth. She'd forgotten how grand the feeling was. "Yes, so much to see and do," she murmured in agreement. Just don't get eaten up by bad wolves, little girl. "So, architecture is an option, then? You get to travel and study all the wonderful ancient buildings."

"I don't know anything about building. Actually, I like what you do better."

Jaymee laughed, startled. "You like roofing better? And how's that going to be part of your world travels plan?"

Grace wiped her face with a dirty hand, smudging her nose and cheek with dust and dirt. Jaymee grinned. She was looking scruffy again. "What use is staring at those structures if I don't understand the work and sweat put into its making? I don't want to admire just the building. That's boring. I want to look at it and see in my mind how they did it, what the builder did to create it, what the laborers worked with. You know how to appreciate that—you know what it takes to build a house. Foundation and structure. Way cool."

She stared at the younger girl in astonishment. She'd underestimated her. Grace wasn't as innocent and wild as she looked. "Well, maybe I'll hire you as a roofer," she told her.

"It won't be way cool when you're dying up on the roof in the heat, Trouble, especially when General Jay is working your butt off," drawled Nick from the doorway. He'd peeked in to ask for a drink and overheard the last part of the conversation. "Believe me, it's way hot."

Grace grinned. "I know. Jed and I had a good time watching you sweat on the roof while we were resting comfortably in the shadows."

Jaymee frowned at that revelation. "How long have you been watching Nick?"

"At least three days," replied Nick, strolling in and grabbing a clean plastic cup from a bin.

"You knew?" Jaymee was perplexed. If he had known, how come he didn't say anything?

He filled his cup with ice water from the five-gallon cooler. "I had a feeling," he explained.

"Like I pointed out earlier, you're obviously out of practice, if you just had a feeling." Jed said softly. He was lounging against the doorjamb. His shirt, like Nick's, was off. He was, Jaymee nodded, tanned all over. "We could have cancelled you."

Nick savored the cold water in his mouth, then swallowed. His blue-gray gaze was steady. "Think so?"

Jed just cocked his head, his own gaze unwavering. "I have the element of surprise on my side. And...you were distracted."

Jaymee dropped her hammer, deliberately obtaining the two men's attention. She straightened up to her full height of five feet two inches. "I'm a little tired of being out of the loop," she said, keeping her voice level, "and I am not a distraction to anybody."

Nick tossed a cup at Jed's direction, which his cousin caught without even looking, since his strange light eyes were studying Jaymee. "Is she always so blind about herself?" he asked Nick as he headed for the cooler.

"Only about herself," Nick answered with a grin. "And, she gets you to give her answers, believe me."

Jed finished his drink and looked back at Nick. "In that case, you'd better think of a way to keep her. If you don't, I might go for her myself."

Nick's eyes narrowed a fraction. "It isn't like you to poach, cousin," he said silkily.

Jed headed towards the door. Jaymee, her mouth hanging open at the exchange, noticed flesh-colored scars criss-crossing his back. Walking back out into the back porch, he said over his shoulder, "I'll do what it takes to keep you on your toes, cousin. I want your switch to be on all the time." He disappeared outside.

Nick gave a succinct curse, and strode after Jed. "Dammit, Jed, this isn't a game..."

The sound of Jed's saw cut through the rest of Nick's angry words. Jaymee stared at the open door, then looked at Grace, who had a big, amused grin on her lips.

What was all that about?" she asked. Surely, Jed didn't say what she thought he said.

Grace arched an eyebrow. "That was testosterone talking."

Jaymee looked incredulous for a moment, then burst out laughing. "I think it's dangerous!"

"Quite potent," agreed Grace. "I don't think I've seen Jed and Kill at each other like that in a long time."

Somehow, that didn't sound very comforting. Better change the subject. "Tell me, Grace, why do you call your father by his name, but Nick is sometimes Cousin Kill? It's strange."

"Jed--Dad--wants me to," explained Grace, twirling a pigtail. "Safer, if less people know how we're related. Kill's just a cool nickname. His buddies call him that sometimes and I picked it up. He calls me Gracie."

Jaymee frowned. "This is really serious, isn't it, this thing with your training and the relationship between your dad and you?"

Grace met her troubled gaze with mocking brown eyes. "Your relationship with Nick is just as serious, you know, Jay."

"How so?" Jaymee bent and picked up the hammer she'd dropped.

"Why do you think Jed is testing Killian? He wants to see how far he can push him."

That was enough to make Jaymee paused in mid-pull of a nail. "I think you lost me on that one. Why would Jed be testing Killian?"

"Because he wants to see how important you are to him, silly," Grace sighed, as if she was wondering at her inexperience with men. "He wants Kill to acknowledge that you're important, like I am to him."

"Why?" Jaymee wondered whether there would ever be a time when she didn't have any questions about Nick and his relatives.

"Because it's going to get you or Killian killed. See? Distraction leads to carelessness, which leads to being possible targets, and right now, Killian is a target, if whoever is after Dad's unit knows that he's still alive."

Jaymee saw the logic behind it, but still couldn't believe that she—boring, dependable Jaymee Barrows—could possibly be involved with people who talked about being targets like it was an everyday occurrence. "You mean," she managed to calmly word out her fears, "since he was a target, then I'd be one too, like you are, because of your relationship to Jed."

No wonder Nick wanted to leave as soon as possible. She understood it now.

"Yeah, but since they don't know that Killian's still alive, you're pretty safe right now," assured the teenager.

"But Jed doesn't want Nick's guard down," Jaymee ventured a guess.

"Righto, and Kill's failing the test."

"How so?"

Grace sighed again. "Jay, you're really blind. Instead of ignoring Dad just now, Kill is out there fighting with him! Basic evasive tactic for Viruses—submerge when being tested."

"Wait a minute, wait a minute." Jaymee threw up her hands in exasperation. "You're losing me again. First, your father isn't interested in me, so he isn't arguing over me. Second, what on earth are 'viruses,' is that what you said, 'viruses'? Third, surely Nick will see through such a stupid test! After all, I just met you two last evening!" That seemed like a century ago.

Grace laughed lightly, obviously amused at something showing in her face. "Maybe Dad likes you more than you think?" she teased.

"What?" Jaymee stared back in consternation. "He wasn't serious, was he? You told me that he was testing Nick, to show him his weakness."

Grace played with her pigtail as she considered for a moment. "Well," she said slowly, but her voice still had laughter in it. "I don't know. Jed doesn't joke. Actually, Jed always means just about everything he says." She took the broom out of Jaymee's hand. "As for the question about Viruses, maybe you ought to ask Nick to explain to you. Here, I'll clean up. You can go out and calm the men down, maybe ask more questions."

She grinned again, a mixture of childish humor and adult observation. Jaymee couldn't believe that a sixteen-year-old, who was also advising her on how to deal with men, was outmaneuvering her. But then, Grace sounded like she knew more about the opposite sex than she would ever get a chance to find out. What did she know about men like Nick and Jed, anyhow? She ran a nervous hand through her tangled curls. She had to take control again, somehow.

"Sorry, girl," she firmly said. "Jaymee Barrows doesn't placate testosterone. They want to make fools of themselves, let them. I've more important things to do. Come on, you're going to learn how to strip the doors down to their natural wood."

This she understood—the certainty of a finished task, the toil behind labor. Not testing and words and arguments. She could never win an argument like that. She eyed Grace thoughtfully. Well, if all the girl got from her father was cerebral food, it was time she was given a chance to enjoy the fruits of hard work. She did seem to enjoy it enough.

"Yeah, let Jed handle cousin Kill," Grace agreed, putting away the broom. "Do you want to take the door knobs off the doors first?"

Jaymee nodded. "Good thinking. You do that while I get the rest of the tools." She tossed a last glance at the back door. "We'll give them an hour, then we'll break for lunch."

A chuckle bubbled from Grace. "I like you, Jay. You shoot straight from the hip. Maybe that's why Dad is after you too. He likes his women tough."

"For the last time, your father doesn't have a thing for me!" She needed to steer the conversation off this topic. Grace was too perceptive by far, and was enjoying this too much for a teenager. She muttered under her breath. "I can't believe this is happening to me."

"Don't worry, Jay. Jed will make sure Kill growls even more than he does when you're around."

Jaymee groaned inwardly. That was all she needed. An angry big wolf to deal with while she was trying to tame him. She groaned again. Did she say 'tame'? There was no taming a man like Nick. To them, she was just a distraction. That really rubbed the wrong way. What did they think she was—a toothache?

She shrugged. At least Grace had answered her questions, which meant that Jed really did like her, enough to allow his daughter to give her information. Thinking like that brought back a frown. All this mental figuring was getting a tad complicated.

\*

Nick didn't see anything complicated about the situation at all. Someone was intruding in his territory and he did what he knew best—attack before invasion. He'd seen his cousin standing too close to Jaymee and talking quietly. He had noticed the way he looked at her when she wasn't paying attention.

When Jed put down the saw to examine the length of pine, Nick quietly said, "I don't need to tell you that I don't appreciate your unusual interest in Jaymee."

Jed fitted the two-by-six piece of pine board into the empty space where the rotten wood used to be. Not looking up, he advised, "Keep her, or let her go."

"Or else?" challenged Nick, as he donned his tool belt. He was angry with Jed, something that hadn't happened for a number of years. His cousin had always challenged him, but never played with his romantic life. Jed had never needed to go after someone else's woman before, and if he hadn't realized by now that Jaymee was taken, he'd better find out now! There was no way that he was going to allow him to even consider Jaymee as fair game.

Jed whacked a six-penny nail into the wood. He glanced up briefly, and mockery glittered in his silver eyes. "Or, I'll do it for you," he informed Nick.

Going down on one knee, Nick clenched the half dozen six-penny nails in his hand. "This isn't going to be one of your head games, Ice."

His cousin kept nailing, his hammer pounding rhythmically, as he secured the two-by-six. "You aren't functioning at top level because you're indecisive. I won't have any of my unit at risk because you've decided to expose your switch, Programmer."

"No one's at risk." Nick's voice was icy, dead certain.

"As long as you're this way, everyone you're with is at risk. Most of all, her. Face it, you can't think straight where she's concerned."

"So you think you can make up my mind for me?"

"No. I'm saying, if you don't, or won't, make up your mind, I'll make up her mind for you. She is, after all, very intriguing."

Nick leveled a dangerous look at his cousin. "Get to the point. What do you want, Jed?"

The other man slapped the head of the hammer on his palm as he met him eye-to-eye. "Just do your job," he responded unequivocally, "and you needn't find out what I want." His voice was soft, stressing the word 'what' with steely delicacy.

"Is that a warning? You'd risk our friendship to have it your way?" Nick tamped down the temper rising inside. A part of him knew what Jed was attempting to do, but he also knew that women found his cousin's dangerous air irresistible. And, the S.O.B. was considered attractive. Would Jaymee find him so?

"Let's just say that I'll do whatever it takes to minimize loss," Jed challenged back with calm arrogance.

Nick never underestimated his cousin's determination. Jed was as lethal as he appeared, as ruthless as they came. He was COS's number one silent assassin, and his reputation was legendary. He always did what he set out to do, and right now, he was warning Nick that he would go after Jaymee himself, if she posed a risk to his men.

"I've been careful," Nick said, deciding that the best tactic for the moment was detached assurance. "The risk is minimal."

"You've been lucky. So far. Unlike Diamond. Use your talents, Programmer, that's all I ask. Write the program, execute the commands, and wrap up all the loose ends. Remove the bugs."

"She isn't a mistake."

"I didn't say that she was the bug." Jed moved back to the pile of pine boards.

Nick seldom lost in anything, and he especially hated losing to Jed. "Dammit, Jed. Stop probing."

"It's my job."

One probe deserved another. "Do you think I'd let you near her, now that you've revealed your intention?" he asked.

Jed only shrugged, absorbed in his work. "Either way, I win. Now you'll be on your toes at all times, won't you—cousin?"

Nick cursed peremptorily, knowing that his unit leader had him trapped in this war of words. He resorted to something General Jaymee taught him. He pounded down nails with satisfying savagery.

# Chapter Twelve

Remodeling the old house was Jaymee's solitary project, somewhere she could retreat and do things that she enjoyed. She was used to being on her own, taking care of problems by herself.

It was, therefore, a new and pleasant experience to have company helping her. Something stirred inside her as she listened to the sounds of work around. The two men outside obviously didn't need her supervision, keeping the air filled with the pounding and buzzing of tools and machines. She had been alone for so long that she'd forgotten what friends meant. She now realized how alone she had become these past years, so intent had she been at keeping her father's business afloat. This was the first time in a long while that someone was doing something for her, and she didn't know whether to laugh or cry over the irony that it had to be three relative strangers who were willing to do that.

As she washed off the brushes she and Grace had used, she studied the two men through the smudgy kitchen window. With the younger girl in the bathroom, she finally had a few moments alone to sort out her thoughts.

Looking at Nick and Jed working outside, Jaymee didn't doubt any of the recent revelations. The two men worked bareback, and even from this distance, she could make out the muscles that rippled under their sinewy male flesh. These two were in superb shape, looking every bit the trained warriors that she now suspected they were. They moved with the easy grace of active people who were used to working together, throwing two-by-fours and tools back and forth as if they'd been at this kind of job for years.

Her gaze was drawn to Nick. Sleek and powerful in a pair of dirty cut-offs, he exuded enough magnetism to give her a mild case of heart palpitation. It never failed every time. She sighed. How could just the sight of bare chest and muscles make her weak like this? She had seen enough half-naked men in her line of work, but that man out there was the only one who gave her bedroom thoughts. She eyed the small masculine buttocks encased in the jeans hugging so temptingly low on his hips.

Very energetic bedroom thoughts indeed. She was turning into a sex maniac where this man was concerned.

Quickly, she shifted her gaze to the other man. Jed was leaner, with a hard, defined body that reminded her of a wild cat. She wondered again at the scars on his body. Besides those on his back, there was one on his side that looked as if its history was painful. Jed, she noticed, was very graceful. Every move he made was deliberate, as if he had very limited personal space, yet the very minimalist moves made her very aware of him whenever he was near her. And those eyes. They were always watching everything…no, she amended, they were stalking, like big animals looked at their prey. If Nick was trouble personified in her imagination, then Jed was danger in the flesh. She had a feeling that Nick's cousin had no compunction when it came to matters of life and death when dealing with the enemy.

They must be talking about something serious by the look on their faces. Apprehension fluttered in Jaymee's stomach. Maybe they were making plans to depart.

Her hand tightened around the brush in her hand. Tonight. Tonight would be hers. She'd forget about her fears and worries and get herself a memory of Nick to carry with her in the lonely nights ahead. Wiping her hands dry, she prepared two glasses of water, and putting a smile on, she stepped out onto the porch.

"Here comes the boss," drawled Nick, brushing back the dark lock that fell over his forehead.

"You two have done enough for the day," she said, handing the cups over. "We've to get ready for Mindy's soon. Wow, you guys accomplished a lot!"

She examined the finished back porch with a critical eye. Despite the argument she and Grace had heard going on outside, the two men had done quite a bit of work. The repairs were finished, and only needed a few coats of water-resistant veneer. They'd even pulled off the rusty gutter around the back of the house.

She grinned, giving the thumbs-up. "Well, if you both ever need another job, you can apply right here." She ran a hand down the well-used banister. "Good work, men."

Nick lifted a dark brow, questioning whether she'd expected anything less. "I'll help you with the counters and the doors tomorrow morning, but Jed and I have to take off sometime in the late afternoon."

Jaymee's smile dimmed. "Sure. Will Jed be going with us to Mindy's this evening? You are still going, aren't you?"

"I wouldn't dare risk Mindy's wrath," assured Nick wryly. "Grace and I are, but Jed needs to borrow the Jeep to do some errands. Can we take your truck?"

"Of course." Jaymee looked at Jed, who was quietly putting his shirt back on. "Are you sure you won't come too?"

Jed shook his head. "I have to get some things ready for the trip tomorrow, but thanks anyway."

"You can still join us after you're through with your errands," Jaymee persuaded. She wanted the two men to be friends again. Maybe a relaxed atmosphere would make Nick realize that his cousin didn't mean what he said.

Nick didn't seem to understand. He interrupted silkily, "Jed doesn't like to socialize."

Jed's lips curled. In an instant, he turned devilishly handsome, his smile crinkling the corner of his eyes. That odd intensity disappeared. Jaymee blinked, swallowing the sudden intake of breath at the amazing change. Sexiness was a family trait for these men, it seemed.

"Perhaps I'll join you later, Jay," he said, his silver eyes frankly appraising her. "That way, I can pick Grace up and take her with me without the need for you to drive her back."

Grace, who was silently sitting on the railing, surveyed the three adults. Her grin was knowing, mischievous. "Yeah, use me as an excuse."

Nick scowled and stalked into the house, leaving Jaymee to stare after him, then at Jed. "What did I do?" she asked carefully.

Jed shrugged. "Give me directions to this place you're going," he said, instead, deliberately diverting her thoughts back to him. After she told him, he walked off toward the woods, heading back to her house to get Nick's Jeep. He called back, without looking, "Behave yourself, Grace Audrey."

"Always," Grace promised, swinging off the railing. She helped Jaymee put away the rest of the tools. "I can't wait for the food," she said, licking her lips in anticipation. "Hamburger sounds absolutely marvelous. Hmmm. With lots of bacon. Oooh, and cheese." She rattled off more ingredients as her appetite grew bigger.

Jaymee laughed. "That's going to be one humongous burger," she teased. "I'll do my best to satisfy your hunger, young lady. Let's go get ready."

First, she had to find Nick. He came out right at that moment, looking as if he had just used the shower. "Thought I'd better leave the bathroom at your place to you girls. I have no wish to compete with feminine beautifying."

Jaymee felt the tension under his teasing words. He was still upset about Jed agreeing to be at Mindy's party. But why? As Grace ran ahead of them in the woods, she mused, "That girl must be the Energizer Bunny." When Nick didn't respond, she paused in mid-stride. "OK, out with it. What's eating you?"

Nick threaded his fingers through hers, his slate eyes intense. "You aren't curious about where Jed and I are going tomorrow."

"If I ask, would you tell me?" Jaymee challenged.

His lips quirked. "No."

She wrinkled her nose in disgust. "So that makes you mad at me? Because I didn't ask, knowing that you won't answer?" She wrenched her hand out of his and turned away so he couldn't see the desperation in her eyes. "I'm a big girl, Nick. I know you have a more important job to do than nailing shingles."

Nick's voice was low, but to her, it seemed to echo off every tree in the woods. "It's for the best, Jaymee. I can't have you and my job at the same time."

"Why?" she cried, letting her frustration out. "Because I'm a...distraction?"

He placed two hands on her shoulders and turned her around gently. "Do you understand how difficult this is for me?"

Jaymee looked at his face, knowing every inch of it by now, from the lock of hair that always strayed onto his forehead to those eyes that could undress her with a look. The lips with that crooked, wicked smile, to the masculine lean jaw line that clenched intermittently whenever he was angry.

Pursing her lips, she asked, "When?"

"Soon. A week at the most."

Less than a week. Jaymee swallowed the angry denial that threatened to burst from her. She glared up at him, hating him for making her feel so lost. "And you'll leave me. Just like that." She snapped her fingers.

Nick wanted to hold her, to take away the anger and pain, but he kept the distance between them. She had a right to be angry, and maybe this first step away from her would lessen the pain. Whose pain? A voice inside his head mocked. Yours or hers? He ignored that voice.

Anger was a good, cleansing emotion, unlike the way she had bottled up her emotions when he'd first met her. Let her be angry. He would rather have her angry with him, than have a wound festering inside.

When he didn't answer, the little hope Jaymee had retained snuffed out. "You told me once that I was afraid of losing control," she told him in a quiet voice. "Yet, it's you who needs to be in control. You're always somewhere outside, standing and watching, while you go through the motions. You're doing it now, for God's sake. Even when we're in bed, I can feel part of you constantly disengaged from me. You're the one afraid of losing control. You're the one who's letting your fears imprison you."

She turned and ran off, leaving Nick behind. He stood there among the sabal palms and giant oaks, hands thrust in his pockets, a bleak look in his eyes.

Her father looked up from the kitchen table when she walked in. There were piles of papers scattered across it. "There's a girl with green hair in the living room," he announced. "She said that she's waiting for you."

Jaymee forced a smile onto her lips. "That's Nick's cousin."

She walked toward him, waiting for a sarcastic reply when she noticed that her father was arranging the bills she had stacked in her office. He didn't look up from his task as she drew nearer. In silence, she watched for a few moments, then bent down and kissed him gently on the cheek. "I'm going to get ready for Mindy's party, Dad."

Bob nodded, not acknowledging the kiss. She went into the living room and found Grace watching television.

"Come on, let's get dolled up, girl."

The teenager looked up and gave her usual impish grin. "Are you going to put on some serious-looking clothes?"

"Does serious-looking mean a party outfit?" Jaymee guessed wryly. "I'm sure I have something that fits you. What's your favorite color?"

"Maroon."

"To go with that green hair?" she teased. She could imagine the look on Mindy's face.

Grace chuckled. "OK. I'll be good. I'll cover it with temporary color."

*

Nick entered the kitchen, closing the door softly behind him. The sight of Jaymee's father only made him feel worse than he already did. Knowing the old geezer, he'd be hounding his daughter even more when he found out that he'd left her. Determined to do at least one thing right, he advanced to the kitchen table. Bob didn't greet him, sparing him only a cursory glance before resuming his chore.

Nick frowned. Damned if the old man wasn't doing office work, arranging bills and filing them. "Busy?" he asked, pulling out a chair. "Need help?"

"Don't you need a shower too?" the old man countered. "After all, you already practically live here, don't you?"

At least the rancor was still there. "It won't take me long to get changed," he replied, picking up one of the stacks. He started arranging them in order. There was a short silence as the two men shuffled papers and files.

"I'll be gone in a week," Nick finally said, as he punched holes in the bills. His eyes met the older man's. "I don't want you to use my absence as a means to hurt Jaymee."

He handed over the papers in his hands. Bob accepted them, and put them away into a ringbinder file.

"Does Jaymee know about your plan?"

"Yes."

"And she didn't hit you upside your head?"

Nick smiled humorlessly. "I'm sure she was tempted, but I have to go."

"Are you coming back?" Bob closed the shoebox with the small receipts and put all the files one on top of the other.

"Not any time soon," Nick admitted. Then, more firmly, "No. I won't be coming back."

Pushing his chair back, the old man stood up. "Beer?" he offered. At Nick's considering stare, he added, "It'll be the only one I'll have tonight. I'm...cutting back."

Nick nodded slowly. Something certainly had changed here. "Thanks."

Bob took two bottles from the refrigerator, and passed one to Nick. They both popped them open at the same time, eyeing each other.

After some nervous coughing, Bob said, "I had me a long thinking yesterday afternoon. It occurred to me that I hadn't done that for a long time." He took a swig. "It isn't easy to come face-to-face with yourself and finding that you don't quite like what you see."

Nick let the small silence settle around them as he took a measured swallow from his bottle.

The older man continued, "What you said the other morning made me look hard at what my daughter has gone through for me. I don't suppose that you'll stay...if ...I apologize."

It took a lot for a man as proud and obstinate as Bob Barrows to apologize, and Nick respected the old man for the attempt to make amends. The trained part of him was already taking note of the change in the other man. The Programmer could certainly manipulate this new switch to make things better.

"I can't stay," he said. To stay would mean to turn Jaymee's life upside-down. "But, you can take care of Jaymee for me."

Bob nodded. "She's my daughter. She doesn't need to work so hard by herself."

"I'm glad we finally agree on something important, Bob." He could even offer friendship, despite the years of pain this man had caused his woman. He could, because he wouldn't be here for her, and she needed a father. A friend. His hand tightened around the beer bottle.

Bob surprised Nick by actually giving him a smile. The wrinkles fanned out, softening the harsh features. "The important thing," he said, finishing his beer, "is to know when to change when opportunity knocks."

How ironic that the old man had stolen his very own line. Nick tossed down the rest of his beverage before he headed to the study to look for the clothes he'd brought last night.

\*

Change, he decided later, must be contagious. He couldn't take his eyes off Jaymee when she came back to the kitchen with Grace. She had changed. His throat went dry at the sight of her, and heat shot down his loins and threatened to set him on fire. He had to curb a growl of frustration. The woman was certainly fighting dirty.

Her hair, a mass of gypsy auburn curls, hung in untamed ringlets down her back—loose, the way he loved it. Several curly tendrils fell across her forehead, bringing attention to her face. She had done something to her eyes—he didn't know what—but they looked bigger and more mysterious. They seemed to be greener than he remembered them. Her lips were a shiny ruby red and the smile she gave him started a cold sweat under his collar.

And was that supposed to be a dress? It was made of some luminous material, jade-green melting into some soft sunset colors and misty gray. It hung off her shoulders and wrapped around every sweet curve of her body until it flared out around her hips, so that with every step she took, the material swayed and caressed her thighs. There wasn't any trace of the roofer tonight. Jaymee Barrows looked one hundred-percent woman. And Nick wanted to eat her for dinner. And dessert. And breakfast. He put a hand to the back of his neck, to wipe away the perspiration.

Jaymee stood at the doorway. She was nervous but determined. Tonight, she was going to teach her big, bad wolf a lesson. The sight of her father and Nick sitting amiably at the table was disconcerting, though, and she was too distracted to really grasp the fact that the two men were arranging her bills, working together.

She wondered whether she'd overdone it. Grace, with the enthusiasm of a sixteen-year-old, had helped her with her hair, using some sort of glaze that made it shine and curl like a professional model's. It felt strange, though, being dressed up like this. It had been so long.

She blushed at the blatantly sexual look in Nick's eyes as he stood up slowly. Her heart drummed an erratic beat as his eyes traveled from her teased hair, all the way to her low neckline, and down to her three-inch heels.

"Jaymee girl, you look beautiful!" Her father stared at her.

She gave her a father a grateful smile, suddenly needing the reassurance that she didn't look like a dolled-up idiot. "Thank you, Dad."

Nick approached Jaymee, those blue-gray eyes intent and penetrating. Grace sidled away with a knowing grin, giving Bob a wink as she sat down on the chair previously occupied by Nick. The old man regarded her with a frown, looking at her now pitch-black tresses.

"I see I'm going to have a busy night fending off other males tonight," Nick said.

Jaymee's smile widened. "They've seen me in a frock before."

"Not for years," her father stated.

"That," Nick declared, as he touched the material, "is not a frock."

"Aw, that's a major party frock," Grace disputed from behind him. "It has Jaymee written all over it. It's a male magnet."

Jaymee laughed. Nick frowned.

"A male magnet," he muttered under his breath.

"Don't you like how I look?" Jaymee asked, gliding away as sexily as she could on her heels. As she headed out the door, she added, "I wonder how the others will like my new look? See you later, Dad."

She sauntered out, not waiting for Nick.

Bob chuckled from his seat. "I get a feeling my daughter is out to have a good time tonight," he said, amusement in his voice. "You had best keep an eye on her."

"I intend to," Nick replied grimly. Yeah, she was certainly out for his blood. And all he could think about was dragging her into a room somewhere and teaching her to tease him like this. He'd wanted her to be angry with him in a different way, but as always, the woman never reacted as she was supposed to. He hadn't expected her to plan revenge.

As he and Grace followed after Jaymee, his young cousin pulled at his sleeve. "You didn't even notice me," she complained.

Nick grinned down at her. "I didn't know it was you, with that black paint you now have on your hair. Can't you stay with just one color a week?"

Grace lightly elbowed him. "Meanie. I was trying not to embarrass you and Jay by getting all the attention at this party."

"Impossible. You always get all the attention, minx."

She made a face at him. "Just for that, I'm not going to tell you what Jaymee's planning to do, besides dance with all the men at the party."

"Wait a minute..." Nick began, but Grace had skipped ahead of him, toward Jaymee, waiting by her truck. "Damn."

His niece did that on purpose, of course. Women.

"Let me drive," he said, when he reached them.

Jaymee shrugged and handed the keys to him, giving him instructions to Mindy's place. Then, she climbed in beside him as Grace opted to sit closest to the window.

"So the wind doesn't mess up your hair," she said, innocently.

Her long, now black, hair made her look even more exotic. She had tied a thin maroon colored braid across her forehead.

Jaymee couldn't help but smile back. The girl had a certain style. Must come from having an unorthodox father. She wondered whether Nick would make an unorthodox father too, and blushed in the evening darkness, glad that no one was watching her. Nick's child. The picture of a black-haired boy with an attitude appeared. She blinked hard. No, she wasn't going to go there. She wasn't going to be sad tonight.

Tonight, she was going to show that his leaving her wouldn't mean a thing. Her pride wouldn't let her tell him how much she would miss him, how much she really cared. What good would that do, anyway? He would still go. He would still believe that she was better off without him. She felt his eyes on her, even as he bantered back and forth with Grace. Let him wonder what she was up to. She leaned against his arm, savoring the muscled strength against her sleeve, feeling his thigh tighten when she deliberately put a hand on it. A secretive smile curved her lips. She might still have some feminine wiles left in her yet.

Mindy's house was already packed with guests. Jaymee hadn't seen many of them for a while and was stopped numerous times as she wandered through the crowded room looking for the birthday girl. She introduced Nick and Grace as they moved on, and deflected the speculative inquiries with ease.

Finally, Mindy caught sight of them and came over to hug Jaymee. "My, my, dressed up in my honor," she drawled, as she looked at her friend with approval. Out of her waitress apron, she looked slimmer and even taller. Flamboyant as ever, she was dressed in gold, with glitter on her eyelids, traces of gold dust on her chest. "Jaymee sweetie, you'd think to not outshine me on my birthday."

"No one can, with all that gold dust on you, blondie," retorted Jaymee, smiling as she hugged back. "Happy birthday. I see you've started without us."

"Hell, we've been partying since the restaurant crowd went home after their Sunday brunches." Mindy slanted a sultry glance at Nick. "Hi, handsome, how about a birthday smooch?" She winked with unabashed suggestiveness.

Nick grinned, bending down. After a naughty glance at Jaymee, Mindy wrapped her arms around his neck and planted her lips on Nick's. The kiss went a little too long for Jaymee's liking, and without changing expression, she calmly stepped on her friend's foot gently, but with increasing pressure.

Mindy finally acknowledged the silent message. "Girlfriend, you're a mean b…" She noticed Grace for the first time. "Who's this?"

Nick disentangled himself, trying not to laugh at Jaymee's glare. "That's my young cousin, Grace."

"Well, hello!" Mindy was popular because of her genuine generosity and her easy acceptance of everyone. She didn't show any surprise at Grace's mixed heritage. "So sorry I missed you, hiding behind this big and tall specimen. Come into my parlor." She waved her arms in a flourish. "Go ahead and get yourselves food and drinks, OK? Deposit all payments—uh, I mean, presents—on the coffee table, my dears. In fact, why doesn't Grace come along with me to the kitchen, so you two can hang around the adults? What would you like to drink, sweetie?"

"Orange juice," all three of them chorused in unison. They laughed at Mindy's questioning look.

"Inside joke, Min," Jaymee explained. "Just get the girl some orange juice."

Mindy curled a friendly hand around Grace's elbow as she led the younger girl away. "OJ, huh? Well, you're in the right state, honey."

Mindy's parties were always casual, boisterous affairs, and this one was no exception. Everyone loved Mindy, and she reveled at the attention. They sang a rousing 'Happy Birthday' and ate the triple-layered chocolate cake. There was plenty of entertainment—dancing, pool, chit-chat, even a game of darts in a corner.

Jaymee found plenty of invitations to dance. She was privately amused because she knew her partners weren't interested in the real her. They were reacting to this new made-up version of her. Of course, she'd done it to get Nick's attention, not theirs, but it couldn't hurt to dance with a few other men. Besides, he didn't ask her for a single dance, and he had plenty of female company since they arrived. Every single woman at the party had breathed down his neck at one time or another.

Even Mindy had pulled her to one side and said, "Jaymee, you have to hang on to him if you want to keep him."

To which she'd shrugged and pretended non-interest. "I don't keep men."

Mindy had rolled her eyes and sniffed, "Silly me, I forgot your men-hating mantra. Come on, Grace, let's check out the men."

Grace had grinned and let herself be tugged away, a plate with the biggest hamburger in her hand. Mindy had obviously taken a liking to Nick's cousin.

Jaymee knew Nick was watching. She knew because she felt his gaze on her, on every man she danced with. She grew a little bolder, accepting a slow dance with an old classmate she hadn't seen in years.

Someone cut in and she looked up in surprise. It was Jed.

"Hi," she said, instinctively putting a little distance between them.

Jed's silver eyes glittered down knowingly. "You're playing a dangerous game," he said, in that soft voice of his.

Her chin went up. "I don't know what you're talking about. When did you arrive?"

"Fifteen minutes or so ago. I've been watching you."

"And Nick too?" she mocked.

"Of course. He's important to me." Jed whirled her around, moving her further away from the crowd on the makeshift dance floor in the room. Seeing her uneasy expression, he told her quietly, "Relax. I won't hurt you."

"So why are you constantly trying to make Nick jealous?" she demanded, annoyed that everyone seemed to be able to read her thoughts from just looking at her. "You're the one playing a dangerous game."

"I have a better reason than yours. I have to know whether he can function without you, or whether he can think when you're dancing with another man." He looked in the mirror hung directly behind Jaymee. "And he's failing the test miserably."

Jaymee frowned. "I don't understand you."

He acknowledged the comment with a small nod. There was a trace of a smile on his lips, but she wasn't sure, since the man rarely smiled. "All I want is for you to know that you can trust me."

She cocked her head. "I trust you with Nick. I know you have his safety in mind."

"You're absolutely right. You can't trust me with you," he told her, reading her thoughts again. "If I could get him off your mind, I would. However, since I can't...."

He gently drew her closer to him as they moved to the music.

"Jed..." Jaymee began, wondering what that last sentence meant.

Jed's eyes held hers for a moment. "I like you, Jay. Under different circumstances, I might even give my cousin a run for his money, but tomorrow, he and I have to go back to where he was nearly murdered. After that, we have to get this unfinished business done before he can return as his real self. As the Programmer, not your roofer boy."

"Why are you telling me this?" She would be calm about this, she told herself. She wouldn't lose her temper. She wouldn't let Nick or his cousin know how close she was to screaming her anguish.

"Because I like you enough to want to help you," he murmured. "He has to make up his mind, but I'll set the virus in motion."

"Virus? What virus?" Jaymee asked in alarm.

"That's what I am. What we're called. Viruses. We're trained to invade the enemy covertly, Jay." He placed a hand behind her neck. "Will you trust me this time?"

Jaymee examined Jed's face seriously. She was afraid of him, but she'd never felt actual danger to herself. It was just the feeling that he was a dangerous man, the kind she wouldn't want to cross. Yet, she would entrust him with Nick's life without hesitation.

"Yes," she answered simply.

"Then, let me kiss you."

Her eyes widened. "What?" She must have heard wrong.

"I'm going to kiss you and you're not going to struggle."

He slowed down to a minimal sway as he bent closer to her. She stared up at him, not even thinking of struggling, as she watched his face come nearer.

He murmured, "Trust me."

It wasn't a friendship kiss. Jaymee felt the probing of his tongue and with his last words echoing in her head, she obediently opened her mouth. He deepened the kiss, drawing a reluctant response from her. She felt strange, but she kissed him back. His hand skimmed her back, and somehow they were still swaying to the music.

He was a good kisser, but he wasn't setting out to seduce her or even to excite her. She could tell somehow; she could feel a part of him disengaged. Just like Nick. No, not like Nick. Nick sent her up in flames. Jed was just...deliberately removed. Yet, she could feel a certain need in him, a certain...

"Sorry to interrupt, but I believe this dance is over." Nick's voice was clipped, furious.

Jed lifted his head slowly, meeting his cousin's angry eyes over Jaymee's head. "Hello, Nick," he greeted, as if nothing unusual was happening.

"I warned you about mind games and Jaymee."

"So you did."

"Do you think I just said it for no reason?"

Jaymee felt very small, standing between the two men. She thought she understood what Jed was trying to do, but right now, she didn't think it was working. "Nick..."

Not looking at her, Nick very calmly took her hands from Jed's shoulders and pulled her close to him. His eyes were hooded as he continued to stare down his cousin.

Jed didn't blink. "I wasn't playing any mind games with Jaymee."

Nick's hold tightened. Jaymee wondered whether he missed the slight emphasis of her name in Jed's answer.

"She isn't available," he said between clenched teeth. "If we didn't go as far back as we do, I'd call you out for what you're trying to do."

"Be sure of what I'm doing before you start anything."

"And what are you doing?" Nick asked, as the tiny muscle in his jaw contracted. "Besides the obvious, that is."

"You figure it out, Programmer. I'm just the point man, after all."

The little confrontation wasn't going unnoticed as Jaymee cast desperate eyes at Mindy across the room. As usual, her friend wasn't much help, giving her the thumbs up for being so wonderfully ensconced in a territorial fight. She rolled her eyes when Jaymee glared meaningfully at her, and finally walked over, a gleeful smile on her face.

"What a nice surprise! Someone I haven't met. Who is this unknown guest? Another relative of yours, Nick?"" She extended a manicured hand at Jed, as her studied look turned into an interested one.

"Min, this is Jed," Nick quietly said. A slow devilish smile crossed his face and he added, "My present to you."

"Ohhhh!" Mindy rubbed her heart. "All mine?"

Jed didn't say anything, as he just stood there and looked at the blonde woman. His face was as inscrutable as ever.

"All yours," agreed Nick. He addressed Jed, his voice now deceptively mild, "I trust you'll take Grace back to the efficiency tonight and we'll meet at the scheduled time?"

Jed didn't answer.

"Don't you worry about him, honey," Mindy cooed, slipping her hand in the crook of Jed's arm and walking him away. "I'll take care of him."

Jaymee stared after them in consternation. Didn't her friend have a drop of sense in her? The man on her arm wasn't to be trifled with! Couldn't she feel that dangerous aura? She was about to go after them when she felt Nick pulling her away in the opposite direction. She looked at his set expression, and gulped.

"Where...are we going?" she asked. "Mindy..."

"We're going home," he told her grimly. "Mindy can take care of herself."

"But..."

"Don't push me right now, Jaymee."

Heedlessly, she went on. "I want to stay," she insisted.

Nick acted as if he didn't hear her, pulling her toward the front of the house, stopping only to say goodbye to the few people who stood in the way. Jaymee reluctantly followed, not wanting to make another scene.

"You can't bully me!" she told him, as she stumbled in the darkness outside.

Nick pushed her into the truck and got in. Then, and only then, did he grab her by the shoulders and capture her lips with his. It was an act of possession, as he thoroughly kissed her until she forgot that she was supposed to be fighting him, and kissed him back. He kissed her until she was out of breath, only allowing her to surface for air before taking her lips again. Over and over, he made his point. Only he, and he alone, could make her feel like this.

"Now," he said, when he finally released her. "I think I won't spank you after all."

It sounded so ominous, Jaymee was silent all the way back to the house, wondering whether it was really wise to unleash the wolf again.

## Chapter Thirteen

Rage and jealousy burned inside Nick as he forced himself to ease up on the gas, slowing the truck down. He couldn't think straight, wanting only to take Jaymee away from that party. He should question his strange behavior, but right now, all he wanted was her.

She hadn't protested any further since his threat, hadn't uttered a single word as she sat there, staring straight ahead. His hands clenched around the steering wheel when he remembered Jed kissing her. It was an irrational anger because he knew deep down that Jed had initiated it, that Jed was testing him. Instead of ignoring it like his head was telling him, he chose to satisfy the jealousy that gnawed at his heart.

Silence suited him fine. He didn't particularly feel like arguing or discussing. Tonight, with her looking so damned beautiful, her hair like some gypsy enchantress, she had given him a glimpse of what he'd miss most—her sweet sexiness mixed with that bulldog determination. He knew what she'd been up to, dancing with all those men. He'd understood her motives, and had given her the space to do it. She wanted to show him that she could have fun without him, and he was equally determined to show her that he wouldn't let jealousy bother him.

Until Jed had appeared and danced with her. Until he had kissed her.

Next thing he knew, he'd crossed the room, a roaring fury howling in his head, and Jed, damn his manipulative soul, had exposed his weakness with his usual cold, surgical approach. Again, he ignored his training to analyze why he acted as he did; instead, he tortured himself with what he saw.

Jed had kissed her. And she had kissed him back.

When they reached her house, he took her by the hand and led her to her bedroom. She stood quietly by the bed, her hands clasped in front of her. Deliberately, he pulled down the window shades and turned on the bedroom lights before walking back to her. Her lower lip trembled slightly, but she didn't say anything as she continued watching him. It was obvious that she was expecting a fight, but it wasn't what he had in mind. It was a shock to know that he couldn't stand the thought of her with someone else. After all, wasn't that what he wanted? To take away her pain and let her live a normal, happy life? Yet, the moment his mind sensed real competition, in the guise of his too-knowing cousin, something primitive had taken over, and all he wanted now was to assure himself that she wouldn't reject him for another.

She just stood there, as he unzipped her dress and slowly pulled the soft material off until it pooled around her feet. For a long moment, he stared down at the lacy, strapless brassiere. Kneeling down, he slid his hands down her legs, savoring the silky feel of her pantyhose.

She just stood there, still in her heels, as he caressed her intimately. Suddenly, he buried his face in her belly, inhaling her soft fragrance.

His voice was muffled. "I don't think I can let you go."

The admission shocked him. Every trained part of him screamed out a denial. Letting go was essential. Letting go was control.

Jaymee's hands were gentle as they framed his face, making him look at her grave, mysterious eyes with their speckled depths. "You don't have to," she whispered.

Nick shook his head. "It has to stop. This wanting. This needing." He stood up and carried her to the bed. Placing her on the sheets, he sat down beside her. "I have to get ready for tomorrow."

Jaymee understood. He needed to be alone. She felt the tension in his body, felt how much he truly wanted to be with her. She remembered how she'd fought a similar losing battle not so long ago where this man was concerned. Now it was his turn.

"Why?" she asked simply.

"Because I cannot let emotions take over. Jed already knows, and he keeps testing me. I have a job to do." One that took him to too many places, too far away. Wanting Jaymee, and needing her, would interfere. Nick could see no way out. "I'll be downstairs in the study, working. Go to sleep."

Jaymee offered no protest as he left the room. She lay awake for a long time, waiting for him, but he didn't come back. Finally, exhausted, she fell asleep.

As the hours ticked away, Nick worked on modifying the programs on Jed's flashdrive, using it as an exercise to release his pent-up frustration. He had to get himself back in control. The next few days alone with Jed would be good for him, giving him a chance to distance himself from her.

It was very late by the time he finished. Jaymee's bedroom light was still on and he hoped that she hadn't waited up for him. He was relieved to find her asleep. Standing by the bed, he stared down at her for a long while, as an unfamiliar deep longing grew inside. She was his to take, he knew it, but he wouldn't take her away from her world. It wouldn't be fair, taking her away from all that she'd built for herself, and for what? For a life of unknown danger with him?

No.

Quietly, he joined her under the sheets, careful not to wake her. She curled against his body like a contented kitten, snuggling trustingly when he slid an arm under her head. The longing grew like pins and needles. Staring into the darkness, he absorbed the pain, refusing to nurse the hunger. It would be so easy to satisfy what his body craved. It didn't help when her hand reached out for him in her sleep, seeking and finding him. He stared in resolute silence into the darkness, ignoring her moving hand, ignoring his own hunger.

He would not give in. He needed his control back.

*

The tension between them was palpable the next day. Jed and Grace had exchanged a telling look and had gone about as if nothing was wrong. The men worked on the siding around the house, cut a skylight hole on the roof, then turned to the countertops in the kitchen and bathroom. Grace helped Jaymee finish the trim work, then they opted to start caulking and cleaning some of the windows.

They went out on the back porch for a late lunch. Jaymee sat on the steps, picking at the weeds as she ate, her mind busy reshaping the back yard, figuring out how to clear the brush back so that it looked more presentable. Nick sat nearby, on the railing surrounding the porch, one tanned long leg dangling by her arm. The urge to lean against it ate at her, and she determinedly concentrated on the food and the weeds. She could feel his eyes on her, burning a hole in the back of her head.

Trying to ignore her own growing frustration, Jaymee turned her attention to Jed, who was sitting on the sawhorse, facing her. He looked at her fidgeting hands with interest, and she stopped moving them.

"How long will you be gone?" she asked casually.

"A few days. Three at the most," Nick answered from above her.

She refused to make any direct comment to him. "Is Grace going with the both of you?" At the men's silence, she demanded, "You aren't thinking of letting her stay at Nick's place without a car or company, are you?"

"I'll be OK," Grace assured her in a lazy drawl. She was sprawled on a picnic blanket a few feet away, sunning herself.

A sudden suspicion formed in Jaymee's mind, and she turned back to Jed, her voice fierce. "Please tell me you aren't going to let her live in the woods by herself."

Jed darted a narrow glance at Nick, who drawled back from the railing, "Told you she doesn't miss a thing."

"You are!" Jaymee was appalled. "No!"

"She needs to…"

"No!" Jaymee stood up, glaring down at Jed. "Uh-uh, not in my neighborhood. You can train her another time, Jed. She'll stay with me while you're both gone."

Grace turned onto her front, propping herself on her folded arms. She didn't say anything, but her brown eyes sparkled in the sunlight as she enjoyed the sight of someone actually daring to oppose her father.

"She's with me because she's in training," Jed told her in a quiet voice, but his face was implacably cold. "If I wanted her happily domestic, she'd be in Ohio with her grandmother."

"Nick…." Jaymee finally looked up at him, appealing with her eyes. Surely he wouldn't agree to let the young girl do this.

Nick studied her as he chewed on an apple, watching the myriad emotions flit over her face. "It's between Jed and Grace," he finally proffered an explanation, not taking any sides.

"You're all insane!" exclaimed Jaymee, agitatedly pacing between the two watching men. She folded her arms and stood in front of Jed.

"Uh-oh…" drawled Nick. "I've seen that look before."

Jed returned Jaymee's glare expectantly.

"I'll make you a bargain, Jed," she said briskly. She paused as he cocked his head. "You let her stay with me, and I'll give her some training." At Nick's soft laughter behind her, she went on earnestly. "I can't bear the idea of her on her own out there. She can work with me, learn how to do some sweat work. I'll run her exhausted with ten-hour days. I'll build her muscles carrying bundles of shingles. I'll even stop her orange juice intake."

Nick fell off the railing laughing, whereas Grace groaned aloud in mock horror.

"No, no, don't listen to her, Daddy!"

Jed's light eyes glittered with amusement, although his expression was passive as ever. "I don't know," he said mildly. "You might kill her with all that training."

"She'll be building calf muscles, biceps, endurance. She'll be..." She stopped, realizing that he'd just given her tacit permission. "Yes?"

Jed nodded. When Jaymee gave a sigh of relief, he turned to Nick, and said without inflection, "She'll be fine."

A muscle worked in his jaw as Nick abruptly stood up. "Let's look at your program before we go," he said flatly, ignoring his cousin's baiting.

"Have you modified it?"

"Yes."

"I have a notepad and laptop in the bag in the kitchen. We can check it out in there."

The two men took what remained of their lunch with them. As he passed Jaymee, Nick stroked her cheek with the back of his fingers. She wanted him to kiss her, but he was still in his strange mood. So she stared back challengingly at him.

"Nicely done," he whispered, and his fingers lingered for a moment before he went in.

Grace sleepily slapped at a fly as she turned on her back again. "That was great, Jay. Jed seldom backs down for anybody."

"That's because he knows that I'll keep my word," Jaymee threatened lightly.

"My last day of freedom, then," sighed Grace, closing her eyes.

"Do you know where Nick and your father are going?" Jaymee didn't want to pry, but couldn't help it.

"Back to where Nick's boat was. Sorry, can't tell you the location."

Jaymee joined Grace on the blanket, putting on her sunglasses. "It's OK, I just need to sort of know."

"I know," Grace softly responded, her eyes still closed. "I go through it too, you see."

For the first time, Jaymee understood the burden of loving someone like Nick. From what she could gather, Grace lived with her grandmother and seldom saw her father. She was a little girl who was forced to grow up fast. She wondered whether she was lonely without her parents, whether she liked what her father did for a living. Which brought her to wonder whether she herself could live like that, knowing Nick was always in some form of danger somewhere, whether she would be lonely.

But loneliness was nothing new to her. She had been alone and lonely before Nick came into her life. As for his lifestyle, she'd love him no matter what he did. She'd love him whether he was Killian or Nick, or whatever he chose to call himself. It was what made him the way he was, and she wouldn't want to change him. She sighed with resignation. It all came to a very dismal conclusion. She wouldn't try to change his mind to leave her. She wouldn't want to change him.

The two men were sitting on the kitchen stools, staring at Jed's laptop when Jaymee and Grace came back in forty-five minutes later. Jaymee trashed all the paper plates and refilled her glass with iced-tea. Grace hopped onto the kitchen counter and watched her father and uncle at work, her quick eyes reading the screen. She cocked her head and immediately the family resemblance with the two men became apparent.

Jaymee hesitated, unsure whether she was in the way. As if he sensed her indecision, Nick whipped out a hand while still talking to Jed, silently asking her to go to him. She placed her hand in his and he drew her close, until she stood in front of him. Taking the glass from her hand, he stole a sip of the ice tea, then set it down on the counter.

"...without the grid. The decoding should work but didn't. Even when I reversed the code, the damned sequences gave errors," Nick was telling Jed, as he crossed his long arms around Jaymee and laid his chin on her head.

"You're missing something," Jed stated.

Nick reached out and hit a few of the keys. "It's there, right in front of me. I just don't see it. Look at this sequence. And this one."

Jaymee looked at the screen. Numbers. Patterns. Color dots. Map-like diagrams.

Jed pointed to one of the diagrams. "This is location." He typed something. Apparently, Jaymee noted, all these Virus-men could type fast. "This is position."

"That information is apparently unimportant enough for them not to hide. They didn't care if we know we're spying on them, Jed. They just don't want us to find out which satellite and how. This computer program they're using is dangerously versatile."

"Of course. Their encryption board is our technology in the first place. It should have been child's play for you to decode them."

"I'm missing something," Nick agreed.

"Unless they have developed a new encryption technology."

"Possibly."

"How long before you can break through?"

"Not long."

"That's too long."

"You have so much confidence in my abilities," Nick came back, wry amusement in his voice.

"The longer that satellite is out there, the more our national security is under siege, and the more others in our unit are in danger."

Jaymee felt Nick's coiled tension, although his voice remained remote. "I know."

"It's definitely something we can use later down the line. If we can figure this out and stop it in time, we can play with the combined tech at COMCEN and create a super program." Jed finally looked at Jaymee. "What do you think, Jay? Can you break the code?"

Her eyes widened and she studiously gave the symbols on the screen a careful lookover. "Looks like shingle codes to me," she jibed. "Manufacturing dates and invoice numbers. And warehouse locations."

She cast a triumphant glance back at the hard man beside her. She could toss strange terms at him like the best of them.

"A password would override all the walls," Jed said, his eyes faintly challenging her to have a comeback for that line.

"With the new ASTM code, the shingles are supposed to withstand category two hurricane winds. Of course," she said with her most serious face on, "I can't guarantee about the walls." She felt the rumble of amusement in Nick's chest as his hands lightly stroked her bare arms.

"All codes are decodable," Nick interrupted the little game, laughter in his voice. "I have the right sequences in one of those strings." He kissed the top of Jaymee's head. "Right, Jaymee?"

"Of course," she gravely nodded. "Don't mix the color codes. The shingles won't match."

The two men finally laughed, even Jed. Jaymee grinned back, rather shocked to see Jed showing his teeth. He had a deep-throated laugh. How sad that he didn't do it often. She turned her head to look up at Nick.

"What, did I say something funny? Mixed codes can cause a major problem, you know."

"Minx." His smile was sexily lopsided, and her heart flipped. God, she was going to miss him. "Think you know everything about codes, hmm?"

Jed turned off the program and snapped the laptop shut. "Good mind reflex, Jay," he complimented. "You could have been an asset in COMCEN."

Jaymee shrugged, picking up the glass of ice tea. She was getting the hang of talking at Jed's level. She gave him her best Nick-stare, measured and bold. "All a mind game, I've learned. No sweat involved. Nothing to show off when completed. Just a lot of manipulation."

Nick chuckled again, obviously enjoying her sudden scornful mood. Jed nodded appreciatively.

"Touché," he acknowledged, a corner of his mouth lifted in mockery. He arched a brow at Nick. "I think we'd better leave to accomplish something, so we can show some sweat when all's said and done."

Nick gently released Jaymee and got off the stool. "You can't beat Jaymee when it comes to making you sweat," he agreed, giving her a suggestive leer.

Jed moved to the backpack, putting away his things. "I have the scuba gear in the Jeep. All I need are your things."

"They're on the front porch."

"I'll get them. Come on, Grace. Help me load the Jeep."

The moment father and daughter were out of the kitchen, Nick kissed Jaymee hard on the lips. She opened to him without protest, desperately needing a final connection with him before he left. She told herself that she wouldn't show her anxiety. She wouldn't distract him, so he would come back safely.

Nick looked into her expressive eyes, the muddied brown and green betraying her feelings more than she knew. He felt that now familiar tightness in his chest, trying to come to terms with his reluctance to leave her. She was doing her best not to interfere with his work, and he was a selfish bastard not to stop giving her hope. Yet, he needed to kiss her, to taste her, before he left.

"Three days," he husked out.

"Promise you'll be careful?"

"Promise."

"One more thing, Killian?"

He stiffened at her using his name. "Yes?"

"Give me one more night when you come back? Just you and me, nothing else?" Her eyes were luminous with unshed tears, but she was determined to let him know that she was prepared for his choice. She forced a light note into her voice. "Then I'll consider your debt over my torn clothes and dirty tee-shirts paid in full."

Nick gave her a long, passionate kiss, his tongue possessing her mouth with such evocative tenderness, she wanted to beg him to stay. He laid his forehead on hers.

"I always pay my debts," he told her. "It's a deal."

Jed was already in the Jeep waiting when they went outside. Grace was perched on the hood, and she jumped off when Nick climbed in. He tweaked her cheek and returned his attention to Jaymee.

"Good luck," Grace told Jed, as he started the vehicle. "I'm sure you'll get the sequences decoded, Cousin Kill. Their computer language wasn't that difficult, even with it in Chinese."

"You've been practicing, I see," her father observed, shifting into gear. "Nick?"

"One minute," Nick said, and turned back to Jaymee, taking the basket she handed to him.

"Hey, Dad," Grace said softly over the idling engine, deliberately waiting till he gave her his full attention. "Tell Killian thanks for the Chinese books he gave me. They have an interesting way of writing."

Jed nodded, and the Jeep pulled away. Jaymee waved, and Nick saluted back. Grace just stood and watched.

"What lovey-dovey things did Nick say to you?" she teased. "You guys were just so sweet."

Jaymee flushed. She wouldn't let a teenager make her uncomfortable. "He was telling me how to access the new program for my invoices in the new computer, that's all."

Grace laughed merrily. "Ah, how romantic."

"I don't know how to do anything with the new stuff and Nick was supposed to teach me," Jaymee retorted defensively. "He knew I'd be trying to use it when he's gone."

Grace linked her hand with Jaymee's in affection. "Well, let's bargain. Orange juice for help with the computer."

Jaymee's eyes narrowed. "How many glasses?" She should have known the darn kid was also computer literate.

Grace grinned. "Negotiable," she offered generously, as they walked back to the house. "This is going to be fun...boss."

Her imitation of Nick's drawl was so on the money that Jaymee laughed, despite missing him already. She would have to carry on, and not think of the lonely nights. Determined, she donned her tool belt.

"Fun..." she drawled back in a similar vein, "is for sissies."

# Chapter Fourteen

Jaymee kicked a stone in moody contemplation as she walked through the woods toward the house. She was sweaty and tired. And she missed Nick. The last two days, without him, had been long and tedious. It was difficult to continue, when everywhere she went made her think of him—sitting in her truck, working on a roof, sitting in her study, even in what used to be her sanctuary, her project-house. It frightened her, this feeling of desolation. How was she going to cope when he finally left her?

Work herself to death, she supposed. That used to be her antidote to pain. Smiling wryly, she kicked at another stone. Poor Grace. She'd worked the teenager hard the last couple of days but she was a tough young thing and absolutely fearless where height was concerned. After going out to buy the right kind of shoes, she'd taken delight in running around on the roof, working without complaint in the heat.

Without the Hidden Hills subdivision, Jaymee didn't have to meet many deadlines. Her workload, with smaller independent builders, was lighter, and she spent more time at remodeling, leaving Dicker and Lucky on the job. She'd sent Grace ahead of her today, to start cleaning out one of the upstairs rooms while she answered some messages on the business line.

It was a mistake walking alone in the woods. It made her think of Nick. She sighed. What didn't make her think of Nick? The sound of broken twigs behind her halted her thoughts. Turning around, she saw two figures coming toward her. Very quickly. Two very well-dressed men, looking absolutely out of place. They didn't seem lost. Or friendly. Her eyes widened at the sight of the gun in one of the strangers' hands. It was pointed at her.

*

Nick stared out at the ocean, wondering what Jaymee was doing at the moment. Working, of course. He smiled wryly. The woman was an incurable workaholic.

Jed looked up from the maps he was studying, his gaze hard on Nick's contemplative stance. "You have to decide sooner or later, you know," he said softly.

Nick didn't deny Jed's unspoken admonishment for letting his mind wander off. He knew Jed already guessed of whom he was thinking. His rejoinder was short.

"There's nothing to decide." His slate eyes followed the flight of a seagull as it swooped into the ocean. Stealing a page from Jaymee's book, he changed the subject. "Two things bother me about the whole mission. First, how did they find me? I was in the middle of nowhere out there, yet they homed in on me as if I personally gave them a call. I know my boat was clean; I double-checked before starting sail. Second, how did they find the others, one after another? I can't accept that we were tracked down so easily."

"It's on my mind too. Emma's boat was checked by Diamond himself."

A muscle worked in Jed's jaw. "He must blame himself."

"He's disappeared," Jed told him, his voice expressionless. "The unit is in disarray."

"And you also opted to disappear in the middle of this mayhem?" Nick turned around, walking back to where Jed was seated. "I'm dead. So is Winters. Diamond's disappeared. You're here. Who's at the helm?"

Jed folded up the maps. "They'll find me eventually. I know they'll send out a tracker. Right now, training Grace is all that matters. And getting this mission completed. I want those responsible cancelled. For Emma. For the others."

Nick nodded. They were all in danger as long as these people knew some way to get to them. "I'll break the code soon, I swear it. I refuse to let those Chinese characters get to me. There's a link in there somewhere. I can feel it."

"Extrapolate," Jed ordered. "That's why we're here. We move from what we know to the unknown."

Nick turned around and kneeled on one knee as he scooped sand through his hand. It felt cool to the touch and he deliberately concentrated on the exercise, scooping a handful, then letting it trickle out. "After getting the encryption code, I made the copies and gave them to Emma to distribute to the rest of our team. Then we spread out, each with one for decoding and backup. That's the last time I saw them. I was out there, waiting for instructions from Command, and I attempted to break the code."

"Did you call Command or try to reach them by computer or phone, so they were able to trace you?"

"No. All I did was the initial decoding interface, and run a random overview. Nothing unusual."

"What warned you?"

Nick dusted his hands. "You know my computers are different from the others. I have my own warning system. There was an incoming missile."

"Incoming?"

"Yeah, underwater."

"So you were targeted by an outside explosive, not prewired."

Nick nodded. "Right, but there was still a tab on the boat for them to know the exact spot to hit. It was too well-planned, as if they were out there hunting for us, knowing they would get us." He ran impatient fingers through his wind-dried hair. "Maybe I need a refresher course in Chinese. Maybe I overlooked some important double meaning. I've tried every damned sequence."

"You can reread those books you lent Grace," Jed suggested.

"She's done with those? She's good with languages, you know. I've seen her memorize those pictograms in one sitting. She probably has the encryption code in her head by now, the way she was staring at the program so intently that afternoon."

Jed's silver eyes narrowed a fraction. "She gave me a message to pass along to you before we left. I didn't think it strange then, because you were talking to Jay, but it did sound cryptic, now that I think about it."

Nick grinned crookedly. "I wonder where she got that from."

"She instructed me to thank you for the books, and to tell you that the Chinese have an interesting way of writing."

"She's your daughter. Was that supposed to have an underlying message?"

Jed repeated the message, then arched a dark brow. "What were the books about?"

"Just essays, reprinted newspaper arti...cles...."

Nick suddenly sat back on his haunches, closing his eyes as he pinched the bridge of his nose with thumb and forefinger.

His curse was short and explicit. Silver eyes met Nick's blue-gray ones when he opened them.

"I assume my daughter has caused some trouble?"

"Trouble," snorted Nick, his mind racing. "Hell, Trouble has been playing her father's little mind games."

"Oh?"

"An interesting way of writing," Nick repeated Grace's message again.

Jed's eyes glittered in the sunlight. "You've already tried right to left, the way they do it. Error, remember?"

"Yeah, but Trouble meant the books and articles I gave her. Chinese newspapers read up and down, Jed." His lopsided grin was rueful. "I'll bet if we just connect the pictograms up and down…." He stood up, his eyes far away. "Let's go. I need to get back to Jaymee's place."

"Not yet. Our plan was to retrace your steps. We'll start with you getting to shore and work our way to your getting the small apartment." Jed stood up, jamming his sunglasses on his nose. "I need that piece of information to assimilate."

"All right," Nick agreed.

Jed's specialty was information assimilation, assessing how the other side thought and compacting massive chunks of information into relevant details. Simplification, followed by the process to extrapolate cause or effect. Very useful for an assassin. No one could get into an enemy's mind like Jed, and certainly, very few could rival the Ice Man when it came to silent elimination.

Jed would find and target the enemy from within. As all Viruses were trained to do, Nick acknowledged. Invade and disappear. That was why all these attacks on them were unacceptable. No one was supposed to know about the Virus Program.

It had to be something tied with the targets and their relatives, Nick darkly concluded. Emma was Diamond's wife. Jed said one other victim was a relative too. Winters was using his brother's boat. Jed. Unlike the others, he didn't have anyone vulnerable. Until now. A sense of protectiveness burned fiercely in him. He had to find these bastards and eliminate them. There was no way he would let Jaymee be jeopardized by unknown assailants who, one day, might link her to him. Even after he disappeared from her life. His eyes darkened at the thought.

*

Jaymee tried to hide her fear. The gun against the small of her back felt hard and cold, and she knew that her captors wouldn't hesitate using it. It was in their eyes, the way they marched her to the house, the swift slap one of them gave her when she made an unexpected move.

She hadn't asked any questions. She had known instinctively that these men were after Nick, that they were looking for him now. For the first time, she was actually grateful that he wasn't anywhere in the vicinity. Maybe things did happen for a good reason.

"Open the door," the one holding the gun commanded.

It shouldn't be locked, but Jaymee took the opportunity to make as much noise as possible. She had to warn Grace somehow. Pushing at the door, she said to her captors, "The house isn't lived in."

"Perfect hiding place," the other man commented, his voice echoing through the empty house. "I wonder why he rented the little apartment when he has this."

Jaymee blinked in relief. Another reason to thank God. If she hadn't argued with Jed, Grace would be in Nick's apartment and these men would have gotten her.

"Decoy, of course," the one holding her replied, pushing Jaymee roughly into a chair. "Now, Miss Barrows, you'll tell us what you know."

"I don't know what you want to know," she managed to say in a steady voice. "Please, do you have to point that thing at me?"

The armed man studied her for a second, then put the weapon away. He was a big man, and his expensive suit didn't hide his physique. He stepped closer, and Jaymee smelled the musky cologne that clung to him. It made her more afraid somehow, and she wanted to vomit.

"Do you understand what I can do to you if you don't cooperate?" His voice was quietly menacing. "I'll break every bone in your body, starting with your little finger."

Jaymee swallowed. She looked at him in the eye. "I still don't know what you want."

"The man you hired recently."

"Nick?" Jaymee feigned surprise. "My new helper? But he's gone."

"Don't lie to us, please. The two men we talked to told us you fired them because you're sweet on this man."

Damn Rich and Chuck, Jaymee silently cursed, even as fear unfurled in her stomach when the big man in front of her moved even nearer.

"I don't really want to hurt you too much," he continued, "but I will, if you won't tell us where he is."

"I'm telling the truth!" She was. She didn't know where Nick and Jed went off to. "He left two days ago, said he was tired of roofing work."

"Just like that." Disbelief in his voice.

Jaymee shrugged. "Transients are like that in Florida. They make cheap labor."

"And easy bed partners?" the other man sneered.

He pulled up another chair, and sat astride it. Leaning forward, he twirled a few strands of Jaymee's hair in his fingers. She forced herself to sit very still.

"Keep your mind on getting our guy, Les," the first man said.

"There are other ways to make her talk."

"No. Go check out the rest of the house and see whether you can find any trace of him, or the board."

Les reluctantly released her hair, and stood up. "What if he's really gone?"

"Then we wait for the next time he plays with the encryption board. We'll get him."

Jaymee kept her eyes blank, trying not to show any emotions that might betray her. She dared not look in any direction, in case they saw clues of Grace's presence. Her heart was beating so loudly, she had trouble paying attention to their conversation. She tried to calm down by counting slowly.

*Nick, don't play with the board, wherever you are.* She didn't fully understand it, but somehow, handling the encryption board would bring Nick danger. The foreboding feeling spread as she realized that she was asking for the impossible.

*Nick.*

It was a hopeless silent scream.

*

Nick felt restless as they reached his efficiency. He wanted to see Jaymee, needed to hold her in his arms. A heavy sinking feeling settled in his gut as he faced the fact that he'd have to live with this yearning for the rest of his life. He could only hope that time would dull the edges.

He clamped down on all thought of personal needs. They had no place in his job.

"This is it," he told Jed. "I laid low for a few weeks. After deciding to remain 'dead' until I could get word to you, I went to look for a job that wouldn't call attention to me being a stranger in town."

Jed cocked his head. "Roofing isn't exactly your forte. I'd thought you'd try out something electrical, for computer parts."

Nick shrugged and gave a wolfish grin. "No openings. Besides, my new job had unexpected fringe benefits."

"A waste of this efficiency, then." Jed took out the key to unlock the door.

"True," Nick agreed, "but under the circumstances... don't move."

The last two words came out in a hiss, as his trained eye caught the signs. Jed stood very still, his hand still turning the knob, the door ajar wide enough for him to walk into the apartment. He nodded in comprehension at Nick's nod toward the doorknob, keeping it turned clockwise while Nick slipped under his arm.

"This isn't exactly what I had in mind when I said we'd to stick close together," Nick commented as he squeezed his muscular frame between Jed's body and the door to peer behind it. "Ahh..."

He was silent for a minute as he studied the device.

"Can you disengage it?"

Nick passed him a mocking look. "As long as you don't release the knob, we'll be fine." Because this was what he was trained to do, the cocky façade of the Programmer fell in place seamlessly, as he slid into the apartment to have a closer look at the little trap laid out for him. He knew it was for him, of course. Eyeing the gadget, he told his cousin, "Five minutes."

"Good. If I may add that Jaymee and Grace are in danger, perhaps you can hurry a little?"

"Damn you, Jed. What have you assimilated from all this?"

"I'll tell you as you work, to keep your nerves steady," Jed said, with the calm assurance of complete confidence that Nick would get them out of this jam.

Nick was already on his knees, studying the contraption wired to the knob. "What do you mean Jaymee is in danger?" His voice was soft, his hands steady.

"Extrapolate."

"Damn you, Jed." Nick slowly took off the plastic cover.

"What happens every time before some explosives show up in your wake?"

Gently. Gently. He unscrewed the panel covering the wires.

"I'm working here. Why don't you tell me?"

Cockiness was essential when walking on the edge. Fear would only breed nervousness. Every COS commando's first lesson was cockiness at all times, especially when death was close.

"What important thing did you do before they found you?"

Which wire? Nick hesitated with his wire-clipper. His hand was very steady as he hummed under his breath.

"I was..." The clipper moved nearer to a wire. He cut through in one clean motion, then held his breath. Adrenaline rushed through, as he knew it would, as it always did. Standing up, he continued, "You may release the knob now."

Jed let go and stepped in to take a look. "Four minutes. You're getting slow."

"You distracted me with a question." Nick breathed in deeply, settling the lightness in his head. "Each time before they found me, I was trying to decode the encryption board." He cursed as realization dawned. "You mean that I have been calling them myself every time?"

Jed nodded. "On the boat. Here, that night I arrived."

"Shit. In the kitchen of Jaymee's house." Nick was already out the door. Oh God. He had brought them to

Jaymee's house. They ran back outside. The Jeep's gears screeched in protest as Nick backed out of the parking lot.

"A homing device triggered every time you tried to break the code. They were counting on everyone to try many times, so they could cancel each one of you." Jed went on with his analysis in the same calm tone of voice, as if Nick wasn't driving at breakneck speed, breaking down all the assimilated information. "Emma and Winters could have been doing the same. You were warned because of your own computer system the first time. You probably sent them a signal from the efficiency, and this time, because you spent the night with Jaymee, you avoided them again. Luck saved you, Programmer."

He didn't add that Jaymee and Grace were the next probable victims.

"I'll kill them if they got to Jaymee and Gracie," Nick said, his eyes on the road.

Jed's eyes were unreadable as he stared ahead. "They lay a finger on Grace, and they are mine. Every single one of them."

Luck. He didn't need luck for himself. Nick cursed at himself over and over as he stepped on the accelerator. A homing device, Jesus. And they'd been gone over two days, ample enough time for the enemy to trace to that location. This wasn't such a big town, and the right people would easily direct anyone to Jaymee's house, if they were asked. For the first time, he forgot about his training. Fear for Jaymee's safety clutched at his heart, at his very soul.

*

Thirsty and weary, Jaymee sat quietly on a chair in one of the upstairs bedrooms. Her two captors had searched every room and Grace's and her tools on the floor had caught their attention. Their assumption, though, was wrong.

"Two sets of tools?" the one with the strong cologne inquired, eyebrows raised. "If he was supposed to be gone, why didn't he take his tools with him?"

If they looked closely, they would realize that the belts were sized too small for a man, but Jaymee hadn't any intention of pointing that out to them. At least Grace was safe. She had no idea where the teenager could be hiding.

"The tools are mine," she told them truthfully.

"Or, he might actually be back soon," the one named Les said, "although I'm getting tired of standing around waiting."

A muffled sound came from inside the other man's jacket, and reaching in, he pulled out a slim cell phone. "Yeah," he answered in a curt voice. "Nothing to report, except that this is a male, probably the leader of the three." He paused, listening to the speaker on the line. "He's still deciphering the e-board. We're now at the last place he used it, but he isn't here." Pause. "I'm still not sure whether he's gone or not." Pause. "Fine, I'll cover the bases. I'm pretty sure that this one is the last of the three, so once we get him, Les and I expect full payment."

He flipped the phone shut. Jaymee eyed him warily as he approached, then slowly circled her. The more she listened to them, the more it was apparent that these men didn't even know exactly who Nick was. They were after three people, and he was one of them.

Didn't Nick tell her that two people who worked with him were dead? Cold sweat ran down the back of her neck. She knew without a doubt that this man was going to kill her too.

"What do you intend to do with me?" she asked quietly. She wouldn't show him how afraid she was.

Something akin to admiration lurked in the stranger's eyes as he looked down at her. "You should be frightened, lady. Your fate is in my hands." He touched her hair that was tumbling around her shoulders in mass disarray, having come loose from their rough handling. "Such pretty hair. Dark flame. Are you afraid of fire?"

Sick to her stomach, Jaymee clenched her hands in her lap. She jutted her chin defiantly, her eyes blazing contemptuously. "Melodramatic threats don't scare me."

He laughed and held on to her hair tightly. "Too bad I don't have time to play with you, lady. I have much to do, just in case your man does return."

"I told you, he isn't going to come back!"

His killing eyes were pitiless. "Then you will die alone," he told her.

*

Please let her be alive. Nick prayed as he drove. Unused to desperate measures, he was forced to acknowledge that, for the first time in his life, he feared failure.

"She should be home cooking dinner for her father right now," he said to no one in particular. "She works like clockwork."

Jed hadn't said anything since making his analysis. He'd turned inward, aloof, preparing himself for battle.

The Jeep made a cloud of dust down the unpaved road and the brakes squealed as Nick turned into Jaymee's ranch house. To his relief, he saw her blue truck there, as well as Dicker's vehicle and another one. Chuck's and Rich's truck, if he remembered right. Yes, he could see them on the front porch, talking to Jaymee's father. Frowning, he searched for Jaymee's familiar figure as he turned off the engine and jumped out. He could hear Jed's steps behind him as he stepped toward the group of men, all of whom had turned at his noisy arrival.

Nick ignored Chuck's sneer when he reached them. She wasn't there. "Where's Jaymee?" Not bothering to greet any of them, he asked Bob, who was standing on the top step.

Before the old man could answer, Chuck interrupted, "Get him off your property, Bob, before he gets you arrested for harboring a wanted man. I tell you, you're going to need Rich's and my help again once he's gone." He eyed Jed, who stood a few feet away. "That one is probably one of his accomplices, man. Look at him. I wouldn't trust them with your daughter, Bob, not after those men said he was a criminal."

He pointed at Nick, as Jed looked disinterestedly back. Nick turned to Chuck.

"What are you talking about?" he asked in a silky voice.

Chuck spat out some tobacco juice, then gave a triumphant smile. "You heard. I told them FBI boys when they came around town looking for a newcomer that may be acting suspicious-like. You came to mind, acting like you're a construction man, when you ain't." He drawled out the acronym to sound like Eff-bee-yai-boys.

"Yeah," Rich chimed in. "They told us they you're a felon, man. We wanted to save Jaymee from the likes of you, so we told the FBI we thought you're probably the one they were looking for."

"You sent them here?" Nick said through gritted teeth. "To find Jaymee?"

Mistaking Nick's anger for fear, Chuck went on, the sneer on his face bigger. "Yeah, once they talk to her, she'll fire you and we'll get our jobs back."

Nick turned to Bob again. "Where is Jaymee?" he asked, enunciating each word in measured control, his eyes glittering in his pale face.

Bob studied the younger man for a moment. "She disappeared into the woods with that green-haired girl earlier, but told me she'd be back to make dinner," he told him, "but she still hasn't turned up."

He frowned, as if realizing that something was wrong.

"She's probably talking with the FBI right now," Chuck cut in again. "They told us they needed to protect her from..."

He never got to finish his sentence as Nick's fist shot out in a blurred move. The other roofers stared down at the unconscious man on the ground, blood coming out of his nose.

"Bob, I need a rifle," Nick said, his voice deadly soft. "Got one?"

"There's a hunting rifle in my bedroom," Bob answered without hesitation, his gaze still on Chuck. "I'll get it."

Nick turned to Rich, who cowered behind Lucky. "If anything happened to Jaymee, you and that scumbag will pay dearly."

\*

She wasn't scared. She was not scared. Not scared.

Jaymee didn't dare move. She couldn't move. And she was sweating profusely under the blanket Cologne Man had draped over her. It must be getting dark. She wondered at the time. As if it mattered. Well, it should. At least she would know what time she died.

Grace. She had to warn Grace to get out of here, but the gag in her mouth wouldn't budge and her hands...no, she refused to think what her hands were holding onto. The blanket was like an oven but she dared not roll over.

It must be at least fifteen minutes since the two men had left her, and still no sound of Grace. Jaymee hoped that she'd escaped. Those men wouldn't think twice about hurting a sixteen-year old, and if they knew who she really was.... She now had a notion of what being Grace must be like, constantly aware of danger.

She shivered despite the heat, knowing that her own chances of survival were slim. The man with the horrid-smelling cologne had explained exactly what he was doing every step of the way, had enjoyed watching her face go whiter and whiter.

Finally, he'd smiled, and said, "Better not make any unexpected moves, my dear. But then, someone is bound to try to wake you when they see you huddled under this blanket, don't you think?"

He didn't mention who he thought might be the one who would wake her.

Grace mustn't come anywhere near her. In desperation, she worked her tongue and teeth furiously against her gag. It moved just a little but the exertion tired her face out after a while, and she felt numb and helpless. Maybe she was imagining that the gag didn't feel as tight as in the beginning. Gingerly, she lifted her shoulder to rub against her mouth, careful not to move her fingers. It hurt as the ropes cut into her flesh, and she struggled between pain and concentration. Her panting made her realize that her gag was finally loose enough for her to make some kind of sound.

What came out of her throat was a hoarse croak, barely audible through the blanket. No one heard her.

\*

Nick didn't like the silence at all. He circled the house under the shadows of the giant oaks, but couldn't see any movement or light from within. His own stomach burned as fearful imagery invaded his thoughts. Was she all right?

Behind him, Jed was as silent as a shadow. Evasive training ensured light feet and quick reflexes. "Wait," his soft voice cut through the quietude of the area as Nick ventured closer to the front porch.

Nick paused, his hands already on the wooden railing, about to heave himself over. Looking in the direction to which Jed was pointing, he saw a red reflector sticker on the eave.

"That's Grace's," Jed told him, coming nearer. "It means danger."

That didn't ease his fear one bit. "I'm going in," Nick asserted.

"No. Red means to stay put. We'll walk around the house again, Number Three."

The sudden use of his code name forced him to act rationally. Nick hesitated, reluctant to follow his leader's direct order. Jaymee's safety was on his mind. Jed's gaze was piercing as he waited, and after a moment, Nick released his hold on the railing. As they circled the house one more time, they noticed more red reflector stickers spaced on various parts along the eaves.

"How did she find time to go around the house to do that?" Nick wondered. "And she would need a ladder to reach that high."

"Not if she was on the roof," Jed suggested.

Nick frowned. Why would Grace be hanging upside-down on the roof pasting reflector tape? Unless....

"Is she still up there?"

"I'm here."

The sound of disturbed foliage made them turn around, and Grace suddenly emerged from a clump of trees, a little out of breath. She had on a camouflage body veil, a one-piece lightweight construction that covered her from head to foot, and the two men wouldn't have made her out from among the trees, if she hadn't spoken up.

"Where did you go?" Jed asked, as he watched his daughter peel off the hand loops, then push the material back to reveal her dark head of hair.

"I followed the two men to make sure that they were really gone before I attempt to get to Jaymee." Grace shrugged out of the mesh.

"Jaymee's OK? Where's she?" demanded Nick.

"She's inside the house." As Grace gave them a synopsis of what happened, she folded the body veil into a surprisingly small square with quick, practiced movements and pushed it into the unobtrusive butt-pack she had on. "The two men are gone now, and I've got their car plate number. It's a rental."

Jed nodded. Nick didn't give him a chance to speak.

"Later," he told Grace. "If Jaymee's in there, why aren't you with her?"

Grace pointed to the reflector stickers. "That was to tell you guys to leave the place alone if you happened to get back before I do. Jay's safe as long as you don't go inside. At least, that's what it looked like to me, when I saw them wiring every door and window before they took off."

Nick's heart dropped into his stomach. Fuck. The damned place was rigged. "Jaymee is in there alone?" He stared at the house, which now took on an eerie, mocking demeanor. "Why isn't she trying to get out?"

Images of her dead inside. No! He refused to think of that possibility.

"I think she's OK," Grace informed them carefully, her brown eyes concerned, as she looked her second cousin over. "I sneaked out of the window in the upstairs room when they forced her inside, and I heard most of the conversation before they closed the windows."

"If every door and window is wired, we're going to need a team here to get inside," Jed noted.

"No, you can go in, Dad," Grace said, and pointed to the roof. "They forgot one opening."

"The skylight hole I cut out," Nick breathed.

"Yes, but I couldn't jump down myself, so I couldn't check on Jay," Grace said, her voice apologetic. "I'm sorry, Kill."

Nick forced his eyes from the house and turned to Grace. He pulled one of her pigtails with affection and knuckled her chin. "You've done enough, Trouble. Now stay out of sight, hmm?"

Grace nodded, then pointed to a ladder lying on its side by the house. Nick gave her a strained smile, and went to get it. As she watched him prop the ladder against the house eave, Grace exchanged a glance with her father.

"Dad, it's the encryption board. It has some sort of tagging device."

"We already figured it out."

"Did you pass on my message to Kill?"

"Yes."

"I've been thinking. I suspect there's a homing device of some sort on that e-board. The signal led them to him and the others. I don't think they were after the Virus unit."

"Too bad for them. Now the unit's going to be after them." Jed said, deadly intent on his face.

"Hired mercenaries," Grace notified him, her eyes gleaming. "I'm very sure of that, Dad. Probably hired by either the Chinese or the people your team took the board from."

Jed's eyes glittered back from his dark, tanned face. "Don't let me stop you from finishing my job for me, little Trouble."

Grace smiled brilliantly, then sobered up. "Cousin Kill will need help down the skylight hole, Jed."

She looked up as the tall, lanky figure disappeared over the peak of the roof.

"Stay at a safe distance," Jed ordered, heading for the ladder.

Grace nodded, then turned and disappeared into the woods.

\*

Jaymee heard the creaking sounds. She recognized what they were, having heard them a thousand times before. Feet walking up a roof. The plywood echoed everything, from the moving feet to something being pried apart. She hadn't any idea what Grace could be doing up there. Then, silence. She strained hard for some more noise but the blanket made it difficult, muffling the quieter sounds. After what seemed an eternity, she finally thought she heard Grace approaching.

As loudly as she could, she cried out in a hoarse, spitless voice. "Don't touch me, Grace! Stay away from me!"

She hoped her words were recognizable through the thick fabric. There was a short pause, then the cover over her slid off very slowly, and she let out a sigh at the sudden cool air.

"Jaymee."

She stiffened. "Oh my God, Nick!" She couldn't see him, slumped in the position her captor had placed her. "Don't move me, OK? Don't!" She quelled the rising panic, trying to make herself intelligible. In as calm a voice as she could manage, she continued, "I think I'll explode if you touch me."

\*

Nick blinked away the red mist of rage that obstructed his vision. This wasn't the time to be angry. After climbing down the skylight tunnel with Jed's help, he'd walked from room to room, wondering where they had put Jaymee, why it was so silent. A quick check had revealed that the main doors and windows were indeed fixed to trigger off if disturbed. Thank God for Grace's quick eyes and thinking.

Jaymee was in this box somewhere, maybe knocked out. Not dead. He refused to accept that.

His heart leapt when he spied the outline of what could be a body under the blanket lying on one of the old sofas upstairs. He knew, from the familiar shape, that it was Jaymee under there. It had to be. The position looked awkward—abnormal—and he felt a great abyss growing, breaking his insides apart, as he rushed toward the shrouded figure.

Oh God. Not a shroud. Shrouds are for...he was about to let out a howl of despair when he heard the muffled noises coming from under the covers.

Urgent sounding. Hoarse, almost inaudible, but absolutely, beautifully alive.

He closed his eyes in relief, blinking back unexpected tears, then hurried to take Jaymee into his arms. Something in the tone of her voice halted his frantic state of mind. She was trying to convey something important. He heard the last part of her urgent warning.

"I'll explode if you touch me."

She was repeating it over and over, like a fervent prayer.

Nick inched the blanket off Jaymee carefully. Taking several deep breaths, he said, in a soothing voice, "Sweetheart, shhhh. I hear you. Shhhh." When she settled down, he continued, "I'm going to turn you over very slowly. You just lie still and don't exert a muscle, OK? Are you hurt in any way?"

He needed to make sure that she wouldn't jerk in pain from some wound he couldn't see. Her voice was thin, exhausted.

"I'm fine, at least, I think I am. I can't feel my hands and feet too much because the ropes are too tight. Nick, go get the cops or something. It isn't safe for you here."

She was so relieved. He was here. Alive and here. His hands were reassuringly gentle on her, moving and turning her over with infinite care, and she gave a sigh as she slowly faced him.

"Don't exert a muscle," he reiterated, in the same soft tone. "Don't think about the danger, just concentrate on my moving you. That's right, baby. Almost there. Good. Now, let me look at you."

Nick kept his face an expressionless mask as he took in the bruise on one of her cheeks and the marks left by the gag on her delicate skin. Her hair was plastered to her face, tendrils damp from perspiration. Her shirt was soaked from perspiration. He fisted at the sight of her small hands tied close to her chest, palm to palm. Her knees and her ankles, too, were crisscrossed with—his eyes narrowed—electrical wires. Her hands....

Jaymee stared up at Nick's face, trying to get past the controlled expression. She realized that he was hiding his reaction from her. She could guess at some of his emotions raging in there somewhere. Loving him for coming into the house for her, she sought to comfort, to reassure.

"It's alright. I'm perfectly fine, as you can see. Now, why don't you go and call the police or whatever department it is that takes care of...bombs." She faltered on the last word.

Nick smiled down at her gently. "And leave you?" He guessed at her motive. "Do you think that I'd leave you here alone, with this thing in your hands?"

"You have to," Jaymee whispered back. "I don't want you hurt." She turned her eyes downward to study the small package in her hands, secured tightly in such a way that any movement of her thumbs would hit the little lever on the module. That Cologne Guy, as she'd dubbed him, had told her exactly what would happen if she accidentally activated it. Desperation made her voice clearer as she begged him to leave her. "If I press down from fatigue, it's going to go off and...please, Nick, get out of here!"

Nick pulled a small case out of the back pocket of his jeans as he locked eyes with Jaymee. His blue-gray eyes were clear and steady. "I'll not do that even if you set it off accidentally. If you go, you'll take me with you."

He opened the case and extracted the small instruments inside.

"Nick, please." She begged him with her eyes, her voice. "You're being unreasonable."

"Don't you have confidence in my skills, babe? I'm more than a big, bad wolf, you know." His voice was teasing, as if it wasn't a matter of life and death at that moment. "You did say I have elegant, clever hands."

Jaymee felt tape being pulled from her skin and she flinched at the sting of skin and body hair parting from the glue.

"Don't move your thumbs, no matter what, sweetheart," Nick continued, the deep timbre of his voice down to a croon. "Really, when I told you I wanted you tied up, I meant in a more spread out position, Jaymee. This one makes access difficult, to say the least."

"Nick, this is no time to joke!" She couldn't believe that he was capable of such calm, even making fun of the situation.

"Is she all right?" Jed interrupted from the doorway.

Nick didn't turn around as he slowly cut the knots and pulled at the tape that bound Jaymee's wrists. "Get out and make sure Grace and you are out of the way," he calmly instructed. "This one will take some time, cousin. If you see my flashlight, come back on the roof to help me get her out through the skylight. I don't trust any of the doors."

Jed, understanding the situation, didn't argue. "We'll be waiting for your flashlight." Then Jaymee heard his fading footsteps.

"Did you miss me?" Nick asked as he continued working at the tape.

Jaymee looked at those long eyelashes, the sensual lips, the stubborn lock of hair across the forehead. She noted the muscle ticking in his jaw. He probably needed distraction more than she did, she realized with sudden insight. The thought of her in danger would affect his concentration. She must keep him from thinking that she was hurt.

"Maybe," she told him, forcing her voice to relax. "But only the nice parts."

She was rewarded with his sexy, crooked smile. He looked at her again. "The next tug is going to hurt. The tape is wound around your thumbs."

She nodded. She understood the consequences if her thumbs jerked from any kind of pain.

"Ready?" he asked, keeping the smile on his face, although his eyes were oddly remote.

"Ready."

She concentrated on her thumbs, stiffening them so that they didn't react from the expected sting. Her breath caught sharply when the tape was ripped away, but she managed to keep her thumbs inert. The air in her lungs hissed out in relief.

"Good girl." Nick picked up another small instrument. "Now, which nice parts did you miss, hmm?"

It was impossible to undo the rest of the knots and tape without hurting her. He had to work while she still held on to the module. Slowly, he pried open the small cover on top of the casing in her cupped hands.

Jaymee closed her eyes, trying not to think of what might happen if something went wrong.

"Your ass," she told him. "It's a nice part."

"Oh yeah?" Nick's eyes narrowed as he studied the electronics in the device.

"Your lips. Your hands. Your chest. Your belly button," Jaymee continued.

"You're forgetting the best part," he reminded her, as he spliced the wires.

She opened her eyes. "Which part is that?" she softly queried.

"The big bang," he said, and gave her a leer. Reaching down, he picked up the tiny snips.

Her smile was brilliant, even though her lips trembled. "Is it going to happen next?"

She looked meaningfully at the snips in his hand. Nick leaned forward, carefully positioning the snips.

"Not if I can help it," he whispered, his head dipping closer to hers. He looked at the module one last time before giving her his full attention. His eyes were unwavering, dilated from the intensity of his feelings. "Don't move your thumbs."

Jaymee couldn't really see him through the tears threatening to come out. His lips were soft and warm against her own cold, dry ones. His tongue flicked across them, wetting her lips and comforting her gently. She didn't mind if it ended this way, she thought in a daze.

"I love you," she told him, as she heard the sharp snipping sound.

# Chapter Fifteen

Silence. Nick counted his heartbeat, his lips still on Jaymee's. Slowly, he straightened up, thinking that Jaymee's tear-streaked face was the most beautiful thing in the world.

"Silence is golden," he gravely told her.

Her smile was tremulous, and the tears flowed again. "You owe me a big bang," she managed through the tears. "I can't deduct that from this week's paycheck."

"I'll pay up," promised Nick. If they got out of this helltrap safely, he added, as he methodically untied her bound wrists.

Her hands and feet hurt even more once they were free, and Jaymee moaned softly as Nick rubbed them with strong, tender hands. God, she loved those hands. And she remembered. She had told him that she loved him, and she knew that he'd heard her. Those words had come out naturally. Her only thought then was if she were to die, she wanted him to know the truth.

"Thank you, my hero," she said aloud, getting off the sofa with his help and stumbling as her limbs refused to support her.

"You can thank me later, boss," Nick drawled, then swung her into his arms. "Let's get you out of here first."

He carried her out of the room, stopped long enough at a front window to flash a light to signal Jed, and moved on back under the skylight.

Jaymee curled her hands around his strong neck, reveling in the easy strength and secured warmth. She had never felt safer. For a while, alone in the house, she'd imagined dying and him never knowing how much she loved him. Now he knew. And she didn't care.

Jed's dark head appeared above them, and minutes later, they were climbing down the ladder off the roof. When she finally stepped back from the house, Nick immediately lifted her off her feet again, and Jaymee didn't protest. She felt weak and needed him close by. When Grace squeezed her hands anxiously, she smiled back at her.

"I'm OK," she told her.

Nick passed Jed a telling look. "Don't go in there. I'm going to have to comb through the whole house to make sure that they didn't leave any surprises."

"No!" Jaymee tightened her hold around his neck. "No, call the police instead. Let it stay like that forever. I don't care. I don't want you in there." The words tumbled out in panicked phrases.

"Jaymee…"

She didn't care that she was at the edge of hysteria. The thought of him blowing up with the house was even more frightening than when she was alone in there, contemplating death.

"No, no, no!" Her voice was adamant, fierce. "If you risk your life in that stupid…empty house, I'll go back in there with you."

"I'll call in a team," Jed suggested quietly.

"Then Command will know where you are," Nick pointed out, as they kept walking. "I thought you wanted a stretch of time to do what you needed."

Jed shrugged. "I'll think of something. Disappear before they show up."

"Please, Nick, don't go in there," pleaded Jaymee, interrupting the two men. She wasn't in the mood to stay out of their business. This was her business now too, damn it!

Nick looked down at the face of the woman who had almost died because of him. The feeling of helpless rage that he was holding in check was threatening to break through again.

She had almost died. And it was all his fault. It humbled him to know that she would have willingly sacrificed herself so he would be safe.

"All right," he relented. "We'll work out an alternative. But no one goes near or into that place till it's swept by a team."

Jed nodded. "Go take Jay home now. We'll talk later."

"Meet me there in three hours," Nick said, his eyes still holding Jaymee's.

He carried her all the way back, hardly out of breath as he made his way through the woods. She clung to him, her hands stroking the back of his neck, her lips occasionally bestowing kisses anywhere they made contact. They didn't say a word in the gathering darkness as he walked, yet their hearts whispered and conversed, knowing how precious each passing moment was.

Bob, Lucky, and Dicker were still at the house when Nick climbed up the back porch and entered the kitchen. Bob's lined face was filled with worry as he took in the disheveled appearance of his daughter, the bruises on her face and arms.

"Good God, what happened?" All three men got up from their seats.

Nick shook his head when Dicker pulled up a seat for him. "I'm taking her upstairs. She needs rest."

"What happened?" Bob asked again. "Are you all right, Jaymee girl? Who were those men Rich and Chuck were talking about?"

"Not FBI," replied Nick, a hard edge to his voice. "Where are those two bastards, by the way?" He wasn't done with them yet.

"Took off the moment Chuck came to," Lucky said. "You OK, boss?"

"I'm fine, thanks to Nick. Don't worry, I'll be back to work in the morning."

"You just rest up. I'll take care of work," Bob cut in. "Go on and take her to her room, Nick. We'll talk about this later."

No one questioned Nick's actions, letting him take Jaymee to her room. They understood that something serious had occurred, recognized that Nick had saved Jaymee from something.

"Don't you worry, Jay," Dicker called after them. "Take tomorrow off. We'll get the roofs done."

Nick carried her straight into the connecting bathroom after he kicked the bedroom door shut. "A nice warm bath first," he murmured. "You need a good scrub, woman. You're all sweaty and dirty."

"You too," Jaymee said. "You can put me down now, you know."

"I want to carry you forever," he said, simply.

Jaymee felt his tension and understood his desire to keep her close to him. They had almost lost each other. "I love you," she told him.

"I know."

He didn't tell her that he loved her too, but she could see it in his eyes. There was a tenderness in them that seemed to make his eyes bluer, and her breath caught at the deep yearning in them. She felt his emotions in the way he held her so tightly against his body. She supposed it wasn't easy for a man like Nick to say those words, not when he had been trying to sever the ties emotionally the last few days.

They bathed each other slowly, touching and exploring. She kissed him, soothing the fury that rose when he saw the ugly bruises on her in better light. He traced every part of her, as if committing her to memory, growling now and then as he found a scratch here, or a cut there. He handled her with the attention of a mate, with such a gentle touch that it made her want to cry.

After the bath, he carried her to bed, babying her, taking care of her every need, as if she were the most precious thing on earth to him. And Jaymee let him. She'd never felt like this before, out of control, yet also still in charge. His hands were demanding, yet caring. His kisses had an urgency that was both passionate and reverent. His mouth found the vulnerable pulse in her neck, coming back to it again and again, as if her heartbeat reassured him somehow. He leisurely explored the hollow in her throat, the dip between her breasts, the womanly curve of her abdomen.

Jaymee returned his touches with the same reverence. His body was strong and powerful, and trembled under her hands. She kissed the back of his neck, traced her lips down the dip of his spine, molded her hands on the male grace of his small buttocks. He turned over for her eager lips, and moaned as she paid attention to the beautifully formed member that grew bigger with every stroke of her tongue and fingers.

Finally, a sheen of perspiration on him, Nick lifted Jaymee astride him, and she pushed down, taking him fully inside her, enjoying this possession of him, taking and giving pleasure, until they were gasping. It was what they needed, what words couldn't describe. They were one and home. Nothing else mattered.

He lay there quietly, eyes half-closed and filled with passion, as he let her set the pace. His breathing was labored, but he didn't move, except for the lazy teasing of his long, elegant fingers on her sensitive nipples until she went crazy for him, moving faster and faster as his fingers moved on down to rest where they met. She cried out when he pushed away the folds that hid her sensitive feminine bud and pushed down on it so that every move she made gave her the utmost pleasure possible.

Nick wished he could make this go on forever. It'd always be imprinted in his brain, the way she looked on top of him, in the throes of passion. Her head was thrown back, with those wild ringlets all over her shoulders, and as she succumbed to her climax, she sagged forward, her hair enveloping the both of them. He loved the fragrance of her desire mingled with her unique scent, and when she opened her eyes as she braced herself on his shoulders, he was willing to drown in the limpid pools of green. She moaned at every downward stroke and sucked in her breath when she slid back up.

She drove him to the point of madness like that, moving so slowly, seeming to draw every ounce of blood to only one point of his fevered body. Every slick ride down brought shudders of need through him. The pleasure made him clutch the sheets. Not yet. He wasn't willing to let go yet. Let her take him wherever she wanted. He wanted to please her.

Her breasts swayed temptingly as she rocked, and Nick reached up for them, caressing them until the nipples were hardened and she was gasping and moving faster. Oh please, faster please. He wasn't sure whether he begged her aloud. It felt so good. Faster, baby, please.

And when her internal muscles began to clench around him, he went rigid, and without thought, held her hips tight as he thrust up in hard strokes. Harder. Deeper. And he was just as lost as she was in the swirl of heat waves that swept through his consciousness as he emptied his whole soul into her.

*

Jaymee fell into a deep, exhausted sleep, and Nick held her for a while before leaving her to go downstairs. She'd told him that she loved him. And he hadn't told her that he....

He banished the words even before they were formed. Didn't what happened today reinforce the dangerous aspects of having a weak link, a switch that every two-bit mercenary could find? The knowledge that Jaymee could have ended up like Emma turned his stomach and hardened his resolve.

But why couldn't he just say those words?

No, he could never leave her if he ever did. He would want to stay. An impossible dream.

"Are you sure it isn't going to be a problem for you to get a team to sweep the area?" he asked Jed in the kitchen. Bob listened to them, sitting quietly at the kitchen table.

"There won't be, if I'm not here and Jaymee doesn't say too much."

"But they'd know that you have been here."

Jed shrugged. "I'll be long gone." His eyes were thoughtful when he looked at Nick. "What about you?"

Nick returned the gaze levelly. "I'll be with you initiating the encryption board, except that this time, we'll be prepared for the bastards." Revenge was going to be very sweet.

"Yes, they'll think that we're still trying to decipher it, but we have to move fast."

They agreed to meet the next morning and after Jed left, Nick sat down at the kitchen table. The old man offered a cup of coffee, and he accepted.

"Seems like we do our best talking at this table," Bob commented wryly.

Nick's lips lifted at one corner. "True," he agreed.

The details he gave didn't tell much, except that Jaymee was caught in the middle and he had to leave, for her sake. Bob didn't ask any questions, much to Nick's surprise.

"As long as you don't leave without saying goodbye to Jaymee, I won't push for more information. That's what happened the last time, you know, when Danny just left. I don't think she can go through another sudden disappearance."

Nick looked at Bob silently for a second. "I won't leave without saying goodbye," he said softly.

Bob nodded briskly. "Now, what else do you want me to do?"

*

Jaymee awakened the instant he rejoined her in bed, and she curled up eagerly against the heat of his naked body. "Where did you go?" she asked sleepily.

"Taking care of details," he gently murmured against her cheek.

She rubbed the sleep from her eyes, wincing slightly at the stiffness in her wrists. "Are you leaving?" Common sense returned, now that she'd rested. If those men had traced Nick here, the next logical step was for him to leave. His sigh was answer enough. "Nick?"

"Hmm?"

"Why is it not possible?"

"Us, you mean?" Nick caressed her supple body, wondering whether he could ever forget the softness of her skin, her unique fragrance. "I can't risk you, Jaymee. I can't have your safety an issue every time someone comes after me."

"Is it often that someone comes after you?"

"No."

"So, the risk is minimal, right?" she insisted.

There was a short silence. "I won't risk you," Nick said in a stilted voice.

"There's risk in everything, you know."

But he didn't want to discuss risks or targets. He wanted to forget, to melt into this woman and dream of sunlight and impossible dreams. He didn't want Jaymee to argue with his decision. It would only muddle his thinking, tempt him to give in to her. He did what the Programmer would do in this situation--evade and divert. It was for the best.

Turning her over, he covered her sweet, pliant body with his, crushing her in his need for her. When she gasped for breath, he kissed her deeply and pushed her thighs apart with his own.

This sweet oblivion. This unconditional surrender. This generous loving. No, he would never forget her.

*

"Forget you?" Jaymee couldn't believe her ears at his words. "Can't you think of something better to say as parting words?"

She wrapped her arms around her, as if that would keep her from hurling herself at him, to beg him to stay. She would not beg. Her chin tilted up and she sucked in air. Her insides were wound tighter than a spool of thread, and her mouth tasted like sandpaper. Somehow, she managed to stay on her feet, although she couldn't quite manage a smile.

Nick just stood there, a remoteness in his expression that chilled her. She realized that he'd already gone away, beyond her reach. And she, too, retreated inside, trying to rebuild the protective wall this man had broken through. Her hand trembled slightly as she reached up to touch him for one last time, pushing back the stray lock of black hair from his forehead, feeling the stubble of his unshaven face, the pulse that beat strongly at his throat. His face remained expressionless but she felt the betraying swallow under her hands. One last touch.

"Take care of yourself," she whispered, her voice stiff with emotion.

His nod was curt and his slate eyes were wintry as they traveled over her, from the top of her auburn hair to the painted toenails. At the sight of them, they flared with a naked longing that disappeared immediately, and when his eyes returned to hers, they were banked, empty.

"Live for yourself, Jaymee. You've been living for others, do it for yourself from now on," he said, trying to sound gentle, when all he wanted was crush her to him.

He kissed her, hard and possessively, then turned and walked to his red Jeep. Not turning back, he started it up and drove off.

Live? Jaymee covered her mouth with her fist, and she had to bite down hard to control the torrent of pain choking out. Forget and live? Just like hoping he'd turn around and come back to her, that request was an impossible dream.

## Chapter Sixteen

All she wanted was to be left alone. But no one would let her be. Mindy bothered her with phone calls. Her father followed her to work. Everyone rained her with conversation, questions, words. It was all strangely disjointed, as if she stood outside observing herself.

She couldn't even escape to her other house. Strangers appeared one day to "sweep" the place, and like a robot, she followed Jed's instructions, giving the password and handing them his note. She didn't mention Nick at all. She couldn't think about him.

A young man showed up to interrogate her, and it took a few minutes before she realized that he was looking for Jed, and not Nick. His description could have fitted either one of them, except for the silver eyes. She'd answered in a detached manner until she remembered Grace, and what Nick had told her about the young girl. So she paid closer attention to the man and his questions. He was young, in his mid-twenties, and very polite but very thorough. When did she meet Jed? How?

Jaymee deflected the questions with the story she and Jed had agreed on, that she'd planned to lease her house to him for a year and he helped with the cleaning and remodeling.

"And you don't know where he is now?" the young stranger asked, a touch skeptically.

His eyes, a warm, magnetic blue, were cool and quizzical as he studied her from head to toe. Like Nick, there was an air about him that hinted of something underneath that friendly demeanor. The way he stood so still amidst the activity of the other "sweepers" also reminded her a little of Jed. He might be a few years younger than her, but she had the feeling that he'd seen a lot more about life than she'd ever known. Another mark against her. No wonder Nick thought she wouldn't ever be "safe" enough for him. She was so stupid to think that she could make it work.

"Nope," Jaymee answered, looking back at him just as coolly.

His blue eyes narrowed, as if trying to gauge her honesty. "I find it strange that you didn't call the police."

"I like Jed." Jaymee cocked her head. "I trust him." And Nick. And Grace.

"And you don't trust me," he stated. When Jaymee didn't refute it, he added, "Why are you keeping information from me? Jed McNeil and I work for the same company. You obviously know more than you're telling, what with a cleaning unit here sweeping your house, after a bomb scare. I'm not here to harm him, or these guys here would have taken me out already. They know me."

He nodded towards the people working around her house. Despite what little Jed had told her, Jaymee liked the intelligence gleaming in the younger man's eyes, knew from instinct that he wasn't sent to harm Jed. However, she'd decided to side with Jed and Grace, and so she stuck with her story.

"All I know's what I told you," she told the stranger calmly. "Florida is full of transients. They come and go. Some I like, and some I don't."

He did smile then, and Jaymee had to smile back. The look he gave her was cocky and confident.

"Nice. But then I wouldn't want it so easy. Less of a challenge. I'll find him sooner or later," he said. "Thank you for your time, Miss Barrows."

She wondered whether he was part of this Virus Program that Nick and Jed were in. No, she decided, as she watched him walk off to his car. He moved differently from the stealthy, lazy stroll that she had noticed in Nick and Jed. And there was an arrogance in the way he looked and walked, that reminded her of a cat on the prowl. She shook her head as he drove off, mocking her own imagination. She hadn't changed one bit, still putting men into animal categories.

Which suddenly brought her full circle back to Nick. Her big, bad wolf.

With iron determination, she forced the mental picture of Nick away. She didn't think she could bear having Mindy call her, or having her father following her everywhere, or going through another awkward conversation with anyone who thought she needed consolation.

All she wanted was to be left alone. Was that too much to ask?

Later, she ordered shingles to be stocked at the other house the coming week, and after the call, ran all the way to the now "swept" place to start work on the roof.

For the next two days, she tore at the old roof by herself, digging up the shingles with a shovel. It was good, methodical work, the kind that exhausted her enough to sleep for a few hours at night. When she'd removed the shingles and original underlayment, she unrolled the tar felt paper over the cleaned-off plywood, fastening it down with simplex nails. The task was a two-man job, really, but she didn't want company. Perspiration poured down her forehead and blinded momentarily, she hit her forefinger with the hammer at full force.

Pain jolted from the finger to every nerve end in her body. Cursing aloud and sucking her injured finger alternatively, she watched the blood blister that had immediately formed. The throbbing shot through her numbness, bringing her whole body alive again. Every feeling she'd tried to block pounced. With a groan, Jaymee sat down onto the roof.

Pain. It ploughed through her like a live current. Physical and mental pain wrapped around her like invisible wires, coiling tighter and tighter until she felt she would burst with the torture. The pain strangled her, made it impossible to move. Hugging her knees, she ground her head against her thighs, moaning and shivering even though it was ninety degrees outside.

Jaymee sat like that for a long time, unheeding of the heat, her eyes unseeing as she stared down at the tangled bushes around the old house. That was what her life was, she realized. An old house in need of repair and new life. So ignored outside, that it was being choked by untended growth. She'd spent eight years working to pay for her past and planning to pay for her future. She'd never lived for herself as in the now, and if Nick had taught her anything, it was to live for the present, to enjoy what she could.

She took a deep breath and slowly got up. She felt as if she was a thousand years old. She leaned on the shovel for support, gathering her strength, making decisions. She had to change, to prune away all the tangled growth in her life, or she was going to end up like this old house. By the time her father came home that evening, she'd already booked the tickets.

"I'm taking off," she announced. "I need to go away." She waited for the protests.

Bob washed his hands at the sink and joined her at the table. "You deserve to go on a holiday, Jaymee girl."

Jaymee stared at her father in undisguised astonishment. A month ago, he would have given her an earful about leaving for a vacation. Somehow, he'd changed these last few weeks.

"Where are you going?"

"Europe," she told him, frowning. "Don't worry, I'm using my own savings." The money she'd put away to remodel her old house.

"You've always wanted to visit there. How long will you be gone?"

"I don't know. A month. Two. Till my money runs out." She paused. "Is it selfish? Can you take care of the business that long?"

"I think selfish is what you need to be right now, Jaymee girl. I've been selfish for too long." Bob shifted in his chair uncomfortably. "I do remember how to run a roofing business, you know, even if I can't get back on the roof. We can hang on till you come back."

"The loans are up to date. The only bills are current ones, and the jobs are lined up..."

Bob interrupted gruffly, "I thought we agreed that you're going to be selfish. Now, tell me about your travel plans instead."

For the first time in a long, long time, Bob Barrows smiled at his daughter and opened his arms. Jaymee slowly walked towards him and hugged her father.

*

The humidity reminded Killian of Jaymee. Sluicing water over his sweaty body after a hard day of hiking reminded him of Jaymee. Eating. Drinking. Sleeping. Every damned thing reminded him of her, and there was nothing for him to do but to endure it.

If Jed noticed his foul mood, he didn't say anything. Her name wasn't mentioned once since they'd left. Their assignment had been completed a week ago after they had trapped their targets, and Jed had relayed electronically to Command the decoded encryption board. He had the satisfaction of personally dealing with them, especially two, whose description fitted that given by Jaymee, down to the smell of cologne.

There was still much to do. The scums who had used Jaymee against him had been mere mercenaries. They had given the names of their handlers, but in the world of covert games, handlers had handlers, and every personal agenda had to be determined before the next move.

Killian watched as Jed cleaned and cooked fish over an open fire. Grace was taking a nap close by, having been thoroughly worked out by her father that morning in a series of exercises. He could only marvel at the young girl's tolerance for pain, for it was pain and endurance that Jed was training her in.

He mulled over his next step. Jed had told him getting those men wasn't enough. He had his own agenda to meet.

Killian understood. There was still Grace to think about and time spent training her meant extra time for Jed to assimilate his information and come up with a solution to the crisis waiting for them back at Command. For himself, this particular mission was over. Time to return to Command Center and be debriefed.

"I'm going back tomorrow," he said. "Is everything taken care of?"

Jed's glance was calculating. "It depends on what you mean."

His attention returned to the fish. Killian sighed. He wasn't in the mood for mind games.

"The hell you don't." He couldn't help the curtness in his reply. Sleep had eluded him for weeks now.

"The satellites are going to be destroyed. The unit is still looking for me, and," Jed paused a beat, then went on conversationally, "Jaymee had left a message where I told her."

Killian wanted to punch something, someone. Even her name was painful to hear. "And?"

"The team came and swept the place, and she's fine, I suppose."

"What the hell do you mean, you suppose?"

He glared at his cousin's cool silver stare. Jed shrugged. His tone of voice was deceptively nonchalant, meant to infuriate.

"I can't vouch for what she's going through or how she is, since I'm not there physically. She mentioned some young man looking for me, and that was all there was to her message."

"She didn't ask about me?" Why did he ask that? He didn't want to know.

"Of course she did," Jed replied, still in that mild voice. "What do you want me to tell her? That you don't care, or that you do?"

"Damn you, Jed."

"You're the one looking damned, cousin." The retort was dry, amused.

"Back off!" Killian all but snarled, then reined in his anger with effort. "What did you want me to do? Take her with me to D.C.? Leave her whenever I take off? I thought, of all people, you would understand the danger." He regretted his outburst immediately. Jed didn't deserve that. Sighing, he attempted to apologize. "I'm sorry. I'm not thinking straight."

Jed was silent as he turned the fish over in the pan. "There are always choices, Nick."

"Yeah, tell Command that."

"I haven't reported to them that you're alive. In fact, you missed a relevant part of Jaymee's message. They're looking for me, Kill. No one else."

The silence that followed was broken by Grace, who sat up in her sleeping bag, yawning.

"What do you mean?" Nick queried carefully, trying to read his cousin's expression.

"You tell me. What do you want it to mean? Is the Programmer dead, or not? Has he disappeared? Enquiring agencies want to know." There was true amusement tingeing Jed's voice now.

To Nick's amazement, Jed started to laugh as he continued to stare at him. His own mind was running a sixty-yard dash to...to what? Freedom. Jaymee. Sunshine. Jaymee.

"What about you?" he asked, his voice a low gravelly rumble. "You said Jaymee wrote that someone was coming after you. They'll get you sooner or later."

Jed shrugged again, his usually harsh demeanor softened by amusement. "I'm not dead, just missing. I know how to keep in touch with them and give them relevant information just to show how much I miss them. They'll find me in a year or so. I'll give that young tracker that long, and if he fails, I'll show up at Command Center like I promised."

"Maybe the tracker will give up." It was entirely possible. Tracking the Ice Man wasn't an easy assignment, and a young tracker probably didn't have the experience or the patience.

"Not likely. I ran a check on him while I was sending in the report. Lance Mercy has an interesting file. Five years in COMCEN and already shot up the ranks like a rocket ship. He single-handedly, it seems, tracked down and revealed the identity of the Beijing Butcher to Command last year."

Nick whistled softly. "Impressive. Sounds like you're going to have fun. The Beijing Butcher and the Ice Man under his belt in five years. I'd like to meet young Mercy some day."

"He hasn't found me yet." Jed looked in Grace's direction. "And he won't, till she's ready."

Nick followed his gaze. "She's special."

"So is Jaymee." Jed actually smiled at Nick. "Give her my love."

"The hell I will." He still held a grudge against Jed for kissing her. "The next time you kiss her, it'd better be a brotherly smack on the cheek."

Jed's shapely lips quirked with mockery. "That is, if she's married to you."

Nick's eyes narrowed suspiciously. "What do you mean now?"

Taking his time, Jed turned the fish over.

"Meat's done," Grace murmured from where she was as she sniffed the air. "Just like Cousin Kill."

Jed slanted a look at his daughter's direction. "Jaymee strikes me as someone who evades anyone who hurt her badly." He sat back and rubbed his chin thoughtfully. "She's probably never going to forgive you."

That did it. Killian stood up in a hurry.

"Hey, Nick."

He turned and scowled down at his cousin. Manipulating bastard. He knew he had been expertly played.

"Do keep in contact, so I know I don't stand a chance with the lady."

And Jed laughed again. Grace grinned at Killian cheekily.

"See ya sometime, cousin Nick," she said, waving.

*

Jaymee didn't contact anyone while she was in Europe. She was, finally, alone. And lonely. Europe was enchanting, beautiful--everything she had imagined it to be. She sat down by a fountain in Piazza Navona, entertained only by a mime who told her in actions that she looked lonely. She'd smiled back and nodded, giving him a tip for such insight. She leaned against the leaning tower of Pisa and wondered how such weakness could survive all its problems. She climbed up the Alps and wondered whether the glaciers were as cold as her heart. She ate without relish the foreign dishes, dutifully trying the different wines, the warm beer, the exotic chocolates, the array of cheeses. Everything.

Every cathedral and museum was a monument of her own deadness. So she went shopping instead, maxing out her credit card. Clothes in Rome. Perfume in Paris. Lace in Venice.

She looked at the superb statue of David and wished she could buy it to take home because it reminded her of someone warmer, sexier, with the big parts intact. Looking at the Greek deities, she wondered whether a fig leaf would look funny on Nick. That had brought out a bitter laugh. It seemed that she couldn't forget, no matter where she was.

And late at night, she still cried.

Home.

Jaymee pulled up at the driveway to her house exactly six weeks after she left for Europe. The evening sun was a giant orange globe, getting ready for fall weather. Other than that, as she looked listlessly around, nothing had changed.

Her father greeted her with a hug. "It was wonderful to hear your voice over the phone," he said, looking robust and healthy. "I sure have missed you, Jaymee girl."

"How's everything? Work OK?"

She pulled the suitcases out of her trunk. She had left with a small bag and returned with three giant ones.

"Oh, we've been busy. Anderson called just a few days ago, in fact, and he says the roofs by Glenn's men are leaking, and he wants us back." Bob laughed. "I told him that he needed to negotiate the price with you when you return. It felt good saying that, after what he did. Everything's fine, in fact...you look different, Jaymee girl. Very good."

She was dressed different, that was all. Her father hadn't seen her in anything more than a work shirt and pants for most of eight years. Now, she was wearing a designer blouse and short skirt. Beneath her outfit, she wore expensive lingerie and French perfume. Even her hair had been cut and restyled. But no amount of change on the outside healed the emptiness she felt inside.

"Thanks, Dad."

She looked around the house after her luggage was brought in. Everything was tidy. The kitchen sink was clean. The tile floor had been mopped. Even the living room had been dusted down. Her father, it seemed, had survived better without her.

"The house looks great."

"I have a...er...housemate now," Bob admitted, looking uncomfortable. "I hope you don't mind, Jaymee girl. I wasn't sure when you were coming back and all, and well, I needed someone to supervise the roofing work. I told him it ain't a permanent position, so..."

"Dad, it's your roofing business too," Jaymee interrupted. Her father was right; he couldn't possibly work like she did. She smiled, thinking that he probably enjoyed the male company. "A clean housemate is always welcomed. Where is he?"

"He...uh...he's back at your house, the one you bought."

She froze. "What?"

"Well, he liked to work and I set him to clear the main driveway to the house for easier access. He..."

"No one touches that house," Jaymee cut in tonelessly. "You shouldn't have let him. Just because I let you know about that place didn't mean I wanted you to work on it."

She saw that her words hurt her father's feelings, but she didn't care. No one was allowed to go where she and Nick had spent time together.

"I didn't know," Bob apologized. "When the delivery men showed up after you left, I just thought..."

Jaymee sighed. She remembered her phone orders for shingles and gravel. She couldn't blame her father for assuming that she wanted work to continue on that house while she was away. After all, she hadn't left any instructions.

"I...I'll just go over there and meet him now, I guess." She had to be polite to this man, for her father's sake. "You seem to like him, Dad."

"Oh yes, sure do. He's been a big help while you were away, and although I wasn't sure whether I liked him at first, I find him...ah...a good man."

"All right, we'll talk more later, but I think I'll drive over there to see how the house is, seeing that you have cleared the driveway."

"Go ahead. I think you'll like it." A small smile touched his lips.

Her little rental car wouldn't have been able to reach the place over a month ago. Now, although the ride was bumpy, she could drive all the way in. She stared at the house as she emerged from the car, not knowing what to expect.

The sound of an airgun riveted her attention to the roof. When there was a pause between the noise, she yelled up to the unseen man.

"Hello!" Damn. In her hurry to get here, she had forgotten to ask his name. "Umm, can you hear me up there? I'm Bob's daughter, Jay."

She heard some answer that she couldn't make out from the back side of the roof and moments later, the familiar sound of someone getting down a ladder. She walked around the cleared up shrubs, taking quick notice of the new coat of paint on the siding before turning the corner to meet...looking up at the descending man, she almost tripped.

Her eyes must be playing tricks on her. Her mouth opened and then closed, as she stared into intense blue-gray eyes.

Nick slowly approached Jaymee, his eyes devouring her. Not seeing her had been torturous, and not even knowing where she was the last six weeks had almost driven him crazy with worry. He should have known to expect the unexpected where Jaymee was concerned. No wallowing in misery for her. No work as usual. The woman had packed up and taken a vacation in Europe! He could only shake his head in disbelief when he'd shown up at her doorstep with flowers in hand, only to be informed by Bob Barrows that nobody knew where she was or when she would be back.

As the weeks went by with still no word from her, he'd wondered whether she would come back after all. In fact, he'd been near breaking point when her phone call came, telling her father that she was returning home. He knew that she would come looking for the stranger meddling with her house as soon as Bob told her. This was her private place, her sanctuary, and she wouldn't want anyone to make any changes without her say so.

He paused, unable to say anything just yet. She looked so beautiful. His eyes hungrily took in every inch of her, from the shiny auburn mane to the sophisticated ensemble she wore, down to the elegant leather shoes. It dawned on him that he'd been so blind, thinking that she'd never leave her safe little world. This woman could fit anywhere, would go anywhere, if she wanted to.

"Hello, Jaymee." Nick broke the silence between them. "You look...sensational."

She had gained some weight, adding a softness to her face. She was the picture of feminine allure, standing there with the setting sun illuminating her glorious curls and haunting eyes. In short, she was the most desirable thing in his life.

"It...is you." Her voice was incredulous.

"Yes," he said, simply.

"Why?"

Jaymee couldn't believe what her eyes were telling her. This must be a mirage. If she moved, he would disappear back into her dreams. Her heart ached at the sight of his familiar face, with those incredibly-lashed eyes. She wanted to reach out and touch him, to push aside that roguish lock of hair.

She wanted to, but she didn't dare. Maybe she was dreaming. Maybe moving would wake her up.

"Because I love you, Jaymee."

She began to shake. Her hand came up to cover her trembling mouth.

Nick's eyes never left her face as he took the last few steps toward her. His voice was pitched low, almost a mutter. "I missed you. These last few months have been hell on earth. Jaymee, I need you."

She didn't care whether this was a hallucination. It was killing her. She pressed her hand harder against her mouth, trying to contain the loud gasps coming from inside her, and she blindly backed away from him. Her sobs were heartbreaking, uncontrollable.

"Oh, God. Don't. Don't cry, baby, please."

In one swift moment, Nick lifted, gathering her pliant body high against his heart. Catching her scent, he closed his eyes for a moment, letting it fill his lungs, his whole being. God, he'd missed her. He could feel her trembling as he carried her indoors, and he wanted to kick himself for hurting this woman so much.

He sat down on the old sofa, with her on his lap, and held her against him, letting her cry. He wanted to kiss her. He wanted to love her. But her tears had him helpless and unsure. He didn't know how to deal with such grief.

"Please stop crying," he finally pleaded, stroking her hair. "I don't want you to be sad. I never wanted you to be sad. All I ever wanted was for you to live a safe, happy life."

"I tried, Nick," Jaymee whispered, looking up at him, her eyes red from crying. "But I'm dead inside. There's a void in me that gets bigger every day. And it hurts. It hurts so much."

He'd felt the same. This was the first time in months that he felt truly alive, and it was because she was in his arms again.

"I'm not leaving you, Jaymee," he told her softly. Seeing her wide, questioning eyes, he explained, "The Programmer is dead, killed by an explosion on board his sailboat. If you will have me...?"

He left the question dangling, his eyes searching. As she digested the news, a slow smile lit her face up. Nick caught his breath. He'd never forget the look in her eyes. Sheer joy. Love. The sunlight to his heart. He smiled back.

"What do you intend to be, a kept man?" she asked.

Nick's smile became wolfish. "The idea does have some appeal. Remind me to inform Jed and my unit when they bother me." He ran a gentle finger over her frown, as he went on, "I won't ever be entirely free from my job, Jaymee, but Jed has given me some choices. I owe him, if he ever needs me."

She understood, and would never ask him to relinquish something he so wanted to do. As long as he was hers, she didn't care. The happiness bubbling inside could conquer anything.

"OK," she simply said. "Now, being a kept man, I order you to kiss me."

His lips were at first gentle, as if he was afraid his passion would crush her, but at her eager response, his kiss became deeper, hungrier. His tongue danced across hers, teasing and loving, telling her without words everything that he was feeling. This, she thought in a fiery haze, was what had been missing in Europe, this feeling of belonging, of being alive.

"I want to show you the house, what I've done." He rained kisses on her eyes, her nose, the corners of her lips. "I did it all by myself, you know."

"Are you looking to hire some help?" Jaymee asked, her hands busy tugging at his tee-shirt to get at the muscled body underneath. "I'm a pretty good roofer."

Nick pulled back and arched a brow down at her. Casting a leer down the length of her designer-clad body, he drawled, "Don't look like a construction worker to me at all, miss." He pulled off one of her heels, examining it with a mocking smile. "Wrong shoes." He threw it over his shoulder, and grabbed her manicured hand. Kissing the tips of pink-tipped nails, he said, "Clean nails, and," he ran a finger up her arm, "no tattoos."

It was so good to laugh again. So good to be alive again. She raked her nails down his chest, and grinned at the sharp intake of breath. "Let me show you how good I am at finding leaks," she invited.

Nick didn't need further encouragement.

\*

Someone turned on the light. Jaymee groaned and turned over.

"I've something to show you, sweetheart. Wake up."

Nick pulled the covers off her nude body, his hand lingering intimately for a moment before determinedly shaking her awake. She groped for a pillow and covered her head with it.

"Tomorrow," she mumbled.

Her tormenter was unrelenting. "It is tomorrow. It's past midnight."

"Go mow the lawn. Or finish laying the roof."

Nick laughed. He'd forgotten about her jet lag, but he pulled the pillow away mercilessly anyway. "Come on, sleepyhead. You can't see this in the daylight."

Jaymee opened her eyes, meaning to glare at him, but he looked so damned glorious sitting there, so at ease without a stitch on, that she could only smile happily back. She still couldn't believe that he was real, that this was happening.

"You need a fig leaf," she murmured.

"A fig leaf," he repeated, puzzled.

"David had a tiny fig leave, but he looked really sexy with it," she informed him, then giggled at the look on his face.

"Who the hell is David?" Nick demanded, imagining some Romeo posing as...oh, that David. He glared down at the grinning woman. "What else did you learn from your European travels, besides admiring nude statues?"

"That those cathedrals need a leak expert," Jaymee replied, her eyes filled with laughter. "You'd be amazed at how many of them leak."

Nick grinned ruefully. How he loved her. Only she would check famous centuries-old buildings for leaks. He held out his hand and after a moment, she fitted hers in his, letting him pull her off the bed. Flipping off the light switch and plunging the room back into darkness, he led her to the back balcony, the one facing the lake. The full moon lit everything brightly.

Jaymee gasped.

The backyard had been cleared while she was gone. A path meandered all the way to the shimmering lake, the dark waters mirrored the star-filled sky above. Moonlight reflected off the white gravel along the way, like twinkling stars in the Milky Way. Never in her farthest imagination had she thought the overgrown bushes of the unkempt yard could hide such beauty. She turned to look at Nick, her heart in her eyes.

In the moonlit night, he no longer seemed secretive or remote. His crooked smile was tender as he lifted her hand to place a kiss on the knuckles. In that wonderful, gravelly voice, he said solemnly, echoing her words from that day when she'd confided in him.

"I hereby give you this path, strewn with flowers and covered with stars that you'll never get lost. I promise to walk with you by your side, Jaymee, all the way to our paradise. I know I've been the cause of much heartache and more trouble than you wanted, and probably more in the future. But I love you. You're my sunshine, my life. My path to the stars. Will you marry me?"

He was in his element, the cover of shadow and moonlight, but his wolf eyes glittered with love and Jaymee felt the swell of emotion beating in her own breast. He'd taken her painful past and given her hope and love in return. He was her future, the only thing that mattered.

"Yes," she replied, her eyes glowing with happiness. "You, Killian Nicholas Langley, are no trouble at all."

THE END

Check out Gennita Low's websites:

http://www.gennita-low.com/

http://rooferauthor.blogspot.com/

http://www.daglowworld.blogspot.com/